SNEAKS

ALSO BY CATHERINE EGAN

SNEAKS

CATHERINE EGAN

ALFRED A. KNOPF

NEW YORK

THIS IS A BORZOI BOOK PUBLISHED BY ALFRED A. KNOPF

This is a work of fiction. Names, characters, places, and incidents either are the product of the author's imagination or are used fictitiously. Any resemblance to actual persons, living or dead, events, or locales is entirely coincidental.

Text copyright © 2022 by Catherine Egan
Jacket illustration copyright © 2022 by Kevin Cornell
Jacket design by Bob Bianchini

All rights reserved. Published in the United States by Alfred A. Knopf, an imprint of Random House Children's Books, a division of Penguin Random House LLC, New York.

Knopf, Borzoi Books, and the colophon are registered trademarks of Penguin Random House LLC.

Visit us on the Web! rhcbooks.com

Educators and librarians, for a variety of teaching tools, visit us at RHTeachersLibrarians.com

Library of Congress Cataloging-in-Publication Data is available upon request.
ISBN 978-0-593-30640-6 (trade) — ISBN 978-0-593-30642-0 (ebook) —
ISBN 978-0-593-48767-9 (intl. pbk.)

The text of this book is set in 12.25-point Adobe Jenson Pro Regular.
Interior design by Jen Valero

Printed in Canada
January 2022
10 9 8 7 6 5 4 3 2 1

First Edition

For James

Monday, September 24

WATCHES
DON'T CRAWL

1

Ben Harp saw the wristwatch scuttling sideways across the hallway, crablike, as he and the rest of his sixth-grade class filed into the library on Monday morning. It was there among the feet of his classmates, and then it was gone.

"Ew! Was that a *cockroach*?" cried Jessica Masterson, who had nearly stepped on it.

"I think it was a mouse!" Audrey Banks clutched Jessica's arm.

Ben had seen it clearly, if only for a second: the leather strap, the round white watch face. The strap had been curling and flattening like a caterpillar, but moving much faster than any caterpillar. A watch crawling across the hall and into the library of its own accord is hard to process at ten in the morning, however. *Cockroach*, his brain stoutly tried to persuade him. *Or mouse*. But he felt uneasy as he sat down on the carpet in the library.

"There's a cockroach on your sweater!" Jae Park yelled at Jessica Masterson; the girls shrieked at him in mock fury.

Ms. Pryce, the school librarian, silenced them with a slight widening of her eyes. When Ms. Pryce first came to their school last year, the kids thought they could get away with anything, because she was new and looked so young, but she disabused them of that notion very quickly. She was a petite woman, the only Black teacher at their school, and the youngest by nearly twenty years. She wore big glasses with red frames and tailored outfits in bright colors. Her clothes said *fun*, but the expression on her face said something else altogether.

"Class, today we are beginning the Livingston history project we discussed last week," said Ms. Pryce. "I want each of you to find a partner, *quietly*."

Even though Ben had known it was coming, his stomach dropped.

This had never been a problem before sixth grade. *Before*, when a teacher said "Find a partner," Ben and Ashok gave each other the thumbs-up, and that was that. They had been best friends since first grade.

But Ashok and his family had moved to Paris for the year, for his mom's research. He would be back for seventh grade, but that still meant Ben had to get through the whole of sixth grade without his best friend.

When Ms. Pryce told them to find a partner, Ben's cheeks grew hot, and he delayed a few seconds, which sealed his fate. By the time he looked around, Ryan Yu and Felix Cross had already moved closer together. Malcolm Church had partnered with Jason Huang. He looked at the other boys in his class with mounting panic. Even Danny Farkas had paired off with Jae Park—not that he would have partnered with Danny

Farkas anyway. Jake Bernstein and Lekan Bassey. That was all of the boys. The girls had made even quicker work of partnering up according to years of habit.

The new girl, Akemi Hanamura, was sitting next to Ben on the carpet. She glanced at him for a second or two, but he felt strangely frozen by the situation and avoided meeting her eyes.

Akemi had made the lethal mistake, during her first week at Livingston Middle School, of beating out Jessica Masterson for captain of the girls' basketball team in tryouts. Jessica Masterson—and the whole town, really—was fanatical about basketball. Jessica Masterson was also the undisputed queen of sixth grade. Akemi was shut out after that. Now she looked resignedly at Charlotte Moss, who had a face like wobbly rice pudding and always smelled of instant noodle soup. Akemi didn't have any other choices, though. She moved closer to Charlotte on the carpet.

"Does everybody have a partner?" asked Ms. Pryce.

Murmured yeses. Ben's no got stuck in his throat.

"Good." Her eyes skated across the class. "Ben Harp—who is your partner?"

"I don't have one."

It came out too quiet. Ms. Pryce frowned, leaning forward.

"I can't hear you," she said.

This time it came out too loud: "I don't have a partner!"

Danny Farkas snickered and then fell silent under Ms. Pryce's frosty glare.

"I forgot that we're an uneven number," said Ms. Pryce. "Join Akemi and Charlotte to form a group of three, please. Class, you have two weeks to complete the project. This will be a lot of work, so I hope you'll all start early, rather than leaving it for the last minute. I want it back Monday, October eighth."

"October eighth?" cried Jessica Masterson. "But we have our first basketball game against Rylant Middle School that day! We need to practice *a lot*—our team isn't very good this year."

She shot Akemi a venomous look, muttering something that sounded like "new captain."

"If you can't balance your extracurricular activities with your schoolwork, you shouldn't be on the team," said Ms. Pryce, handing out work packets. "Ben Harp, join your group, please!"

Danny Farkas smirked at Ben. Ben missed Ashok worse than ever—Ashok, who seemed, whenever they texted each other, to be having such an *amazing* time in Paris, who actually *liked* his new school and had already made new friends, just three weeks in.

Akemi smiled brightly at him. Charlotte gave him her standard blank, rice-pudding stare. He felt, for a moment, so lonely and miserable that he almost forgot about the watch crawling into the library.

2

Ms. Kennedy was frantically searching her desk when they returned to their classroom. The worst thing about sixth grade was that Ashok was gone. The second-worst thing was having Ms. Kennedy for homeroom and language arts. Her baseline was a slow, simmering fury. She had frizzy dyed-red hair, her ankles puffed out around the edges of her shoes, and she smelled like stale coffee. Unhappiness came off her in waves and hung in the air of the classroom. They breathed it in all day.

"Has anybody seen my watch?" she cried as they returned to their desks. "I left it *right here!*"

She gestured wildly at the stacks of papers and folders, the coffee-stained mugs, the pens and rubber bands and chains of paper clips all jumbled together on her desk.

Ben thought queasily of what he'd seen outside the library. But it was impossible to say: *Yes, I saw your watch crawl right past Jessica Masterson's feet and into the library about an hour ago,* so he said nothing. *Cockroach or mouse,* his brain insisted. *Watches don't crawl.*

"No, Ms. Kennedy, I haven't seen it," said Briony Moore

earnestly. Briony Moore was the biggest suck-up in all of Suckupdom. "Do you want us to look for it?"

Ms. Kennedy stared at her desk for a moment like it was her worst enemy and she was getting ready to lay a curse on it. Then she turned that same look on them. Ben sank down into his seat.

"Open your workbooks," she said menacingly. "We're doing *reading response.*"

*

Akemi caught up with Ben as he was getting his bicycle after school.

"Hi," she said.

"Hi."

She was the same height as him. Her black hair was cut in a neat bob, and she had a frank, cheerful expression. If she hadn't been so dumb as to beat Jessica Masterson in that one-on-one basketball face-off, she'd probably have made friends here easily. Charlotte Moss came lolling along behind her, mouth slightly open. They made an odd pair—Akemi in her trendy sportswear, Charlotte in her pleated skirt and high-buttoned blouse, like a 1950s schoolgirl.

"So—the Livingston history project," said Akemi. "Should we start it today? This Agatha Bent person we're supposed to interview lives pretty close. I mean, everywhere in this town is close, I guess." She rolled her eyes. "Charlotte found her address online."

The project had two parts. They had to interview some-body, chosen by Ms. Pryce, who had lived their whole life in Livingston, and write a report on that person's memories of the town and how it had changed. And they had to research a monu-ment or building in town, which they could choose themselves.

Ben wanted to say no. He wanted to be alone and think about the crawling watch. His brain was trying a different tack, and was now telling him: *Hallucination. A weird virus has infected your brain and might kill you.* He opened his mouth, but he couldn't think of an excuse, so what came out was: "Sure, okay."

"Great! Let's go!"

Akemi beamed, and Charlotte Moss stared at him bleakly over Akemi's shoulder.

*

According to their work packet, Agatha Bent was seventy-nine years old. She had worked as a receptionist in the town hall for more than forty years, and had lived in the same house on Winslow Street for half a century. Ben thought she sounded like the least interesting person in the world. Ms. Pryce had added a note that Agatha Bent had been hit by a car recently and was recovering at home.

Akemi never said much in class, but on the walk to Agatha Bent's house she proved to be extremely chatty. She peppered Ben with questions about where he lived and if he'd lived anywhere else and if he liked Livingston and what he thought about Ms. Pryce and Ms. Kennedy and their scary principal, Mr. Susskind. He decided not to tell her about his and Ashok's theory that Mr. Susskind was an alien sent to Earth to learn about humans.

Finally, he thought to ask her where she'd moved from.

"Boston." She looked a little wistful when she said it. He wondered if she had a best friend in Boston who was now stuck partnerless in class without her. "I didn't want to move here. I liked my school and everything back home."

"So why *did* you move?" asked Charlotte.

"My dad wanted a change," she said, and paused, like she wasn't sure this was the right answer. Then she said, "He got a job at the university."

That was no surprise. Livingston was a small college town; most of their class, including Ben, had at least one parent who worked at the university, which dominated the town center.

"Here it is," said Charlotte, checking the address she'd written on the back of her hand.

The red paint on the front door was chipped, and a grinning little garden gnome lay tipped over on its side among the bushes that pressed up against a wobbly-looking porch. There was no doorbell, just an old brass knocker. Ben propped his bike up against the porch railing.

The moments that transform our lives are often so small that we recognize them only when we look back. There was no way of knowing that Agatha Bent would change everything for them, or that, if they'd thought to ask, she could have explained exactly why a wristwatch was crawling across a hallway on its own. Still, Ben experienced an odd sense of foreboding, a slight flutter in his chest, as Akemi reached up and banged the knocker against the door.

3

The person who opened the door was definitely not a seventy-nine-year-old lifelong resident of Livingston. He looked like the kind of camp counselor who would try too hard to get everybody *super excited* about a canoe trip in the rain. He had blond hair, a tan, and bright blue eyes. He was wearing hospital scrubs, and he opened the door wide, beaming at them with all his white teeth, a dimple in one cheek.

"*Hi!*" he said.

"Hi," said Akemi, looking startled. "Um, we're looking for Agatha Bent."

"Oh, *really?*" he said. "Is she *expecting* you?"

"Not exactly," said Akemi.

"We're from Livingston Middle School," said Ben. It occurred to him only now that they should not have showed up unannounced. "We're supposed to interview her for a project. But . . ."

The young man considered them for a moment, and then

he said, "*Cool*, she didn't tell me about that! Hey, let me just check if she's awake. Do you guys want to come in?"

They shuffled into the foyer, which smelled like dog pee.

"Sorry about the *smell*," said the young man, rolling his eyes. He disappeared down the hall, leaving the three of them standing there.

"Ms. Pryce probably checked to make sure none of the people she picked are psychos, right?" whispered Akemi.

"We should have called first," said Ben, feeling awkward.

"It smells bad," said Charlotte.

The young man bobbed back into the hallway.

"*Hey*, thanks for waiting! Come on in, Agatha is totally excited to meet you guys! I'm Simon, by the way. I'm her carer."

They followed Simon-the-carer into a musty sitting room that smelled even more strongly of dog pee, mixed with a fruity perfume.

Agatha Bent, surrounded by pillows and draped in confusing layers of fabric, turned off the television and patted the quivering miniature poodle in her lap—presumably the source of the pee smell. She did not look anything like what Ben expected a seventy-nine-year-old ex-receptionist to look like. She had a platinum-blond updo, scarlet fingernails, and a full face of makeup. She looked like she was on her way to the theater instead of watching TV with her dog. The window at the back of the sitting room overlooked an unkempt lawn and a broken fence that bordered a large, derelict house with boarded-up windows. The house out back was familiar, though Ben couldn't place it.

"How *won-n-n-n-nderful!*" cried Agatha Bent. "Children!"

"Right? How *cute* are they?" Simon went and pointlessly rearranged the pillows around her. The gray poodle barked shrilly at him. There was a wheelchair folded up and propped against the chair Agatha was sitting in. "Do you kids want something to drink? Like, some *milk?*"

"No thanks," said Ben.

The other two shook their heads as well.

Akemi seemed to have momentarily lost the power of speech, and so, after an uncomfortable silence during which Simon-the-carer and Agatha Bent just stared at them expectantly, Ben cleared his throat and said, "Um, we have some interview questions for you, Ms. Bent. It's for our Livingston history project at school."

"Agatha! You didn't even tell me!" Simon swatted her shoulder playfully, sending the poodle into another fury of barking and snarling. "It's like you're a movie star. People coming here to interview you."

Agatha Bent ignored him.

"Sit down, children," she said, waving at the sofa. "Do call me *Agatha*, please! Get them something to drink, would you, dear?" She directed this at Simon, who smiled beatifically and sailed out.

Ben, Akemi, and Charlotte perched on the edge of the sofa. As soon as they sat down, the poodle jumped off Agatha's lap and started yapping at them, the tags on her pink collar jingling.

"Oh, stop that!" said Agatha indulgently. "This is my

13

puppers, Poubelle. She gets terribly jealous. She thinks it's *her* sofa, the little love."

"Poubelle?" said Ben. "Doesn't that mean . . . 'garbage can'?"

"It's *French*, dear," said Agatha condescendingly, as if the French couldn't possibly have garbage.

"I think it's French for 'garbage can,'" said Ben. Ashok's parents were from Quebec. They spoke French at home with Ashok, and Bengali to each other when they didn't want Ashok to understand. Ben had picked up a fair bit of French over the years.

"I don't think that can be right. *Belle* means 'beautiful,'" sniffed Agatha.

"Yeah, but—" Ben started.

Akemi elbowed him in the ribs, and he shut his mouth. Agatha looked annoyed.

"So, maybe we could ask you some questions," said Akemi, taking the work packet out of her backpack.

Simon came back in with a tray holding three glasses of milk and a plate of crackers. The poodle was barking more insistently now, making it difficult to talk.

"We can just stand up," said Ben.

The three of them rose.

Poubelle jumped onto the sofa and peed on it.

"I love children," said Agatha dreamily. "So full of *life*."

Ben took a glass and sipped at the milk, which turned out to be cream, and was also sour. He gagged, but there was nowhere to put the glass down.

"Um, when were you born?" Akemi asked Agatha, propping

the worksheet awkwardly on a folder in the crook of her arm so that she could take notes.

"That's rather a *personal* question," said Agatha, frowning.

Ben looked over Akemi's shoulder and quickly read out the next question.

"What is the biggest change you've seen in Livingston over your lifetime?"

"Ah," said Agatha. "When Lyon's Chocolate Shop closed down in 1974, I thought: That's it—this town won't ever be the same. March 5, 1974. I remember it like it was yesterday. A very sad day. I *wept* and *wept*. But then I took action! My letter to the editor about the decline of the town, the closing of small businesses, was published in the *Livingston Chronicle* on March 17. I'm sure I have a clipping somewhere."

Akemi looked at Ben. He nodded encouragingly. She sighed and wrote: *Chocolate shop closed 1974.*

4

Half an hour later, the three of them burst out into the sunshine, gulping in the fresh air. Simon waved cheerfully from the door. They waved back, rounded the corner, and exploded into hysterical laughter—even Charlotte, and Ben wasn't sure he'd ever seen her laugh before.

"Those are the *weirdest* people I've ever met in my life!" Akemi howled.

"Their dog is *so gross*," added Charlotte.

Ben loved dogs, and it pained him to hear any dog described as gross, but even he had to admit that Poubelle was short on charm.

"*Poubelle* does mean 'garbage can,'" he muttered.

"We definitely got the worst interview subject," said Akemi, once they had all recovered somewhat.

"How many times do we have to go back?" asked Charlotte.

"We asked most of the questions on the worksheet," said Akemi. "But we still have to come up with some questions of our own. She said she'd show us her photo albums if we come back tomorrow. Maybe we can finish interviewing her then. We should say we're allergic to every kind of snack, though. Those crackers looked as old as Agatha Bent."

At the corner of Finch Street, which ran parallel to Winslow, Ben realized why the house backing onto Agatha's had looked familiar. It was an old heritage house—two hundred years old or more—that had been under repair for as long as he could remember, its fence covered in yellow tape warning people to keep out, the windows boarded up, and big planks hammered over the front door. He could see the gate from here.

Charlotte plunked herself down at the bus stop. "Bye," she said abruptly, her face going expressionless, like a curtain coming down.

"I thought you lived by the elementary school," said Ben.

He had a vague memory of Charlotte walking across the street to a white house, where her grandmother was always waiting on the porch. Danny Farkas used to tell everyone that Charlotte had been such an ugly baby her parents had run off but her grandmother couldn't see well, so she didn't mind. In fact, Ben had no idea why she lived with her grandmother, or where her parents were.

"I moved," said Charlotte, not looking at him.

She took two barrettes with big white bows out of her pocket, pinned back her fair hair, and then licked her thumb and set about furiously rubbing Agatha Bent's address off the back of her hand.

"Well . . . see you tomorrow," said Ben, but Charlotte didn't reply, having gone off into some Charlotte-world of her own.

Akemi and Ben walked on together—Ben pushing his bicycle because it seemed rude to ride off without her.

"Your school is so small," Akemi was saying. "At my old school, there were four classes for each grade, and twenty-eight kids in each class."

Ben wondered if it would be better or worse to be in such a sea of kids. If Ashok were with him, he figured he wouldn't mind either way. He felt the need to explain to Akemi why he'd had no partner. He didn't want her to think he just had no friends at all, even though he sort of didn't anymore.

"My best friend moved to France this year," he said. "Just for a year, but that's why . . . I mean, it's really different now that he's gone."

Akemi nodded. "I miss my friends too."

He glanced at her sideways and said, "You probably shouldn't have beat Jessica Masterson in that basketball face-off."

She snorted. "I figured that out by now."

They reached his house, and he said, "Well, this is where I live."

It was a ranch house, with faded yellow siding that had probably been a cheery color when it was new. His parents had let the front lawn turn into a sea of wild grass and dandelions, but the neighbors had complained—it was an eyesore, they said, on their block of otherwise neatly mowed lawns. They even brought a petition over, demanding that the Harps keep their lawn to the neighborhood standard. That was actually what the letter said: "the neighborhood standard." Ben's parents had found it hilarious. They put the petition on the fridge, howling with laughter, and then ignored it, but Ben had been so overcome with shame that he borrowed Mr. and Mrs. Dorian's lawnmower every few weeks and took care of it himself. The Dorians gave him cookies afterward, which made him feel even worse, like the cookies were a judgment on his parents. He thought his parents were flaky and irresponsible too, but he hated seeing other grown-ups come to that conclusion.

Akemi was just standing there, staring at his house. He wondered whether she was waiting for him to invite her in.

"See you tomorrow," he said.

She looked a little disappointed, but she waved goodbye and kept walking, and he wheeled his bike over to the garage.

5

As soon as he turned his key in the lock, Ben heard the creak of the couch springs in the living room, and then the *click-clack* of Morpheus's claws as he came to greet him, tail wagging. Morpheus was an enormous shaggy black mutt, and he had been Ben's constant companion his entire life. Just a few years ago, he would tear along next to Ben while Ben rode his bike, but the dog seemed to have gotten old all at once last year. Now he was bothered by arthritis, and he couldn't see well. He spent most of his time sleeping, but he still loved to walk around the block—slowly—with Ben.

Ben's seven-year-old brother, Leo, was at the kitchen table doing his homework and eating M&M's by the fistful out of an enormous bag. Ben and Leo were both named after inventors—Benjamin Franklin and Leonardo da Vinci, respectively. Leo was an elfin, golden-haired boy whom teachers and other adults tended to fawn over.

"How come you're so late?" Leo asked. "I had to make my own snack!"

He shook the bag of M&M's forlornly, like he'd had no choice but to break out the candy. His friend Christina's dad always picked him up from school and dropped him off at home.

"I had a school project," said Ben.

Their mother's voice came from the basement: "Ben? Is that you?"

"Yes. Hi, Mom!"

"Put down your backpack! Put it down!"

Lily Quist clomped up the stairs and appeared in the doorway wearing their father's pajamas, her blond ponytail askew, a big streak of grease and a lunatic grin on her face. This was exactly why he didn't like to invite people over—except Ashok, who understood how weird his family was.

He put down his backpack. His mother had a black ball, the size of an egg but perfectly round, in the palm of her hand. She whistled once, and a lens like a tiny eye popped out of it. A blue beam of light fastened on Ben's backpack, swiveled around the room, fixed on the backpack again, and then flashed. His mother giggled and tossed the ball in the air. The lens clicked down inside it again, and eight little legs popped out of the ball as it landed. It looked like a robot tarantula as it zipped over to Ben's backpack, grasped the strap with its two front legs, and started to tug. Morpheus whined and backed out of the room in a hurry, his tail between his legs.

"Hmm. Too heavy," said his mother. "What do you have in that bag, bricks?"

"Books, Mom," he said. "For school, where I go all day? What *is* that thing?"

"The Fetcher!" yelled Leo, who was still wildly enthusiastic about every new gadget their mother built. "Can I show him, Mom?"

"Go for it."

Lily whistled again. The Fetcher's legs shot back into its body, and it rolled over to her. It was sort of cute, Ben thought. Creepy-cute.

"So, what you do is, you point the beam at the thing you want it to fetch, and then it goes and fetches it for you," explained Leo, sliding off his chair and picking up the Fetcher. "Like if I want an apple, I can point it at one of the apples."

Leo held the Fetcher in his palm and whistled. The lens sprang out, and the blue beam emanated. Leo pointed the beam at an apple in the fruit bowl on the kitchen island. The lens swiveled and then fastened on the apple again, the beam flashed once, and Leo dropped the Fetcher. Its legs shot out of its body as it landed, and it ran straight into the bottom of the kitchen island with a metallic *thunk*.

"Oops," said Leo.

A thin cable shot out of the Fetcher's round body and suctioned on to the bottom of the countertop, hauling the Fetcher upward. The Fetcher flipped onto the kitchen island, detaching the cable and swallowing it up again, rolled up to the fruit bowl, rolled around it, popped out its legs, jumped on top of the fruit bowl, and speared the apple with a little metal prong that shot out of its side. Then it just sat there with the gored apple, as if it was exhausted.

Both his mom and Leo turned delighted smiles toward Ben. "Wow," he said, trying to look enthusiastic. "That's . . . so cool!"

It *was* cool. Everything his mom made was cool. It was just that none of it exactly worked the way it was supposed to, and he couldn't understand how the things she built were useful. When he was Leo's age, Ben loved to tell people that his mom was an inventor. He'd stopped telling people, though, because it was hard to answer the question "So, what has she invented?"

Before Leo was born, their mom had made a lot of money selling the patent for a voice-activated back scratcher. The company that tried to market it was sued when one of the back scratchers malfunctioned and scratched up all the walls in the buyer's home. She hadn't sold anything since then.

"It didn't actually *fetch* the apple, though," said Ben. "It just kind of . . . stabbed it."

"It's a work in progress!" said his mom cheerfully. "We're halfway there!"

The Fetcher pulled its little spear out of the apple and rolled back onto the counter with a weary thud.

"Anything fun happen today?" asked his mom, but he could tell she wasn't actually going to listen to his answer. She picked up the Fetcher and whistled sharply three times. A panel flipped up so she could tinker inside it.

"Nope," he said. "No fun at all."

Looking at her with the Fetcher, Ben suddenly felt a flood of relief: Ms. Kennedy's watch must be a robot watch! It was strange, yes, but nowhere near as strange as the alternatives. It was exactly the kind of senseless thing his mom would design—a watch that could crawl around on its own. Its programming must have malfunctioned. He felt a weight lift, and he was able at last to put the unsettling question of the crawling watch out of his mind.

Ben's phone pinged in his pocket. He knew without checking that it would be Ashok. It was late in Paris, but Ashok often stayed up with his e-reader under the covers and sometimes sent Ben photos of places he'd been during the day. His mood lightening even more, Ben took his phone to his room.

✱

Ashok: Check this picture out! Totally famous bookstore called Shakespeare and Company. All these really famous writers used to come here. It's like a maze of books inside. My dad took me after school.

Ben: Nice. I just had to interview a weird old lady for a boring project.

Ashok: The town history project you told me about? I'm so glad I'm missing that!

Ben: Yeah, you're lucky.

Ashok: Who's your partner?

Ben: . . . Malcolm Church.

Ashok: If he ever invites you over, say no. His older brother is a total psycho. I went to his house one time in 4th grade, and his brother tried to get us to drink bleach.

Ben: I remember that! I don't know how Malcolm even lived to be 11 with that guy as his brother.

Ashok: Seriously.

Ben: I wish you were still here.

Ashok: Me too. I mean, Paris is awesome, but I wish we could hang out. We'd have so much fun if you were here too.

Ben: Yeah.

Ashok: I'm going to sleep. Say hi to Leo and Morpheus.

Ben: OK. Text me tomorrow!

TUESDAY, SEPTEMBER 25

THE BOOK
OF KEYS

6

"Ben. I accidentally blew up my oatmeal again!"

Ben opened his eyes. Leo was bending over him, breathing in his face. Morpheus's tail thumped twice, and he wriggled up the bed to lick Ben's chin. The old dog usually slept at the foot of the bed, and he didn't get up until Ben did, but at the first sign that Ben was awake, Morpheus was always overcome with excitement, squirming like a puppy.

Ben dragged himself out from under the tangle of his bedcovers and helped Morpheus off the bed—his arthritic hips meant he couldn't easily jump on or off the bed by himself anymore.

"Sorry!" whispered Leo. "I tried to tell Mom and Dad, but . . ."

"I know," groaned Ben. "It's fine."

The three of them went down the hall to the kitchen together. Their dad was dressed in his embarrassing spandex cycling gear. His office at the university was a short bike ride away, but he dressed for it like he was competing in the Tour de France. He was putting chicken and some mysterious jars of things in the slow cooker—which meant they would have an actual dinner of sorts tonight—and talking loudly about a rival scholar who was completely wrong about something that had (or hadn't?) happened in Greece thousands of years ago between two philosophers who definitely did (or didn't?) exist. Aaron Harp was a professor of Greek classics at Livingston University. Their mom was sitting on one of the high stools at the kitchen island, totally wrapped up in whatever he was saying, stirring her coffee mechanically as it cooled. Lily Quist certainly poured a lot of coffee, but in his eleven years of life Ben had never seen her actually drink any of it.

Leo had tried to microwave oatmeal for himself, but he'd forgotten to cover it, and it had exploded all over the inside of the microwave. Ben wiped it up and fixed Leo another bowl while Morpheus waited patiently by the back door. He really *did* understand why Leo had woken him up. It was basically impossible to interrupt their parents when they were talking. They just tuned out the rest of the world. When he was in a good mood, Ben liked how much they liked each other, but other times he felt as if they liked each other so much they forgot that other people existed—their kids included. They sometimes told a story—which they found hilarious—about going out for dinner in winter when Ben was a baby. They had bundled him up in his snowsuit and then forgotten him on the living room floor. They went to dinner, realized halfway through that they'd forgotten him, came rushing home, and there he was, asleep on the floor in his snowsuit, with Morpheus sitting next to him. They laughed like crazy when they told this story, and his mother would say, "We were *so* sleep-deprived," but Ben thought that was a lousy excuse. He didn't think there was anything funny about being left behind in a snowsuit as a baby. Mostly, the story made him grateful to Morpheus—the only one he could really count on.

✳

After dropping Leo off at the elementary school, Ben cycled fast down the hill to the middle school and locked his bike up outside just as the starting bell rang. He sprinted inside and slid into his seat as the last resonance from the bell was fading away. Ms. Kennedy was standing in front of the class, arms folded over her pilly cardigan. The principal, Mr. Susskind, was next to her.

"Class, I've asked Mr. Susskind to come and talk to you about *honesty* and about *personal property*," she said between gritted, coffee-stained teeth.

Ben glanced over his shoulder at Akemi. She waved with her fingers and shrugged.

"Ha-ha-ha, yes, that's right," said Mr. Susskind, his chest puffed out. "Honesty—very important! And . . . moreover . . . respect! Respect for the property of *others*. Now, ahem, Ms. Kennedy's clock has gone missing, boys and girls. . . ."

"My *watch*," she snarled.

"Ab-so-lu-te-ly, her *watch*, ha-ha-ha. Does anybody have an idea of what might have happened to Ms. Kennedy's *watch*?" He held up one long finger. "Honesty!" he repeated. "And *respect*!"

Ben and Ashok were only half joking when they theorized that Mr. Susskind was an alien. He seriously gave Ben the creeps. He strutted around the school in a perfectly pressed suit, chest sticking out, bald head shining, with this rigid, too-wide grin on his face that never reached his eyes. When he talked, he inserted a totally humorless laugh—*ha-ha-ha*—at random, inappropriate moments, and sometimes he paused before responding to something, his eyes unfocused and a blank look on his face, like he was beaming the message back to the mother ship and waiting for instructions on how to proceed.

Ben looked at frumpy, furious Ms. Kennedy, who came up to the principal's shoulder, and at bulky, grinning Mr. Susskind, and tried to imagine what they had been like in sixth grade.

It was impossible.

"My watch was *on my desk,*" said Ms. Kennedy. "And now it is *gone.* Somebody in this class knows what happened!"

Mr. Susskind looked skeptically at the chaos of Ms. Kennedy's desk.

Ben really wished somebody else had seen the watch and that somebody else would say, *This is going to sound crazy . . . but I think that watch is a robot watch and just crawled off and went to the library.*

Nobody said anything.

"Well!" Mr. Susskind grinned toothily. "I know you'll all keep your eyes *peeled.*"

He said it like he was relishing the idea of peeled eyeballs. Ben wished for the millionth, billionth time that Ashok were here, so they could exchange *a look*. Then Jessica Masterson screamed.

Mr. Susskind startled—an exaggerated, seconds-late startle—and Ms. Kennedy went "*Shh!*" so loud that spit flew out of her mouth.

"*Rat!*" shrieked Jessica Masterson, pointing at Akemi. "In. Her. *Pocket*."

Akemi froze. She was wearing a sweatshirt with a zippered pouch in the front. It was partly unzipped, and a little gray head was peeking out, its agile nose sniffing at the air.

Akemi gently pushed the head down and zipped her sweatshirt shut, but Ms. Kennedy was already in front of her desk.

"I saw it!" hollered Jessica Masterson. "I feel like I'm going to throw up. She has a *rat* in her *pocket*! That is *so gross!*"

"*Miss* Hanamura, do you have a *rat* in your *pocket* in my *classroom*?" Ms. Kennedy's purpling cheeks trembled, like her face might actually be about to explode.

"Sorry," said Akemi in a small voice. "It's my pet."

Ms. Kennedy swiveled to give Mr. Susskind a bug-eyed *You deal with this* sort of look.

"You'd better come along to my office with your, ahem, *pet*, Miss Hanamura," he said. "Unhygienic. Ha-ha-ha."

Akemi followed the principal out, her face a mask of misery. Jessica Masterson had a satisfied smile on her face.

"I *mean*," said Ms. Kennedy, looking out over the class as if they might all be secretly harboring rodents in their clothing. "A *rat*! What is the *matter* with you people?"

7

At library hour, Akemi looked like she'd been crying. Ben sat down with her and Charlotte at one of the tables, but before he could ask her what had happened, Ms. Pryce came over and asked them if they'd chosen a monument or building to research.

"Not yet," said Ben.

"But we started the interview part," said Charlotte. "We went to see Agatha Bent yesterday."

"You went to her *house*?" asked Ms. Pryce, after a brief, shocked pause.

They nodded.

Ms. Pryce looked so appalled that Ben's stomach turned over. It took her a moment to find her voice again.

"Didn't you *listen* to what I said yesterday? Didn't you read the instructions? You were supposed to call her and set up a meeting in a public space, and tell *me* when and where. How did you get her address?"

"Oh," said Ben. "Oops. Um, we looked it up. I thought

it was kind of weird, going to a stranger's house. I mean, afterward I thought of that."

"I wish you had thought of it beforehand," said Ms. Pryce. "If you had read the instructions . . ."

Charlotte had a funny look on her face, and Ben had a feeling that maybe she *had* read the instructions but hadn't bothered to say anything.

"Well . . . How did she seem?" asked Ms. Pryce, in a slightly calmer voice.

How to describe Agatha Bent?

"There's this young guy—a nurse, I guess—who takes care of her," said Akemi. Her voice sounded soggy and muted.

"And her dog pees everywhere," added Charlotte.

"But she was conversational? Mobile?" asked Ms. Pryce. "She was the victim of a hit-and-run accident recently. I wondered whether I should still include her. . . ."

"She seemed okay," said Ben. "She has a wheelchair, but she was definitely, uh, conversational."

Ms. Pryce looked as if she was going to say more, but then something caught her eye. She turned away from them abruptly and strode off between the stacks.

"What happened with your rat?" whispered Ben.

"He's in a box in the principal's office," said Akemi. Her voice shook a little, and she blinked away tears. "I tried to tell Mr. Susskind that he can chew his way out of a cardboard box and that I should just take him home if I wasn't allowed to keep him with me, but he said I couldn't leave school. Now I'm scared he's going to get lost."

"Why *did* you bring a rat to school?" Charlotte asked, not bothering to lower her voice.

Akemi shrugged miserably. Ben thought he understood. If he could get away with having Morpheus with him at school—if Morpheus could fit in his pocket!—he would absolutely bring him. Charlotte Moss might be used to being friendless, but it was a new experience for him and for Akemi.

Ms. Pryce came dashing back out of the stacks with something wriggling in her hand. She ducked behind her desk. Ben saw her other hand reach up to grab a bottle of water sitting there. He frowned and looked around, but nobody else seemed to be paying attention. When she stood up, she was closing her purse, and her hands and sleeves were wet.

"Class, I need to put something in my car," she said, as unflappable as ever. "Please stay right where you are, working on your projects."

She strode out of the library, clutching her purse in both hands.

With a strange feeling in the pit of his stomach, Ben went to the window that overlooked the parking lot.

"What are you doing?" asked Akemi, following him.

"What is *she* doing?" he said. He could have sworn it was the strap of a watch wriggling in the librarian's hand.

He watched her trot briskly across the parking lot, unlock her car, and put something in the glove compartment.

She locked the car door and glared up at them in the window. They ducked out of sight and hurried back to their table.

8

Ben and Charlotte did their homework in the library after school while Akemi had basketball practice. Charlotte finished everything well before Ben did, and then began writing columns of numbers and letters very fast. He didn't ask her what she was doing. At three-forty-five, she slammed her notebook shut, and they went to meet Akemi outside Mr. Susskind's office. She came out beaming and relieved.

"He's so good," she said, a little tearful. "He stayed right in the box. He was probably scared out of his mind."

Outside, the clouds were low, threatening rain, and wind was gusting in the treetops. Akemi unzipped the pouch of her sweatshirt, and immediately the little gray face peeked out again, nose twitching at the air. Ben often wondered what it would be like to be a dog, the world a symphony of smells more than sights. It looked like rats took in the world through their noses too.

"This is Larry," she said. "He doesn't want to come out. He's too nervous."

"You named your rat *Larry?*" said Ben.

"I have three of them," she said. "Larry, Curly, and Moe."

He raised his eyebrows at her.

"My best friend in Boston is *obsessed* with the Three Stooges. She basically begged me to do it," laughed Akemi. "They're all boys, obviously—otherwise, I would have, like, a hundred rats by now. That happened to my friend who got two gerbils. The guy at the pet store *promised* they were both girls, but actually they weren't, because a few weeks later there were eight little pink babies in the cage! They tried to separate the boys and the girls, but it's pretty hard to tell with baby gerbils, and so a couple of months later they had . . . I don't know, I think it was close to thirty gerbils in total. Every single kid in my class got a pet gerbil that year. Rats are *way* smarter and friendlier than gerbils, though."

She was grinning as she told the story, but then she broke off suddenly and covered Larry the rat with one hand. Jessica Masterson, Audrey Banks, and Briony Moore had just come out of the school.

"What kind of freak brings a disgusting *rat* to school?" said Jessica Masterson loudly as they crossed the parking lot. She tossed her long dark hair.

Jessica's mom was an actress starring in a long-running TV soap opera in Argentina. She'd gone back to Argentina when Jessica was still a baby, leaving her father heartbroken, according to Ashok's parents, who gossiped about this sort of thing over dinner. Jessica's dad had left LA, moved back to his hometown of Livingston with baby Jessica, and married a towering blond ER doctor when Jessica was in preschool. Jessica looked exactly like a miniature version of her glamorous mother, whom she visited during school holidays, returning with cases full of fashionable clothes.

"I should bring my cat, Estrella, to meet *your* pet sometime," she added over her shoulder, looking right at Akemi.

Akemi looked stonily at a point somewhere over Jessica Masterson's head and said nothing.

"She is *so creepy*," Jessica said to her friends as they walked on, laughing.

"I can't believe she hates me just because I'm better than her at basketball," said Akemi in a low voice. "Why does everybody here worship her, anyway?"

"I don't know," said Ben uncomfortably. "I mean, not everybody worships her."

The weird and slightly complicated thing for Ben was that he and Jessica had been best friends when they were little. They'd gone to the same day care and preschool. He used to go to her house all the time, where her nanny would make them amazing snacks and they could run up and down the long, beautiful halls or play on the enormous playset in her backyard. He even remembered Estrella—not the kind of cat you'd really expect Jessica Masterson to have. She was a huge, wild-eyed, snaggletoothed creature, possibly the ugliest cat he'd ever seen, and Jessica adored her. She used to dote on Morpheus too, and they'd play with him in Ben's backyard, when he was too little to be ashamed of his parents or the untidy house.

Jessica and Ben had entered their first day of kindergarten holding hands tightly for courage. All year, they sat next to each other and shared their lunches and played super-powered hamsters at recess. In first grade, he made friends with Ashok, and she started playing with Briony and Audrey. By second grade, she never even looked at him anymore. For the last few years, she had basically acted like he didn't exist.

"So, we're going to Agatha's house again, right?" said Charlotte Moss.

"Ms. Pryce wasn't happy about us going to her *house*," said Ben.

"But if she's recovering from a hit-and-run accident and using a wheelchair, we don't want to make her go anywhere, and if they wanted to ax-murder us, they would have done it last time, so I think it's safe to say they aren't psychos," said Akemi. "We should just go to her house, like she said, and finish up. We could see her photo albums today."

"I wouldn't bring Larry," said Ben. "Poubelle doesn't seem like she would be rat-friendly."

"I'll drop him off first," said Akemi.

They lingered a bit longer at the edge of the parking lot, without needing to agree out loud that they didn't want to catch up to Jessica Masterson and her friends.

"How is it at basketball practice, anyway?" Ben asked.

"They all hate me," she said flatly. "I'm supposed to be the captain, but they act like I'm not even there, and nobody passes to me unless Ms. Pond makes them."

"Maybe you should just quit," suggested Charlotte. That was what Ben had been thinking too, but he was glad it was Charlotte who'd said it and not him, because Akemi rounded on her, furious.

"I'm *good* at basketball! I made captain because I'm the best one! Why should *I* quit because *they're* being jerks?"

Charlotte shrugged, unfazed. "I'd quit if it meant they'd leave me alone," she replied. "Jessica Masterson can seriously ruin your life."

Akemi rolled her eyes. "She can't ruin my *life*," she said. "That's stupid."

"You don't know Jessica Masterson," said Charlotte rice-puddingly.

They heard a short, sharp curse word, and they all jumped.

Ms. Pryce was standing next to her car, one hand raised to her mouth, like she could put the word she'd said back inside. There was a hole a few inches wide right through the passenger door.

9

"Is everything okay, Ms. Pryce?" called Akemi.

Ms. Pryce spun around. She had her red raincoat over one arm and her car keys clenched in her other hand.

"Yes, fine," she said. She began walking up and down the parking lot, peering under cars.

The watch, thought Ben wildly. *She's looking for the watch.*

He found his voice, and trotted after the librarian. "Can we help?" he asked.

"No," she said curtly. "Thank you, Ben. You'd better get home."

She walked away from him fast, looking under every car.

"What is she *doing?*" whispered Akemi, joining him.

He wanted so badly to tell them what he'd seen, but he couldn't think of a way to say it that didn't sound like he was either a liar or out of his mind. Charlotte surprised him, though.

"In the library this afternoon, right before she said she had to put something in her car, I saw her jump on something, grab it, pour water on it, and stuff it in her purse," she said calmly.

"But what was it?" said Akemi, open-mouthed.

"I'm pretty sure it was Ms. Kennedy's watch," said Charlotte, and Ben felt relief wash through him. He wasn't the only one who'd seen it!

Akemi started to laugh, turning toward Ben, and then stopped when she saw his expression.

"I saw it too," he said. "It was crawling on the floor outside the library yesterday. By itself."

"You guys . . . are *messing* with me!" Akemi's eyes went wide with outrage.

Ben shook his head. "I thought I was imagining it," he said. "But I think it must be a robot watch or something."

Charlotte looked thoughtful.

"Admit it, you're lying!" said Akemi.

He shook his head.

"Oh, whatever! I do *not* believe you."

"What do you think made that hole in her car door, then?" said Charlotte.

"I don't know!" said Akemi. "Not a *watch*! Maybe she has a pet. Rats can chew through almost anything, you know."

"Not car doors," said Charlotte.

"Probably not," admitted Akemi. "Not that fast, at least. But there's no such thing as robot watches."

"My mom is an inventor," said Ben. "She makes weird stuff like that all the time."

That made Akemi pause. "What kind of stuff does she invent?"

"Stuff that's cool but that nobody actually needs," he said, thinking of the Fetcher. "She could definitely make a crawling watch."

"Wow." Akemi looked impressed. "Okay. But even if Ms. Kennedy had a robot watch, wouldn't she *know* it could crawl off? And why would Ms. Pryce pour *water* on it and put it in her car? And how would it make a hole in the door and escape?"

"I have no idea," admitted Ben.

They watched Ms. Pryce finish her hurried circuit of the

parking lot. She stood next to her car for a long time, then got in and drove away. The lump in Akemi's sweatshirt was wriggling now.

"Come on," she said, though she sounded annoyed with both of them. She probably still thought they were messing with her. "I have to take Larry home."

10

Ben left his bike locked up at school, and they walked to Akemi's place—a condo near the highway. She took off the key that she wore around her neck and let them in.

"My dad won't be home till later," she said.

The apartment was barely furnished. There was nothing on the walls. It looked like it was still waiting for somebody to move in. Akemi took them straight to her bedroom, which at least looked like a proper lived-in room, with pictures of friends pinned to a big corkboard, stuffed animals, and clothes and books strewn about. Charlotte examined the photographs on the corkboard. One corner of the room was taken up entirely by an enormous cage that was taller than Ben, with multiple levels covered in fleece, little wooden hidey-huts in the corners, and chew toys everywhere. Akemi opened the doors, and two more rats—one dark gray with white feet and one white with gray markings—came rushing out and onto her arms and shoulders.

"Hi, Curly! Hi, Moe!" Akemi made kissing faces, and the rats went up on their hind legs to lick her cheeks. She unzipped her sweatshirt, and Larry scrambled up onto her shoulder and down her arm into the cage. He ran around the cage sniffing everything, up and down the ramps, as if to make sure it was all still there, and then climbed into a fleece hammock hanging from the ceiling. The other two chased him and sniffed him all over.

"Tell them all about your day, Larry!" said Akemi cheerfully, closing the cage doors.

In the kitchen, Akemi emptied a bag of caramel popcorn into a bowl. They ate standing at the kitchen counter, since there were only two chairs.

"Does your mom work at the university too?" asked Ben finally.

"She died," said Akemi, too fast, like she'd been expecting the question and wanted to get the answer out of the way. "Almost a year ago."

Ben had no idea what to say. "Oh," he whispered. "Wow."

That was definitely the wrong thing to say. You didn't say *Wow* about somebody's mother dying. He stared at the bowl of caramel popcorn.

"So that's why my dad wanted to move," said Akemi, still talking fast. "He didn't want to be in places that reminded him of her. Plus, it's cheaper here. She was sick for a long time."

Charlotte didn't say anything. She just kept shoveling fist-ful after fistful of caramel popcorn in her mouth, her eyes fixed on Akemi's face. The crunching made Ben want to scream at her. He found his tongue.

"That's too bad," he said. "I mean, that's really sad."

"Yeah." Akemi nodded, and whisked the bowl away. "Let's go."

The awkwardness faded once they were outside again. It was starting to spit rain, and they ran most of the way to Agatha Bent's house, Akemi and Ben racing to the end of each block and then waiting for Charlotte to catch up, her face placid and inscrutable. By the time they arrived, it was raining in earnest. A package was lying next to the porch, getting wet. Probably the mail carrier had tossed it at the steps and missed. Ben picked it up.

"I wonder where those stamps are from," said Charlotte, peering at the package over his shoulder.

"*Hi-i-i!*" said Simon-the-carer, swinging the door open and flashing his camera-ready grin at them all. "Come on *in*, you guys!"

11

They followed Simon into the living room. Agatha Bent was in the same chair, Poubelle in her lap. Poubelle lifted her head and growled, but it was mostly drowned out by Agatha hooting, "How lovely to see you all again! Ben, Akemi, Charlotte—have I got your names right?"

Ben was pretty impressed that she had.

"I'll get a snack for you kids," said Simon, winking at Charlotte, who stared at him blankly.

"No thanks!" Akemi exclaimed. "Please, no snacks, thanks!"

But Simon had already sailed out.

"We brought in your mail," said Ben, handing Agatha Bent the damp package.

Her eyes widened, and one hand flew to her heart as she took the package from him. She started to tuck it under one of the blankets draped over her, but Simon had soundlessly reappeared at her side.

"I'll put that on your desk," he said.

"It's quite all right, Simon," she said, hanging on to it. For a moment, they seemed to be engaged in a wordless tug-of-war over the package; then he pulled it out of her grasp and glided back out of the room while Poubelle bayed noisily.

Ben and Akemi exchanged a confused look.

"I don't suppose any of you children know Morse code," Agatha whispered.

"I do," said Akemi brightly. "My best friend in Boston . . ."

She stopped. Agatha Bent was tapping in a funny rhythm with one lacquered fingernail on the arm of her chair, nearly drowned out by Poubelle's indignant racket.

"My old photo albums are right there," she said, in a false,

45

fluting voice, pointing at a stack of albums on the sofa with her other hand. "Do have a look!"

Charlotte opened the big album on top. There were faded pictures of two girls in frilly dresses sitting on a wide porch, and one of a man in glasses standing next to his bicycle.

"What do you think of *that?*" trilled Agatha Bent, one beady eye fixed on Akemi, who was staring at her tapping finger with intense concentration.

"Snacks!" said Simon, reappearing again with a tray, which he put down precariously on the small folding table next to Agatha's chair. Poubelle snapped at his hand.

"Bad dog," he said.

Agatha Bent had stopped tapping. "Simon," she said. "Aren't there more photo albums in my room, on the big bookshelf? Be a love and get them for me?"

He gave her a shrewd look, nodded, and headed upstairs.

Poubelle fell silent, and Agatha's finger started tapping again, faster.

"Ben," murmured Akemi. "Go and distract Simon, okay?"

"*What?*" he said. "What do you mean, *distract* him?"

"I don't know. Just . . . do it."

Baffled, he walked into the front hall. He saw a black bag by the door, and the package he'd brought in sticking out of the bag, the top of it torn open and folded over. Simon was already coming down the stairs with a stack of photo albums in his arms.

"She says there's one more," said Ben, panicking. "With . . . a green cover. She asked me to help you find it."

"I don't think there's one with a green cover," said Simon. He looked a little miffed, but he turned and went back up the stairs, past some kind of electric lift attached to the railing that Ben assumed was for Agatha to get up and down the stairs—an actually *useful* invention. Ben followed him into Agatha Bent's south-facing study. It was lined with books. The window by her desk had a view over the town. You could see the university clock tower from here, the one that appeared on all the postcards.

"Wow," he said. "Nice room."

"Pretty sure I got *all-l-l-l* the albums," said Simon, scanning the bookshelves. "It's nice of you guys to come over and talk to her. I think she gets lonely with just boring old me for company."

"Well, it's homework," said Ben, and then he thought that sounded churlish. "She's . . . interesting."

"Yeah, her family has been in Livingston for generations. Really fascinating," said Simon. "She's a nice lady, but she needs to train that dog." He looked around the room once more. "Do *you* see a photo album with a green cover?"

Ben shook his head.

"O-*kay!*" said Simon. Ben went out of the room ahead of him. Well, he'd distracted him, hadn't he? When he reached the top of the stairs, he saw Akemi kneeling next to the black

47

bag and pulling out the package. He whirled back to stop Simon from rounding the corner and seeing the same thing.

"Wait! I . . . uh . . . I really need to use the bathroom!" he said.

"It's right over here," said Simon, leading him back along the hall and opening the door for him. "Just come on down when you're done."

Ben shut himself in the bathroom and stared out the window at the old heritage house, his heart pounding. What the heck was Akemi *doing?* After an acceptable amount of time, he flushed the toilet, washed his hands, and went back downstairs.

Akemi already had her jacket and backpack on.

"We have to go!" she said, unnaturally cheery. "Come on, guys."

"Come back soon!" trilled Agatha Bent.

Simon waved them off at the door again. It had already stopped raining. As soon as they rounded the corner, Ben said, "What was *that* all about?"

Akemi's face was shining. She looked caught somewhere between elation and terror. "She wanted me to take the package," she said.

"*Why?*" asked Ben.

Akemi shrugged. "No idea. She was tapping in Morse code. She tapped 'Distract Simon. Take package.' Isn't that crazy?"

"But why would you *do* it?" said Ben. "It's stealing her mail!"

"Not if she told me to do it," said Akemi indignantly. "It

seemed like *he* wanted to steal her mail and she didn't want him to have it. He put it in his bag, when he told her he was going to put it on her desk, and he'd *opened* it!"

"Maybe he was going to take it up later," said Charlotte, looking at her watch.

"Or maybe you got the code wrong!" said Ben. "I mean, now what are you going to do with it?"

"I don't know. If we go back tomorrow, I can ask her. In Morse code! I mean, come on, that was *so cool!*"

Charlotte plunked herself down at the bus stop on Finch, her face going pudding-blank again. She got out her giant barrettes with the white bows and started pinning her hair back.

"So . . . where *do* you live now?" Ben asked her, puzzled.

"Pennington," she answered, not looking at him.

"Oh." Pennington was the next town over. "Why do you still go to school here, though?"

"They didn't want me to have to change schools and make new friends."

She said "friends" with a little acid bite Ben had never heard from her before.

"Who is 'they'?" asked Akemi. "Your parents?"

"My bus is coming." Charlotte sounded relieved, like she didn't want to talk about it. She looked at her watch again, and muttered, "I'm so late. They're going to be mad."

Akemi walked with Ben back to the school to get his bike. This time, when they reached his house, he invited Akemi inside.

12

They sat cross-legged on the floor of his bedroom and stared at the package. Agatha Bent's name and address were written in a slanted hand with blue ink. The package had been ripped open and then folded shut again. Akemi was fiddling with the torn, folded end of it. Morpheus lay at Ben's side, tail thumping on the carpet, nosing at Ben's hand whenever Ben stopped patting him.

"It could be something important," said Akemi.

"Or she could be senile and we shouldn't be stealing her mail," Ben pointed out.

"I mean, it's already been *opened*," she said. "If we just look at what's inside . . ."

Ben opened his mouth to tell her no, then closed it again. He was curious too.

"Brazil," he said, looking at the stamps.

Akemi hesitated a second more, and when he didn't say anything, she reached into the package.

There were two things inside it. One was a slim book with a worn navy cover. The other, wrapped in a cloth, was a copper wheel attached to a small wooden base, which fit easily in

Akemi's palm. The wheel looked like a toy ship's wheel, with an arrow at the top. She turned the wheel with a finger, and it clicked as it moved. There were tiny markings all around the wheel, and when Ben looked more closely, he saw they were Roman numerals, going all the way up to one hundred. Letters along the bottom of the base spelled out *vocorotam*.

Ben opened the book carefully. It looked very old. The pages were soft, covered with faded handwriting. A loose page fell out of the book—this one covered with the same thick, slanted writing as on the package. Ben unfolded it.

"What does it say?" asked Akemi, still spinning the clicking wheel.

Ben read it aloud to her:

Dear Aunt Agatha,

As you can see, you were right! Peter Gael—or somebody else—did make a copy of The Book of Keys. *It was harder to find than I'd expected. When your cousin in Rio de Janeiro died, her stupid children sold almost everything, but I finally tracked it down at a rare-book dealer's! They thought it was some kind of obscure, avant-garde poetry.*

I know you'll think it reckless of me, trusting the only remaining Book of Keys *to the mail system, especially as I've already sent the directions. I meant to bring the book back in person, but now I'm sure that I am being followed, and I believe the book is*

*safest off my person as soon as possible. I'll give them
the slip before taking this to the post office.*

*I've been able to confirm what we suspected:
Sabrin escaped a few months ago from the supposedly
impenetrable prison designed for him in the Aleutian
Islands. The top brass at the Gateway Society have
been keeping it very hush-hush as they try to track
him down. We are in more danger than we
thought.*

*I send you this only for safekeeping until I get
back, along with a vocoro, which your cousin's eldest
son still had in his possession, not knowing what it
was. I hope you have hidden the directions well. We
are being watched, Agatha—do not doubt it!*

*May the seal remain ever closed and all the
Sneaks on the other side of it.*

*Love, as always,
Colin*

Ben and Akemi stared at each other. Then Akemi let out a
shriek of delight, and said, "She's a *spy*! Or her nephew is? This
is amazing! We have to hide this stuff and find out what she
wants us to do with it."

"It does kind of seem like that, doesn't it?" he said, trying to
make his voice sound normal.

"*Seem* like it? Ben—impenetrable island prisons and people

being followed and some secret society! What is this book, anyway? *The Book of Keys.* It looks old."

She took it from him and opened it to the first page.

"Look at this," she said.

He read over her shoulder.

> *The Mouth of the Seal*
> *Is Molded to Hold*
> *The Blood of the Young*
> *The Flesh of the Old*
> *The Breath of the Servant*
> *The Tears of the Bold.*
> *When All Four Be Swallowed*
> *Behold—Uncontrolled—*
> *Chaos Unfold.*

"Well, that's just creepy," said Akemi.

"Most of this makes no sense," she added, flipping through the rest of the book. She stopped at a page to read a bit. " 'A tearoom with high ceilings and gold wallpaper. Pour the jasmine tea into the silver bowl on table one for Constellations. Pour the mint tea into the silver bowl on table two for the Rose Garden. Pour the black tea into the silver bowl on table three for the Armory.' It just goes on and on like that." She flipped through some more pages. "Descriptions of . . . rooms, and stuff you do to get to other places."

"It's in code," said Ben. "It must be."

"You're right!" she said, looking up at him, her eyes shining.

"So what do we do?"

"Hide it," she said firmly. "And then we have to go back and talk to her. Figure out what she wants us to do with it."

Ben thought of Agatha Bent's lacquered nails and upswept hair, the snarling, pink-collared poodle on her lap.

"She doesn't seem like a spy, does she?" he said.

"Spies probably *shouldn't* seem like spies," said Akemi. "Tomorrow, let's make a plan, with Charlotte. We *have* to get to the bottom of this."

She grinned at him—a huge, happy grin—and it was impossible not to smile back.

✱

Ben: You are not going to believe what happened.

Ashok: ?

Ben: First of all, Ms. Kennedy has a robot watch that crawls around on its own. It went missing, and Ms. Pryce found it and put it in her car, and it tore a hole in the door and got out.

Ashok: Very funny.

Ben: I'm not joking! Also, we were interviewing that old lady for the Livingston history project and she basically told us to hide her mail from her nurse, so we took it home. I'm going to send you a picture of the letter inside.

Ashok: Ben. It's literally the middle of the night.

Ben: Oops. Sorry.

Ashok: Ben, this is Ashok's dad. Please remember the time difference.

Ben: Okay. Sorry!

TO CALL UPON
THE LOCKSMITH

13

In the lunch line, Ben thanked Mrs. Helios for his slice of warmish cheese pizza and grabbed a container of chocolate milk, then headed toward Ryan and Felix's table. They'd always been friendly, even though he didn't share their obsession with yōkai-sen cards. Malcolm Church and Jason Huang were sitting with them as well, because Malcolm had just got a new deck of cards and wanted to battle. Ben remembered with a twinge of shame that he'd lied to Ashok and said that Malcolm was his partner for the Livingston history project. He didn't really know why. It had just seemed too complicated to explain about Akemi.

"Ben!"

Akemi and Charlotte were at the next table, and Akemi was waving him over. He hesitated, briefly self-conscious, but then decided that, honestly, he'd rather sit with Akemi and Charlotte and talk about what they'd found yesterday than watch Ryan, Felix, and the others yōkai-sen dueling, like he did every lunch hour.

"I was just telling Charlotte about the book," said Akemi eagerly as he plunked his tray down. "Did you bring it?"

He nodded. "What are we going to say to Agatha?"

"First we need to distract Simon," said Akemi. "He was definitely trying to take the package away from her, and he opened it before putting it in his bag!"

"He's going to know you took it," said Charlotte.

"He can't prove it!" said Akemi. "The dog could have dragged it somewhere."

"He'll *know*," repeated Charlotte.

"Well, what is he going to say? 'Give back the package I was stealing?' We'll just play dumb if he mentions it."

Ben frowned. "Why would he want to steal her stuff anyway?"

"Who knows? That's what we need to find out!" said Akemi. "Here's the plan. We go there today. One of us distracts Simon, and then the other two tell Agatha that we have the book and that little wheel thingy, and we ask her what she wants us to do with them. What do you guys think?"

"Sounds good," said Ben, his nerves jangling in a not-unpleasant way. "How do we distract Simon?"

"I'll do it," said Charlotte. "I have a big scab on my elbow. If I pick at it, it'll bleed a lot. Then he'll have to get me a Band-Aid or something."

"Gross," said Akemi.

"Perfect," said Ben.

✱

Ben left his bike propped against the porch again. They knocked on the door for a long time before Simon opened it.

He looked a little ruffled, and stared at them for a moment like he didn't know who they were. Then he broke out the smile and the dimple and said, "It's the inimitable Charlotte and her crew!"

Charlotte gaped at him, stunned. Ben was waiting for him to invite them in, except he didn't.

"We came to ask Agatha a couple more questions," said Akemi.

"Yeah, she's . . ." Simon ran a hand through his hair. "Well, actually, she had a bad fall and had to go to the hospital."

"Is she going to be okay?" asked Ben. He knew falls could be serious for old people.

Simon winced. "I *hope* so, but she's not doing too great right now. She hit her head."

They stood there on the doorstep, shocked and uncertain.

"What about Poubelle?" asked Ben. He peered around Simon, into the hallway. There was stuff lying all over the stairs and on the landing at the top—clothes, papers, shoes, books, a camera. It was like a tornado had just gone through.

"I'm taking care of Poubelle until Agatha's better," said Simon. He was looking at them closely all of a sudden. Ben could have sworn he was looking at their backpacks.

"Okay, tell her we hope she gets better soon," said Akemi, backing down the steps. She tugged on the strap of Ben's backpack.

Charlotte was still staring up at Simon moonily.

"Do you have a Band-Aid?" she asked.

She held up her elbow, which was oozing blood. Something strange flickered across Simon's face. Ben assumed it was disgust at first, but it wasn't—not quite.

"We'll get you one at *home*, Charlotte," said Akemi urgently.

"Of course I've got one. Come on in," said Simon, opening the door wide. Charlotte stepped inside.

"*Charlotte!*" said Akemi.

"I need a Band-Aid," said Charlotte.

Akemi looked at Ben. He didn't know what to do, but he was terribly conscious of the book and the little wheel in his backpack.

"We'll wait out here," he said.

Simon's voice turned cool. "Okay. Be right back."

He closed the door. Akemi and Ben stared at each other.

"We shouldn't have let her go in there alone," whispered Akemi.

"I know," said Ben. "But what were we supposed to do? I'm going to look in the back windows."

"What? Why?" yelped Akemi.

"Did you see how messy it was? Something isn't right. If they aren't out in two minutes . . . maybe we should call the police or something."

Calling the police seemed ridiculously dramatic, but every warning signal in Ben's body was going off now. His skin was tingling, the hairs on his arms were standing on end, his blood was pounding through his veins. He crept around the side of the house and along the tangled bushes at the back, then peeked in the living room window. The room had been ransacked. The cushions on the sofa had been torn apart, their stuffing bursting out of them, the shelves emptied, the drawers pulled out of the chest and strewn on the floor, their contents spilled everywhere. Ben tiptoed farther along, to the kitchen window. The kitchen was a disaster too, every cupboard open, jars and cans and cutlery and smashed crockery scattered across the floors and counters, as if somebody had gone through the cupboards very quickly and angrily, pulling everything out with no concern about the mess.

There was no sign of Poubelle, either.

He suddenly had the distinct feeling that *he* was being watched, but when he looked around, all he could see were the boarded-up windows of the heritage house on the other side of the broken fence. He hurried around to the front of the house, arriving just as the door opened and Charlotte came out with a big Band-Aid on her elbow, and a look on her face that Ben couldn't interpret.

"Thanks for stopping by, you guys." Simon started down the steps toward them, then stopped. He glanced at the mail carrier across the street and the man mowing his front lawn two houses down. He seemed to be considering something. After a brief pause, during which Ben felt frozen with panic, Simon said cheerfully: "I'll let Agatha know you came. It'll mean a lot to her."

Ben grabbed his bike. As soon as they got around the corner, Akemi yelled at Charlotte: "Why did you go in there? He was acting weird!"

"I'd already picked the scab," Charlotte replied, unruffled. "I needed a Band-Aid. The place is really a mess."

"Did you see Poubelle upstairs?" asked Ben.

Charlotte shook her head.

"I think he tore the house apart looking for the package," said Ben. He couldn't quite believe it, and yet he couldn't think of any other explanation.

"He asked me about it," said Charlotte.

"What do you mean?" said Ben, horrified.

"He said Agatha was asking for the package in the hospital, but he couldn't find it. He asked if we'd seen it after bringing it in."

"What did you *say*?" asked Akemi.

"I said no, but he didn't look like he believed me."

"He must have thought we gave it to Agatha and she hid it," said Ben.

"What if she's really asking for it?" said Akemi.

"Maybe we can visit her in the hospital and find out," said Ben. "Let's ask Ms. Pryce tomorrow."

"Should we tell Ms. Pryce about all this?" asked Akemi in a small voice.

Ben wasn't sure how to answer. Maybe that was the right thing to do—tell a grown-up. It was easier to imagine telling Ms. Pryce than any other teacher, or his parents. She might actually take them seriously. Then again, she might take all this away from them, and it was too strange and thrilling to let go of just yet.

"Not yet," said Charlotte, as if echoing his own thoughts. "Let's wait."

"Wait for *what?*" said Akemi.

"Until we know what's going on," said Charlotte.

"Agreed," said Ben.

14

Ben and Akemi left Charlotte at the bus stop on Finch Street and went to Ben's house again. Leo and his best friend, Christina, were building a fort in the living room out of blankets and boxes. Morpheus was sitting glumly in the hall, his favorite couch having been co-opted to serve as one wall of the fort.

"Come on, Mo, we'll take you to the ravine," said Ben, fetching Morpheus's leash. The ravine, as they called it, was really just a meandering path, lined with trees, between two steep, scrubby slopes, but Morpheus loved to amble along it, sniffing at tree roots and barking noncommittally at squirrels he would once have chased.

As they walked, Ben and Akemi came up with every theory they could think of for what the little wheel could be: a gear in a top-secret machine, the controller for some kind of spy drone, a communication device, a family antique worth billions. They twisted it around and around, and it clicked gently, but nothing happened.

"It says 'vocorotam,'" said Akemi. "But in the letter from her nephew, he calls it a 'vocoro.' It must be the same thing, right?"

"I guess so," said Ben.

Ben's phone chirped. It was Ashok:

IS THIS REAL? Send me more!

Ben grinned. That morning, he'd sent a photograph of the letter from Agatha Bent's nephew, Colin, that they'd found in the book. He'd explained about her tapping in Morse code, and all the descriptions of rooms in the book, which must be another kind of code. Ashok was obsessed with codes.

They circled back to Ben's house, and Ben said goodbye to Akemi. Christina's dad was there to pick Christina up, trying to coax her out from under one of the boxes in the living room. Lily Quist stood next to him with her hands in her pockets and a fake smile stuck on her face. She was wearing normal pants, but her feet were bare, her toenails were painted metallic gold, and she had her sweater on backward.

Regular-looking-and-acting dad-of-Christina finally hauled his daughter, screaming and kicking, out from under the box, and thanked Lily for having her. Lily bobbed her head up and down energetically, her grin stretched to the breaking point. Ben's parents had no idea how to interact with people besides each other.

Ben went straight to his room to photograph pages from *The Book of Keys*, sending each one to Ashok. After the creepy poem about "the mouth of the seal," the whole book was just descriptions of rooms or sometimes outdoor spaces, with baffling instructions. The first page said, "A room that inspires peace and rest of the mind, with many of the classics available to read in comfortable chairs, and a chess set in the center. For the Glass Maze, white knight takes black pawn. For the Staging of *Antigone*, check with rook. For Coordinates, checkmate in one. For A Room with a View, black queen takes white knight," and so on. He photographed it and flipped to the next page.

"Museum Room, high windows, clay heads on stands. Roll the dice on the marble stand next to the bust of Cleopatra. Roll 1 for the Speaking Ducks. Roll 2 for the Enigma. Roll 3 for the Apothecary's Chamber." There were rolls up to twelve. The next page was possibly the weirdest. "The Speaking Ducks—a pond upon which twenty ducks make their home. For the Garden of Eden, answer the question the first duck asks of you. For the Portrait Gallery, reply to the second duck in Spanish. For the Wax Museum, answer the third duck backward."

Each place described in the book had at least twelve sets of instructions that led to another place in the book, and some of them had as many as twenty possible instructions. There were a hundred pages—or places described—in total. It would be possible, Ben thought, to map it out, but with thousands of possible routes, and to what end? What could it possibly mean? Morpheus sat next to him, his head heavy and warm, resting on Ben's thigh.

There was a tap on the door. Leo's tousled blond head peeked in.

"So is that girl, Akemi, your new friend?" he asked.

"Mm-hmm," said Ben, sending the picture of the Speaking Ducks page to Ashok. If anyone could break this code, it would be Ashok. Ashok was excellent at puzzles and codes.

"Angus Tubman told me that in middle school boys and girls don't really play together anymore," said Leo.

"What does Angus Tubman know about anything?" said Ben, turning the page and taking a picture of it.

"Yeah," said Leo, sounding relieved. "Because Christina is my best friend in the world. We won't just *stop* being friends in middle school. Except you used to be friends with Jessica, and she never comes over anymore."

"We stopped being friends way before middle school," said Ben. "Because she's a jerk."

"She was nice when we were little, though."

Ben was surprised that Leo even remembered; he was just a toddler when Jessica used to come around. It was true that Leo had loved Jessica, though. One of their favorite games back then was surgery-hamsters, where they pretended to operate on Leo, a baby hamster, while he lay very still, trying not to giggle. When Jessica was four years old, her cat, Estrella, had eaten her hamster, Gordie, and Jessica's way of grieving was basically to pretend to be a hamster every day—for *years*. Jessica was nothing if not committed.

He flipped another page and paused. This one was different from the others. There were no instructions. "A room with four pillars and a deep well, within which lies the seal over the gap." There was nothing else. The letter had mentioned a seal too, hadn't it? He snatched up the letter and looked at it. "May the seal remain ever closed and all the Sneaks on the other side of it." Whatever *that* meant. The creepy poem about chaos unfolding at the beginning of the book had started out mentioning the seal too—"The Mouth of the Seal / Is Molded to Hold / The Blood of the Young / The Flesh of the Old." So what *was* the seal?

"Why are you taking pictures of that book?" asked Leo.

"To show Ashok."

"Couldn't you just mail him a copy?"

"I don't think there is another copy."

"Oh. What is it?"

"Just a book I thought he'd like."

Leo watched him quietly for a minute longer and then said, "Can I have Morpheus in my room tonight?"

Ben looked up, surprised. Leo was leaning on the doorframe, chewing a fingernail.

"Why?"

"I have bad dreams sometimes."

For a moment, Ben wanted to say no way. Morpheus was *his* dog. He was the one who took care of him. And Morpheus *wanted* to sleep with Ben. But he looked at Leo's pale face and the hollows under his eyes and said, "Sure, yeah."

"Thanks." Leo sat down next to him, patting Morpheus. Morpheus's tail went *thump-thump* in acknowledgment. "At school, there's something I don't like," he said, picking at the carpet with one hand.

But Ben barely heard him. At the end of the book there were a few blank pages—he'd noticed that yesterday—but one of them *wasn't* blank, and what he saw there made him sit bolt upright. "Whoa!" he whispered.

No more descriptions of rooms. Here was an enlarged sketch of the little wheel surrounded by Roman numerals. Above it was written "The Vocoro," and underneath: "To call upon the Locksmith, XVI–LV–XI."

"What does that mean?" asked Leo, peering at the page.

"I don't know."

Ben could hardly breathe. He photographed the page and sent it to Ashok.

✳

Ben: Sorry about last night.

Ashok: I forgot to turn the volume on my phone off.
It's fine. I just blamed you.

Ben: Thanks a lot! Now your dad will hate me.

Ashok: No, he won't. My parents love you. But if he catches me texting late at night again, I'll be in so much trouble.

Ben: Sorry. So what do you think? Can you figure out the code?

Ashok: I'm not sure it's a code.

Ben: What else would it be? It's called *The Book of Keys,* but it's just descriptions of places and weird stuff you do to get to other places.

Ashok: It sounds like a video game. The most boring video game ever. Unlocking entrances, basically.

Ben: It looks really old. I'm sure it's not a video game.

Ashok: I know! I'm just saying that's what it reminds me of. Also, that wheel called the "vocoro" in the book? On the base, it says "vocorotam," right? I was googling and getting Latin, so I broke the word in parts. *Voco* is Latin for "call," and *rotam* is "wheel." So it's like a calling wheel, basically—they probably just call it "vocoro" for short. Did you try the numbers underneath the picture? What do you think a Locksmith is?

Ben: I don't know. I'm sort of scared to try it.

Ashok: No kidding. But this book is about opening something, and a Locksmith sounds like it would be someone or something that opens something too.

Ben: But opening what?

Ashok: Only one way to find out.

WHAT CAME DOWN FROM THE TREE

15

At lunchtime, Ben didn't even look at the table where Ryan and Felix were yōkai-sen dueling; he just sat down next to Akemi with his tray and got his phone out to show her and Charlotte the picture he'd taken of the page he'd found last night, with the drawing of the vocoro, the Roman numerals, and the phrase "To call upon the Locksmith."

"It looks like a combination lock," said Charlotte, examining the picture.

"That's it!" said Akemi. "It *is* like a lock! We should try it!"

"But what do you think it means, 'call upon the Locksmith'? What if it's something bad?" said Ben, his heart thumping fast. "Shouldn't we find out more first, like what the Gateway Society in Agatha's nephew's letter is supposed to be, or what the *seal* he's talking about is?"

"I tried," said Charlotte. "I didn't find anything online. I mean, there are lots of gateway societies, but nothing that seemed like it would be connected to all this."

"If there's really some *locksmith* that comes, we can just pretend we're dumb kids who found the wheel and did it by accident," said Akemi. "Don't you want to know what happens?"

"I do," said Charlotte.

Something jabbed Ben hard in the back. It was Danny Farkas's elbow. Danny was a gangly, unkempt blond kid with lips so chapped they bled. He had been mean—like *Watch out for that kid* mean—ever since kindergarten, when he bit and pushed. He wasn't really friends with the sporty boys like Jake and Lekan and Jae, but he hung on the fringes of their group, doing anything to make them laugh. He'd always saved his most vicious taunts for Charlotte, who was an easy target.

"Sitting with your new girlfriends, Benji? Ratgirl and Noodle-Breath?" jeered Danny.

Ben slipped his phone back into his pocket.

"Get lost, Danny," he muttered.

"Noodle-Breath is dressing up for you these days! Velvet skirts, fancy shirts! Your grandma started shopping at a new store, Mossy? Upscale grandma-wear?"

It was true, Charlotte dressed differently this year. She'd been wearing shapeless floral dresses since kindergarten, but this year it was long skirts, starched blouses, and ankle socks, so that she looked like she was going off to a formal church event. She stared into space like she couldn't hear Danny. It was pretty convincing. Charlotte had always had the ability to seem somehow absent even when she was right there. Akemi, however, was red-faced and furious.

Danny knocked his lunch tray against the back of Ben's head before going two tables over to sit with the boys he idolized. Ben hoped that meant he was done, but Danny yelled: "You're really popular with the freaky girls!"

Ben, Akemi, and Charlotte sat in horrible, awkward silence for a moment. Ben took a mechanical bite of mac and cheese, chewed and swallowed, and then said in a voice that he hoped sounded natural and unconcerned: "He's such an idiot."

"Your school has a lot of those," said Akemi, her voice strained.

"Your old school didn't?" asked Ben.

"There were more kids, so maybe it was easier to avoid the mean ones," she said. "Or maybe I just never noticed it as much."

She looked as miserable as he felt, but Charlotte Moss, who was presumably used to this kind of thing, just looked like rice pudding.

Danny Farkas was making loud, dramatic kissing noises in their direction now. Everyone said you should ignore bullies and they would stop, but Charlotte had been ignoring Danny for years—really, pro-level ignoring—and yet he never got tired of picking on her.

Ben didn't want to go sit with Ryan, Felix, and the others, though, because then Danny would think he'd won. He understood a bit better why Akemi was staying on the basketball team. He looked at Akemi and Charlotte, and said, "Okay—let's do it. We'll go to the park after school, and try to call the Locksmith or whatever."

They both brightened immediately. Danny Farkas was

still making kissing noises, but suddenly Ben didn't mind it as much. They were dealing with something much bigger than Danny Farkas.

✳

On Thursdays, they had library right after lunch. Ms. Pryce approached them while they were looking at pictures of buildings downtown and trying to pick one to include in their project.

"You've covered a lot of the interview questions already," said Ms. Pryce, looking at their work packet.

"Yeah, but we don't know if we can finish it. Agatha Bent is in the hospital," Akemi said.

Ms. Pryce dropped the work packet, visibly rattled by this news. She pushed her glasses up on her nose and said in a not-at-all-normal voice: "What happened?"

"Her carer said she fell. It sounded pretty serious," said Akemi. "She hit her head."

"We were hoping we could visit her in the hospital," added Ben.

Ms. Pryce stared at him. He tried to look innocent, just a regular kid who wanted to . . . visit an old lady he barely knew in the hospital. If only they could talk to Agatha Bent, they could ask her about the book and the wheel.

"I'll call the hospital and ask how she is," said Ms. Pryce.

*

"Aren't you going to wait for your girlfriends?" Danny Farkas hollered at Ben, giving him a shove in the hallway at the end of the day.

It was official, thought Ben unhappily. Danny Farkas had decided, with his flawless bully's instinct, that Ben without Ashok was an undefended target.

Akemi had basketball practice again, so Ben and Charlotte went to the library to wait. They did their homework mostly in silence, but it wasn't an awkward silence. Charlotte was just used to spending time inside her own head, Ben decided. When she started scribbling columns of numbers and letters, he asked her: "What are you doing?"

"Playing chess," she said.

He laughed in surprise, and she looked up at him, deadpan, then quirked a tiny smile, realizing he wasn't laughing *at* her.

"How do you play without a board?" he asked.

"I imagine the board in my head," she explained, and moved the paper so he could see it. "The board is like a grid labeled one to eight along one side, and *a* to *h* along the other. So if I write 'BRc3,' it means I'm moving the black rook to the square c3. And I use an *x* for one piece taking another, so, like, 'BRxWQ' means black rook takes white queen. I mean, I'm playing both sides, obviously."

This made no sense to Ben, but he didn't press it.

"Do you play in tournaments and stuff?"

She nodded. "I'm really good," she said. Not bragging, just stating a fact.

"There's a room with a chessboard in *The Book of Keys*," he said. "And the instructions or whatever are all chess moves."

He took out the book to show her. They studied it in silence for a bit, until Ms. Pryce was done with the eighth-grade book club and came over to their table.

"Any news about Ms. Bent?" Ben asked, quickly tucking the book away in his backpack.

"She hasn't regained consciousness," said Ms. Pryce, looking very grim. "It doesn't bode well. At her age . . . Well, I'll go and visit this afternoon."

"Can we come?" asked Ben.

"I don't think that's a good idea," she said, giving him an odd look.

"It's three-forty-five," said Charlotte, checking her watch. "Basketball's over."

They gathered their things and went to meet Akemi outside the gym.

"I guess you miss Ashok," said Charlotte. Her voice turned wistful. "Does he like Paris? It must be amazing—seeing another country like that."

Ben looked at her in surprise. "He's having a good time, yeah," he said.

"I wish I could go to Paris," said Charlotte. "I wish I could go *anywhere.*"

Then she fell abruptly silent, looking off into the middle distance. Jessica Masterson had come out of the gym with her friends, her long hair swishing down her back. Briony glanced at Ben.

"Waiting for Ratgirl?" she asked him, quickly looking to Jessica Masterson for approval. Briony sucked up to teachers all the time, but she sucked up to Jessica Masterson even more. Ben ignored her. Audrey laughed, but Jessica Masterson did not deign to look in his direction.

What would Ashok think, if he came back next year to find that Ben had become an isolated bully magnet? He should probably be trying to hang out with Ryan and Felix more, just give in and buy a deck of yōkai-sen cards. It wasn't a very appealing thought, though, and he forgot about it as soon as Akemi came out of the gym. Her head was down, and she was walking slowly, but when she looked up and saw them, she broke into a smile.

"Thanks for waiting," she said. "Let's go to the park and try this vocoro thing."

✳

Enderway Park was thickly treed in the south, with a pond at the bottom of a gentle slope. Beyond another tangle of bushes and trees there were a playground, swings, and a soccer field. The three of them stopped among the thickest bunch of pine trees, where they could just barely hear the traffic from Slocum Street and the highway north of the park. The ground was a blanket of soft pine needles underfoot.

Ben took out the little copper wheel, the vocoro, and held it in his palm. His heart was thundering in his chest now.

"Like a combination lock," said Akemi.

"I know."

A part of him didn't actually believe that anything would happen. But when he thought about Ms. Kennedy's watch tearing a hole in Ms. Pryce's car, Agatha Bent tapping in Morse code, her ransacked house, the book and the letter, he knew that all of these things must be building toward . . . *something*. The ordinary world had come unhinged somehow, and while he dreaded finding out just *how* unhinged, a part of him couldn't stand the suspense anymore, either.

Peering closely at the tiny numerals, he twisted the wheel to the right and stopped with the arrow pointing at XVI. Then he twisted backward, *click click click click*, to LV. And then forward again, *click click click click*, around to XI.

Nothing happened.

Ben felt sick. It hit him only at that moment how much he'd wanted something to happen, as scared as he was.

"Maybe we didn't do it right," said Akemi. Her voice was tight and strange, almost like she might cry. He realized she'd wanted something to happen as badly as he had. Maybe even more.

"I'll try again," he said.

But Charlotte had stepped back and was squinting at the treetops.

"There's something up there," she said.

16

Ben looked up through the branches of the enormous pine tree next to them. A flicker of blue light played around the top of it for a moment, but it was gone so quickly he couldn't be sure he had even seen it. There *was* something in the tree, though. A shape, a shadow? It was hard to tell. The treetop swayed, and the branches rustled.

"It's big," said Charlotte. Her voice was low.

The shape started moving down the tree. There was another flicker of blue in the sky above it.

"Maybe we should go," squeaked Akemi.

"No," said Charlotte.

Ben glanced at her. Her face was set, intent—not rice-pudding-ish at all, for once. Her gray eyes shone.

He looked back into the thick web of branches. The dark shape was moving down the tree very quickly now, small branches cracking out of its way. Akemi grabbed his arm and squeezed. He was ready to turn and bolt when he saw what it was.

A man. Just . . . a man. He reached the bottom branches and jumped lightly to the ground. He had a silver briefcase in one hand. He brushed the pine needles and bits of bark off his pants with his other hand and looked around with a bemused expression on his face, and then his eyes fell on the three of them, frozen before him in shock.

"Ah," he said. "Hello."

He didn't even look like a scary tree-climbing man. He looked . . . normal. Almost unsettlingly normal, in a Livingston kind of way. He was wearing a gray suit, as if he'd been on his way to work. He was an average height and build, and he had neat, sandy-colored hair, a fair complexion, and an entirely unmemorable face.

"Can I help you?" he asked mildly.

"Um," said Akemi.

A branch broke high up in the tree. They all looked up. Blue light was playing around the treetop again.

"Oh, dear," said the man. "Something got through. The edges are tricky these days. We'll need to be quick, I'm afraid. Where *are* we?"

"Enderway Park," whispered Akemi.

"Hmm."

The man put the silver briefcase down at his feet and took what at first glance appeared to be a folded handkerchief out of his pocket. He shook it, and it unfolded seamlessly into a large, translucent map. It was fine and clear, webbed with glowing lines and curves and markings in the same electric blue that had flashed in the sky above the tree.

"Dear me," he said, frowning at the map. "There hasn't been any trouble *here* for some time. Well?"

"Um," said Akemi again.

"Are you a . . . Locksmith?" asked Charlotte.

"I believe that's *your* term for me," he said, smiling affably. Another loud crack came from up in the tree, and his smile fell away. He looked them over. "You're all very short. Are you . . . *children?*"

Akemi nudged Ben, and he held out the vocoro. "We found this," he began.

"Fine, fine," said the man, with a worried glance up into the tree. "But have you seen any Sneaks about?"

"What?" They gaped at him.

"I thought that was the colloquial term here. Malsprites, then?"

They stared at each other and then back at him.

He looked vaguely annoyed.

"I honestly *don't* have a tremendous amount of time," he said. "We're massively understaffed and dealing with a collapsing universe that risks bringing down its neighbors at the moment. Nowhere near here—don't look so worried—but it's *not* an ideal moment for me to step away. Sneaks! Interdimensionally evolving mischief-makers, posing in *this* universe as ordinary objects? Are you telling me you've never heard of them?"

"Our teacher's watch!" cried Ben, as this last bit sank in. "It was crawling around . . . the librarian put it in her car . . . and it tore a hole in the door."

"A regular watch, of the sort people wear on their wrist?" asked the man.

"Yes," said Ben, nodding vigorously. "I mean, not *regular*, because it crawls around."

"Sounds like a Level Two—possibly evolving into a Level Three. Not overly concerning. But even so, you'll want this."

The man handed Ben the silver briefcase. Ben took it, baffled. Another crack came from about midway up the tree this time, followed by a resonant growl. Ben thought he saw a large shadow forming among the branches, but then it dissolved.

"You *are* the Liaisons for this gap, I assume?" said the man.

"The what?" said Ben.

"Yes," said Charlotte.

Ben and Akemi stared at her.

"Do you know how to use the briefcase?" asked the man.

They shook their heads.

The man sighed.

"What *has* the Gateway Society come to? Well, if you see a Sneak wandering about, catch it. Water will paralyze them for a minute or two, so it's good to have some handy—I assume you know *that*, at least? No? What kind of training *do* you get? Never mind. Water, if possible; another liquid will do, if not. Solids obviously are not very useful, as you've seen with

86

the car door—they don't have much trouble getting through solids. Throw water on the Sneak, put it in the case, close the case, twist this knob here. Simple. That will funnel the Sneak right out of this universe and back to the gap, and then you can retrieve the original object, whose form the Sneak borrowed, from the case. Even if the Sneak doesn't look like it will fit in the briefcase, don't worry, it *will* fit. Remember—all Sneaks feed on fear, so you want to stay as calm as possible when facing one."

"We only just started our training," said Charlotte. "Can you explain, uh, how we can tell if something is a Sneak?"

The pine tree was beginning to sway. There came another groaning, rumbling roar from its branches. Akemi's grip on Ben's arm tightened. The man gave his map a shake, and it folded up to handkerchief size again. He tucked it neatly back in his pocket.

"If you see a pencil sharpener behaving oddly, or growing hair or some such thing, you might guess that it is *not* a pencil sharpener," he said, a note of sarcasm coming into his voice now. "Look for the visible flaw! There has to *be* one. A Sneak can't be a perfect copy. Hmm, I don't much like the thought of a Sneak running around this close to the gap. If they're coming back *here*, they are almost certainly here for Morvox."

Something midway up the tree was twisting about the trunk but still obscured by the branches. The groaning was getting louder and louder. Ben's brain was screaming at him to run, but he couldn't move his feet.

"What gap?" said Charlotte, almost hungrily. "What's *Morvox?*"

The man stared at them. "Hang on. . . . *Are* you the Liaisons?"

"Yes," said Charlotte firmly.

Ben and Akemi swiveled to gape at her again.

"I don't remember the Gateway Society employing children. Aren't children supposed to be . . . ah, weak, or unintelligent? Due to being so young and so small?"

"We're not weak or unintelligent!" said Charlotte, indignant.

Smoky tendrils emerged from the tree, serpent-like, extending toward the man. The end of each one formed a wide mouth full of glinting teeth. Akemi let out a hoarse scream, but Ben could not make a sound. He was frozen in place.

The man looked behind himself at the waving, eyeless heads—multiplying, solidifying, *lengthening.*

"I'd better get rid of this thing before it figures out how to take real physical form here," he said. "Use the briefcase to get rid of any Sneaks you see, call me if there is a more serious problem, but please *don't* call if it isn't *very* serious, and get in touch with whoever is your superior at the Gateway Society and tell them their training program needs improvement. My name is Damon, by the way."

The reaching tendrils broke apart and exploded, roaring out of the tree like a giant swarm of bees. Damon reached into his pocket as the swarm descended on him. There followed a flash of light so bright it seemed to erase the whole world.

When Ben was able to open his eyes, he found he was on the ground, clutching the silver briefcase to his chest, face pressed against the pine needles. Akemi and Charlotte were lying next to him. Charlotte had her hands clamped over her ears. They were both very pale. Damon was gone, and so was the shadowy whatever from the tree.

Ben rose shakily to his feet. Where Damon had been standing, there was a perfect circle of blackened pine needles, smoking slightly. Ben crouched next to the ring and put his hand to it. The pine needles were hot. They crumbled to ash under his touch.

"What . . . just . . . *happened?*" said Akemi.

17

"Why did you tell him we were some kind of liaisons?" Ben asked Charlotte as they left the park.

"Didn't you want him to explain stuff to us?" she replied. "Now we know way more!"

Her face was glowing. Ben had never seen her look so happy. He was still feeling very wobbly, and he wasn't sure what to do with any of the information they had. None of it added up to anything that made sense.

"We should call him again tomorrow and ask more questions," said Charlotte.

"He told us *not* to call him, though," said Akemi. "Unless there's an emergency."

"Maybe there *will* be an emergency," said Charlotte, almost hopefully. She looked at her watch and sighed.

They reached the bus stop on Finch Street just as the number two was rumbling toward them. Charlotte waved and boarded the bus. As it pulled away, they could see her through the window, pinning those giant ribbons onto her hair, still smiling.

Akemi and Ben fetched his bike from school and walked to his house in a daze. They took Morpheus around the block, repeating everything the man had said over and over to each other—mostly just to confirm together that it was real, it had *happened*.

"We should have asked him what the Sneaks *want*."

"There are other universes," said Ben, just to hear the words out loud. They paused and stared at each other while Morpheus peed on a fire hydrant. "There are real, other universes, and we just talked to someone from . . . not our planet."

His stomach flopped over.

"When we moved here from Boston, I thought this town was going to be boring," said Akemi.

An odd snort burst out of her, and the next moment they

both doubled over with uncontrollable laughter. Morpheus looked up at them patiently while they howled and howled, barely able to stand.

"I can't believe this is happening," said Ben, when they had recovered somewhat.

"We *have* to talk to Agatha," gasped Akemi. "The book was supposed to be for her. She'll know what's going on."

"I hope she wakes up soon," said Ben. "Hey, do you think Ms. Pryce is part of the Gateway Society? Damon said to pour water on the Sneaks to paralyze them, and that's what she did with the watch. So *she* knows what Sneaks are."

Akemi's jaw dropped. "You're right!"

They came back around to his house and said goodbye. As soon as she was gone and Ben was alone with this strange secret, it felt unreal again, impossible. He messaged furiously with Ashok while Leo polished off another bag of M&M's.

Lily Quist came upstairs in paint-spattered jeans and an inside-out T-shirt; she peered into the empty slow cooker, as if hoping dinner would materialize. A few minutes later, Aaron Harp came bursting through the door, and almost immediately was halfway into an anecdote about an ancient, erudite professor falling asleep in a meeting and snoring so violently that his dentures fell out.

Eventually, they ordered clam pizza from Perera's. Lily Quist tried to get the Fetcher to bring everyone their pizza, which resulted in half the slices on the floor, much to Morpheus's delight, and a very cheesy, messy Fetcher.

"Oh, well," said Lily. "It's a work in progress!"

"I'll clean up!" Aaron declared extravagantly—which really just meant putting the pizza boxes in the trash, since Morpheus had cleaned the floor with his tongue.

It was the kind of evening Ben normally found comforting: everybody just being their cozy, messy selves in the cozy mess of their home. Tonight, though, everything was normal, but nothing was normal at the same time. His secret sat inside him, clogging his chest and souring his stomach. He tuned out his parents talking about a detective series they were obsessed with, coming up with elaborate theories, while Leo looked back and forth between them, eyes wide, like if he paid enough attention, he might finally figure them out. As soon as he'd finished his pizza, Ben slipped down the hall to his bedroom to look through *The Book of Keys* again.

✱

Ashok: This is basically the biggest scientific discovery in the history of the world!

Ben: It's not like it's my discovery. Some people already know about it. Like Agatha Bent, and probably Ms. Pryce, and whoever else is in the Gateway Society.

Ashok: I bet the government knows and they're keeping it secret. If you tried to go public, they'd discredit you and make you look like some dumb, crazy kid.

Ben: I don't want to go public! I just want to know what's going on!

Ashok: I've been studying *The Book of Keys,* and I'm pretty sure it's a map.

Ben: A map of what?

Ashok: I don't know. But it's all about getting from one place to another. Maybe all these rooms and places in the book are meant to represent other universes.

Ben: If it's a map, where's the starting point? Where are we on the map?

Ashok: That's what I can't figure out. I started making lists of possible routes, but there are thousands of them.

Ben: It still has to be in code, right? I mean, a universe isn't actually, like, a chess room or whatever.

Ashok: Maybe. I can't figure out what the instructions mean. But if I'm right and the places in the book represent universes, it could be the answer to interdimensional travel!

Ben: What about the seal? There's one place where there's no way to get anywhere else. It just says there's a well with the seal inside—did you notice that? This guy Damon was talking about Sneaks like they were trouble, and at the end of Agatha's nephew's letter he says, "May the seal remain ever closed and all the Sneaks on the other side of it"! So it seems like the seal is what keeps Sneaks out of our world.

Ashok: Except they are definitely in our world. Or one of them is, anyway. But the clues in the book must be the keys to get from one place to another, whether it's universes or something else. I mean, it's called *The Book of Keys*—it's right there in the title. I don't know how you're supposed to activate the keys, but we'll figure it out.

Ben: I'm not trying to activate any keys! I don't actually want to go to another universe.

Ashok: Wimp.

Ben: Very funny.

FRIDAY, SEPTEMBER 28

POUBELLE

18

Ben couldn't think where to hide the book, the vocoro, or the silver briefcase, and he was reluctant to part with any of them—as if they might disappear, along with this whole strange mystery, if he left them. So he stuffed all three items into his backpack with his books and homework folder in the morning. He'd barely slept, and his whole body felt tense and jangly.

His dad was already in his cycling gear. He was stretching in the foyer while Lily leaned against the wall, stirring the coffee that she almost certainly wouldn't drink and telling him about her plans for the Fetcher.

Aaron headed off toward downtown on his bike while Ben and Leo coasted down the hill toward the elementary school, which was one block over from the middle school. Ben waited impatiently while Leo locked up his bike in slow motion.

"So, Christina's dad will pick you up?" he asked, like he always did, just to make sure. Every now and then Christina's dad couldn't drop Leo off at home, but his parents never remembered to mention it to Ben, and poor Leo had been left waiting outside the school a few times.

"Yeah," said Leo. "Are you mad about something?"

"No," said Ben. He tried to stop bouncing on his toes and scowling. He just wanted to get to school and talk to Akemi and Charlotte.

Leo was staring at the elementary school like he'd never seen it before.

"I don't feel like going to school today," he said.

"Well, you have to," said Ben.

"I know," said Leo in a small voice.

"Come on, Leo, I'm going to be late."

"There's something I want to tell you about," said Leo.

"Later, okay?" Ben tried not to sound as exasperated as he felt. Leo had the worst timing. "I have to go."

"Okay. Bye."

Leo set his little shoulders and marched toward the school. Ben hopped back on his bike.

✳

The school day felt interminable. As soon as the final bell rang, Ben, Akemi, and Charlotte hurried to the library to ask Ms. Pryce how Agatha Bent was doing, but she had already locked up and left. Charlotte trudged off to Friday chess club, where, according to Jason Huang, who also went to chess club, she mostly just massacred the chess coach in game after game. Ben and Akemi walked out of school together, ignoring Danny Farkas's taunts.

"You should give me your phone number," she said once they were safely away from the school. She handed him a piece of folded paper. "I wrote mine down for you. Just in case something happens this weekend, you know?"

"Okay," he said, taking the folded paper. "Do you have your own phone?"

"No—it's a landline. But my dad never picks up, so you'll get me, for sure."

Ben scrawled his number on a corner of the paper, tore it off, and gave it to Akemi.

"Want to come over?" she asked. "We could play with my rats!"

"Sure."

They skirted the park, and decided to have a look at the spot where Damon had come down the tree. The charred circle of pine needles had been scuffed up, and there were a few broken branches, but everything looked very ordinary.

"It really happened, right?" said Akemi, looking up the tree. "I keep thinking it can't be real."

They walked east through the park, toward Akemi's place. Ben kept hearing rustling in the bushes. Squirrels or birds, he told himself, trying not to be paranoid, although it sounded like something bigger. Then he saw a gray shape in among the bushes before it flashed out of sight, and his heart lurched. It was *definitely* larger than a squirrel. And it seemed to be following them.

"Did you see that?" he asked Akemi in a low voice.

"What?" Akemi looked around.

He heard a low whine.

"Uh . . . what kind of animals live around here?" asked Akemi nervously. "It's not, like, a coyote or something, is it?"

"I don't think so," said Ben. He paused, and then crouched down on the trail, peering into the bushes. There was another whine, very close, and then . . . the telltale jingling of dog tags. A black nose poked out of the bush.

He could see the outline of the little body behind it. "Poubelle?" he said tentatively.

The poodle gave a yip of recognition and leaped out of the bush. She was still wearing her pink collar with its tags, but she had burrs and leaves all over her, and she was trembling with fright. Ben dropped to his knees and patted the little dog, who leaned against his legs and shook and shook.

"How did she get here?" said Akemi.

"I think Simon ditched her," said Ben grimly. "She wasn't at the house on Wednesday. She must have been out here for a couple of days. Poor doggo."

He took his water bottle out of his backpack and poured some water into his cupped palm. Poubelle lapped it up frantically, so he kept pouring until the bottle was empty.

"What are we going to do?" said Akemi. "We can't leave her here!"

"Of course we won't leave her here," said Ben. "I can't believe he dumped her in the park! That pretty much proves it. The guy is *definitely* evil."

Poubelle whimpered. Ben took off his jacket and wrapped her up in it, lifting her into his arms. She was still trembling, but she didn't struggle.

"I'm going to take her home," he said. "I'll come over some other time, okay?"

Akemi pushed Ben's bicycle, and Ben carried Poubelle. She wasn't heavy, but still his arms were aching by the time they reached his house.

"I don't know how Morpheus is going to feel about this," said Ben as Akemi propped his bike up against the garage.

"What about your *parents?*" said Akemi. "My dad would freak if I brought a dog home without asking!"

"We'll see how long it takes them to even notice," answered Ben. It came out bitter, though he hadn't really intended it that way.

Akemi looked at him, surprised, but said nothing.

19

After devouring some kibble, Poubelle yapped at Morpheus for a full five minutes while Morpheus sat on the sofa, staring at her mournfully. Then she huddled in a corner of the living room, tail between her legs.

"How come we have a new dog?" asked Leo.

"We're just taking care of her for a few days," said Ben. He went to check if his dad had put anything in the slow cooker that morning, but it was empty.

"Hey . . . what if Ashok came back and he didn't like Akemi?" asked Leo, trailing into the kitchen after him.

"Why wouldn't he like her?" asked Ben distractedly.

"I just mean, if it did happen—like, if Ashok came back and told you not to be friends with her, what would you do?"

"Ashok wouldn't tell me not to be friends with someone," said Ben.

There were hot dogs and buns in the freezer. He got them out and put them in the microwave to defrost. He was starving.

"I just mean *if* he did," said Leo.

"Leo, why are you asking me all these dumb questions?" Ben snapped at him.

Leo looked like he'd been struck.

"Sorry," muttered Ben. "There's a lot going on right now. I need to think."

Their dad came bursting in the back door, wild-eyed. He always entered every room like he was an EMT arriving at the scene of an emergency.

"Hi, boys!" He stared at them like he couldn't quite remember who they were. "Where's your mom?"

"Basement, I guess," said Ben.

"Great!" said his dad. "Oh, hot dogs. Hmm. Why don't we order Chinese food?"

"Sure," said Ben.

Poubelle came skittering into the kitchen, yapped at Aaron Harp, and skittered back out. Their dad stared after the dog in confusion. Then he turned his attention to Leo and ruffled his hair. "Good day, kiddo?"

"Not really," said Leo. "What do you do if your friends don't like each other?"

"Hmm," said his dad vaguely.

Their mom came clomping up the stairs. She was wearing her own pajamas this time, thick work gloves, and a pair of pink rain boots coated with some kind of powder. Poubelle reappeared in the kitchen entrance, looking panicked. Morpheus followed, like he didn't want to miss the action. Poubelle snapped at his ear. Morpheus barked once, loudly, in her face, and she jumped right into the wall in fright.

"I'm going to EnVision next Thursday!" Lily cried, hurtling straight toward her husband. "To demonstrate the Fetcher!"

"Lily!" he shouted, dropping his bag. "You'll blow them away!"

They threw their arms around each other. She kept talking into the shoulder of his cycling shirt. "I need to finish the new model by then. It's going to be a totally crazed week."

"Just tell me what you need. I'm on it," he said, kissing the top of her head.

Looking at them hugging and happy, Ben suddenly wanted to tell them everything. But how would he begin? Would they even believe him? Was there anything they could do?

"Something weird happened," he said, his mouth very dry all of a sudden.

"Sounds like the title of my autobiography," chortled his mom.

"We should get champagne and celebrate!" said his dad.

"Too early to celebrate—I don't want to jinx it," said his mom. "It's been a long time since I pulled anything off. This might be another dead end."

"Nope," said his dad. "The Fetcher is genius. Right, boys?"

His mom grinned at them. Then she noticed Poubelle.

"Did we get another dog?" she said.

"I was just thinking that!" crowed his dad. "I thought I must have forgotten!"

"I'm taking care of her for a friend," said Ben. "For a few days."

"As long as I don't have to be involved!" said his mom.

His dad was on the phone to the Szechuan restaurant on Barry Street now, pacing around the kitchen island as he talked. Aaron Harp almost never stood still, unless he was talking to his wife.

"Well . . . you just need to take her out to pee when I'm at school," said Ben nervously. "Like, kind of a lot. And you should praise her and give her treats whenever she goes, because she's not really house-trained yet."

"Are you kidding me?" His mom stared at him. "This week is going to be bonkers, Ben! I can't take care of a poodle that needs to go outside all the time!"

"It'll take you thirty seconds!" said Ben. "I'll text you from school to remind you."

"Sweetie, I'm not going to be taking *any* breaks this week, not even thirty-second breaks! Why would you agree to something like this without *asking* me?"

"Would you even remember if I did?" he yelled.

"Why are you *shouting?*" she asked, taken aback.

"Because you never listen to anything I say!"

"Ben, that's not a nice tone," said his father, looking up from the phone. "Your mother just got some amazing news. This isn't the time to be selfish."

"*Selfish?*" Ben could feel his temper rising like a boiling kettle in his chest. "Are *you* seriously going to lecture *me* about being *selfish?* Half the time I can't tell if you even remember I exist!"

Leo put his hands over his ears. He hated conflict.

Aaron Harp looked briefly stunned. Then he said in a curt, dismissive voice: "If you're going to have some kind of fifth-grade version of a tantrum, why don't you just go to your room and spare us the drama?"

"I'm in *sixth* grade!" Ben shouted.

But his dad had turned away and was talking on the phone again, a finger in his other ear. Lily Quist turned on the tap and stared at the running water, apparently for no reason except to look at something other than Ben.

He stormed down the hall to his room, slammed the door, jumped onto his bed, and punched his pillow as hard as he could, but it didn't make him feel better. He felt hot and slightly sick. He didn't have a lot of stamina for anger. It burned itself up so fast inside him, leaving him hollowed out, scorched to the skin. And he didn't know how to fight with his parents, who were endlessly upbeat and preoccupied. They gave him nothing to push back against.

Ashok always insisted Ben was the lucky one, because he was allowed to have a dog and because his parents were so "relaxed"—that was Ashok's word for it. He loved coming to Ben's house. They could come and go as they pleased, eat what they wanted, watch TV or play video games all day. "My parents treat me like I'm a baby," Ashok would say in frustration. Ashok's parents had a million rules, and while Ben didn't envy that part, he *did* envy Ashok, in ways he could never quite put his finger on. He didn't want his parents to enforce a bedtime or ground him if he got a bad test score. But he loved Ashok's house, where everything was neat and organized and smelled nice. One of his parents cooked a real dinner every night, and they used cloth napkins, which felt fancy. They knew the names of Ashok's classmates and helped him with homework projects.

Ben's parents had praised his independence all the time when he was younger. He couldn't remember a time when he hadn't fixed his own breakfast and lunch, gotten himself ready for school, kept track of important school dates on the calendar, and done those things for Leo too, once Leo came along. "He's basically the parent in the family," his dad would brag to friends, laughing, and it was a joke, but also it wasn't, and sometimes Ben felt like he'd been conned. He'd lapped up their approval in place of attention, but the more he did stuff for Leo, the more he thought, a bit resentfully, *Nobody ever did this for* me *when* I *was seven.*

He didn't want his parents to be nosy or controlling, like Ashok's parents, and so he wasn't sure *what* he wanted exactly. He already felt ashamed of his outburst. His mom had every right to be mad that he'd brought home a dog that wasn't house-trained when she had a busy week ahead of her. His anger always came out at the wrong moments, when he couldn't justify or explain it. But he didn't feel like apologizing, either.

He grabbed his phone to text Ashok. There was a soft *whuff* at the door. He opened it and Morpheus came in, with Poubelle right behind him. Morpheus lay down on the carpet. Poubelle sniffed at Ben's stack of comics and then peed on them.

✷

Ben: Did you get my messages?

. . .

Ben: Ashok? Are you asleep? I need to talk to you.

. . .

Ben: You're usually still up reading. Where are you? Call me!

. . .

Ashok,

I guess you went to sleep already. I sent you a million messages but sending an email in case your parents took your phone. Call me as soon as you wake up! Seriously!

Ben

SATURDAY, SEPTEMBER 29, and SUNDAY, SEPTEMBER 30

SNEAK ATTACK

20

Ben set his alarm for every two hours that night, so he could take Poubelle into the backyard to pee. She still had one accident on the newspaper he'd put in a corner of the room, but other than that the night was uneventful.

In the morning, his mother was already in the kitchen, bouncing around in normal clothes, her hair in a semi-neat ponytail. She'd forgotten the argument from the night before, of course.

Leo was using a spoon to dig rivers of milk between the mountains and valleys of his oatmeal, and setting up little fleets of raisins.

"The flood came all at once, wiping out half the continent," he muttered, pouring milk over it all. "Only the sea creatures survived." He set some slivered almonds afloat in the milk.

As soon as Ben appeared with the two dogs behind him, his mom said, "Hey, watch this!"

She balanced the Fetcher on her palm and gave two short whistles. The blue beam fixed on Ben, and she tossed the Fetcher in the air. Legs burst out of it as it landed on the kitchen island, and it raced over to Ben. A little pincer hand shot out of its belly, holding a note. Ben took it and unfolded it. *I love you, Ben!* said the note. Maybe she hadn't forgotten their argument.

"It can pass notes? That's cool," he said.

"It's still got a few bugs," said Lily, delighted with herself. "But I'll have it perfected for the meeting with EnVision. We can do a demonstration for your friends sometime, if you want!"

"Christina will want to play with it forever," said Leo, and then his smile fell away and he smashed the oatmeal hills he'd been mounding back down into the milk.

"Uh-huh," Ben said, distracted. Ashok would have loved it, of course—he always loved seeing what Ben's mom was working on. But Ashok was in Paris, and he and Akemi and Charlotte had other things to think about.

Suddenly his mom was looking right at him.

"You must really miss Ashok," she said.

Lily Quist was so much in her own world most of the time that these moments when she got motherly and empathetic freaked him out a little. He knew she was trying because of his outburst last night, but it just felt weird, and he couldn't decide whether to be pleased or annoyed.

"Yep," he said. "It's okay."

"His new best friend is a girl called Akemi," piped up Leo.

"Oh yeah?" said his mom, raising her eyebrows and staring at him, like a person doing an impression of being *really interested*.

"She's not my best friend," muttered Ben.

He spent Saturday texting and emailing Ashok, with no response, and taking Poubelle out to pee, rewarding her with treats each time. She only peed once indoors all day, in the corner of the kitchen. Ben took both dogs down to the ravine—they seemed to have reached a kind of truce—and thought about calling Akemi, but he didn't know what he'd say. At home, he lay on his bed reading and rereading *The Book of Keys* and the letter Agatha Bent's nephew had written, but no matter how many times he read them, he couldn't make sense of it all. He stared at the vocoro and wished he could call on Damon again and make him answer questions, like Charlotte had said, but Damon hadn't been too happy about being called the first time.

The day passed—one slow, anxious, lonely minute at a time. Ben felt as though he'd never been so aware of time. That night, he set his alarm for every two hours again. Poubelle didn't have any accidents in the room, and in the morning he rewarded her with a strip of bacon on top of her food.

His mom was at the kitchen table, wearing the same outfit as the previous day, her hair messier, her face drawn and exhausted. The kitchen table was covered with notes and diagrams, and the Fetcher was disassembled in front of her. A cold cup of coffee sat at her elbow.

"Did you go to bed last night?" he asked.

"Huh?" She looked up at him blearily. "Oh! Is it morning already? Wow. I should probably get some sleep."

"Mom, do you actually *drink* coffee?"

"Well, I like the smell of it," she said absent-mindedly.

His phone rang. His phone hardly ever rang since Ashok had moved away. It was eight in the morning.

"Don't answer that!" yelled his dad, charging down the hall in his pajamas. "Marketing scammers!"

Ben rolled his eyes and answered his phone.

"Hello?"

"Uh . . . hi! Is it too early?"

It was Akemi. Relief and joy washed through him so fast he felt almost light-headed. There was still no word from Ashok at all. He felt forgotten and alone. Akemi's voice was like a lifeline.

"It's Akemi," she added nervously when he didn't say anything.

"I know! I mean, hi!" He left the kitchen because his parents were both looking at him curiously, and went down the hall to his bedroom.

"So . . . did your parents notice that you brought home a dog?"

He laughed. "Yeah. It took a few minutes, though. My mom isn't too happy about it."

"Wow. It seems like they just let you do whatever you want."

"Mostly they don't care," he agreed.

"I just can't stop thinking about all that stuff Damon told us, and the book," she said.

"I know. Me too," he said. "Do you want to look at it? I could bring it over to your place."

"Let's meet at the square. I got a bike yesterday!"

"Great!" he said. "I can come now. I mean, after I have breakfast."

The square was downtown, just east of the university campus. The public library was at the north end of it, and boutiques and restaurants surrounded the broad green lawn with a playground and splash pad at one end and a fountain in the middle. At the northwest corner of the square, a comic shop and an ice cream store were right next to each other, which made it a popular destination.

"Do you have Charlotte's number?" she asked.

"No," he said. "I didn't even know she'd moved."

"Okay. Well, let's meet at ten o'clock at Fussy's Ice Cream," she said.

He hung up feeling a million times better.

21

"Take Poubelle outside every two hours, and as soon as she goes pee, give her a treat," Ben explained to Leo.

"What if she doesn't go pee, though?" said Leo anxiously.

"Keep her outside until she does," said Ben, suppressing his irritation. He had been taking care of Morpheus completely when he was younger than Leo, but Leo acted like any responsibility was such a big deal. "I won't be gone long."

"Okay," said Leo.

"You and Christina can play with her," said Ben.

"Christina's not coming over," said Leo.

"Really?" said Ben, shouldering his backpack with the briefcase, *The Book of Keys*, and the vocoro inside it. Leo and Christina played every weekend.

"She's mad at me," said Leo forlornly.

"Oh. That's too bad." Ben felt like a jerk, but he really didn't have time for this right now. "I'm sure she'll get over it. Nobody could stay mad at you."

"Christina's really good at staying mad, though," said Leo. He rubbed Poubelle's head. Poubelle wagged her little tail. She was much calmer than she'd been at Agatha's house, following Morpheus everywhere and tentatively sitting next to him on the sofa. Luckily, she hadn't peed on the sofa yet, but Ben had covered it with towels, just in case.

"I wish I could go with you," said Leo, following Ben to the door.

"I know," said Ben. "But somebody needs to take care of Poubelle. You got this. I'll be back soon!"

He left before Leo could say anything else to make him

feel bad about leaving. He rode through falling leaves to the square and locked his bike on the racks outside the comic shop. There was a shiny lime-green ten-speed already there, and he wondered if it was Akemi's.

He was so eager to see her that he burst straight into Fussy's and looked around, but she wasn't there, and his heart plunged in disappointment. His eyes fell on Jessica Masterson, Audrey Banks, and Briony Moore sitting at a table together. The other two hadn't noticed him and were chattering away, but Jessica was staring right at him with a pinched expression.

He turned around and walked back out. Akemi was on the sidewalk a little farther down, waving.

"Sorry," she said when he joined her. "I didn't want to go in there and have to sit by myself, ignoring them."

"It's fine," he said. "We can sit outside. I don't really feel like ice cream."

"Right. It isn't hot enough," she said, relieved.

They walked across the square together and found an empty bench, and Ben took out *The Book of Keys*. They pored over it, reading bits aloud to each other.

"Let's go over everything that we know for sure," said Akemi. "One: there are multiple universes. Two: there are creatures called Sneaks that can get into our universe and borrow regular objects to use as kind of like a disguise. Three: there are gaps between universes? That guy Damon kept talking about the 'gap' here, and he called the Sneaks 'interdimensionally evolving mischief-makers.' So they're basically . . . aliens from the gaps in between universes, right?"

"I guess so," said Ben. "And there are different levels of Sneaks. He said Ms. Kennedy's watch was a 'Level Two' and might be evolving into a 'Level Three.' Also, he said they feed on fear, and there has to be a visible flaw. So even though the Sneak borrowed Ms. Kennedy's watch and looks like a watch, there's something not right about it."

"Well, it can crawl, and that's not right."

"He was saying a pencil sharpener might act weird, or grow hair, if it was actually a Sneak. But I couldn't tell if he was being sarcastic."

"We know there's an organization called the Gateway Society that deals with this stuff," continued Akemi. "And they had someone called Sabrin in a special prison in the Aleutian Islands. . . ."

"But he escaped," said Ben.

"And Agatha Bent is probably part of the Gateway Society. Her nephew too. And maybe Ms. Pryce. There's something called 'Morvox,' and that's why Sneaks are here. The book is some kind of a map, and mentions the seal that keeps Sneaks out of our universe, but we don't know exactly what it's a map *of*. Do we know anything else?"

Ben shook his head. "We need to find the Gateway Society. Unless we can talk to Agatha, we don't know who we can trust. Like, why did Ms. Pryce give us Agatha's name in the first place? She was definitely freaked out that we went to her house."

"We should call the hospital and ask for her," said Akemi.

At that moment, Jessica Masterson appeared before them, hands on her hips. She was flanked by her friends, arms folded over their chests. They looked like a parody of an album cover, thought Ben.

"*So*. Having a nice morning?" she said, her voice sickly sweet.

"Um . . . yes?" said Ben, hurriedly closing *The Book of Keys* and stuffing it in his backpack.

"You two are hanging out a lot these days," said Jessica.

"We're working on our project," added Ben, and then wondered why he was making excuses to Jessica Masterson for hanging out with Akemi.

Jessica tossed her gleaming hair. "Where's the third Stooge?"

"The what?" said Akemi, looking startled.

"She means Charlotte," muttered Ben. Akemi probably thought Jessica was referring to her rats.

"That weirdo is finally cracking up completely," said Jessica. "Nice for her that her only friends don't even notice."

"What are you talking about?" said Ben.

"Charlotte *losing it*, dummy," said Jessica. "Well, have a *fantastic day* together."

She strode off, Audrey and Briony behind her.

"What was *that* all about?" said Akemi. "I know she doesn't like me, but still. That was just weird. And what is she talking about, saying Charlotte is losing it?"

"I have no idea," said Ben. "Charlotte has always been . . . Charlotte. Come on—at least we can go get ice cream now."

They got up. Akemi grabbed his arm, right above his elbow, and squeezed.

"Ow!" he said. "You *have* to stop doing that!"

"Sorry," she whispered. "Don't look behind you."

"Why?" he squeaked. "What's behind me?"

"Simon is over there. He's a ways back, but I think he's watching us."

Ben's insides turned to ice.

"Seriously? Do you think he saw the book?"

"I don't know. Come on, let's walk this way," said Akemi, and they made their way quickly across the square, toward the library. "Don't look behind you. I don't want him to know we know he's there."

Ben glanced over his shoulder.

"I *said* don't look," hissed Akemi.

She was right—it did look like Simon. He was wearing a blazer, sunglasses, and a baseball cap. Ben recognized his easy, gliding walk.

"Let's get to our bikes," muttered Ben. "There's a side door to the library, by the bathrooms. We can go in the front and loop back."

They went up the big concrete steps and into the library, straight through to the children's section at the back, where the bathrooms were, and out the side. They hurried down the lane back to the square and ran for their bikes.

"He spotted us!" gasped Akemi as they unlocked the bikes. Simon must have followed them closely in the library—he was coming down the lane straight toward the square, walking very briskly now.

They jumped on their bikes and pedaled madly down Elm Street, turned left and then right. Ben made sure to lead Akemi on a convoluted route, in case Simon had a car and was looking for them.

"He's definitely after the book, right?" panted Akemi when they reached his house and got off their bikes.

"Remember Agatha's nephew said in the letter that he was being followed? He thought the book would be safe with Agatha, but it seems like the people who were after it had already gotten to her too. The question is, *Why* do they want it? What does it do?"

He thought about Ashok's theory—that it was a map to other universes.

"We *really* need to talk to Agatha," said Akemi.

✳

Feeling anxious that Simon might still be roaming the town looking for them, Ben and Akemi put their bikes away in the garage, out of sight. In Ben's room, they called the hospital's front desk. A nasally voice answered.

"We want to visit a patient named Agatha Bent," said Ben.

"Date of birth?"

"Uh . . . mine, or hers?"

"The patient's date of birth."

"Oh, I don't know. I'm not sure."

"Are you a relative?"

"No. We're . . . students. We know her, we visited her . . . before. At her house."

There was a pause.

"What is your age?" she asked.

"Eleven," said Ben. Akemi shook her head at him. "I mean, twelve," he said, and then cringed. Akemi rolled her eyes.

"Name, please?"

"Benjamin Harp."

"Please hold," she said.

Ben waited, listening to a depressing pop song. He thought a hospital should play more cheerful music. When the nasally voice returned, it was slightly gentler.

"Who did you say you were? I can leave a message for the patient, but visitors are currently limited."

"Um, Ben Harp," he said. "Can you tell her that Ben and Akemi and Charlotte want to visit her?"

"I'll pass that along," said the voice.

"Is she . . . okay? Is she awake?" he asked.

"I'm afraid I can't share that with you."

He hung up, despondent.

22

They spent the rest of the day with the dogs and looking through *The Book of Keys*. Ben's dad made lasagna for dinner, and Akemi called her dad to ask if it was okay if she stayed. They all sat around eating like a semi-normal family, with only one tangent, when his parents got into a heated argument about the capacity of AI to mimic human emotion.

"The human mind *is* essentially an imperfect machine!" Lily Quist cried, dripping lasagna sauce on her jeans, and Aaron Harp bellowed, "No *robot* can *experience* true *love!*" A brief pause followed this proclamation, and then his parents fell around giggling. Ben rolled his eyes at Akemi, who was laughing along. After dinner, Ben and Akemi took the dogs down to the ravine.

"They're pretty weird," said Ben, once they were out in the fresh evening air.

"Everybody thinks their parents are weird," said Akemi, grinning at him. "They're nice."

Ben thought about Ashok's parents again, with a little pang. He missed having dinner at their house, and how they would interrogate him about school and listen to everything he said, like it was the most interesting thing ever. Ashok would sit there, cringing, but Ben had kind of enjoyed it.

"What about your dad?" he asked Akemi, and then wondered if phrasing it that way was like poking a wound labeled "Dead Mother." But Akemi seemed to want to talk.

"He's just . . . really busy," she said. "Before my mom got sick, my parents were always fighting. I thought they were going to get divorced, for sure. When they sat me down, all serious, to tell me something, I figured, Oh, here it is, they're splitting up. But instead, they told me my mom had cancer. They stopped fighting with each other, they stopped nagging me about stuff, they were just . . . I don't know. It was like my mom was concentrating so hard all the time, like she could keep herself alive that way, and my dad was so scared. I heard him crying in the bathroom sometimes. She must have been scared too, but she didn't act scared."

Akemi paused for a long moment, and Ben felt like he should say something, but he didn't know what. Akemi's voice was weirdly flat when she started speaking again. "She died, anyway. My dad and I went to a grief counselor together for a while. That was kind of good. But we really moved here because it's cheaper, and his new job pays more. My mom had life insurance, but most of it went to her hospital bills. The longer you take to die, the more it costs. Now he just works and sleeps, basically, and sometimes he makes these speeches to me about how everything will be fine and he'll always take care of me or whatever, and I'm, like, Okay, but I never even see you."

"Wow," said Ben, staring at their shoes striding along in unison. Why couldn't he ever think of anything to say other than *Wow?*

"I was so mad about moving here," said Akemi. "My mom was gone, and he was making me leave all my friends too. I did my best at that stupid basketball tryout because I thought I'd make new friends on the team. But instead, Jessica Masterson made sure I had *no* friends here." She looked at him sideways. "But now I have you."

A wave of sadness hit Ben, thinking of how Ashok had still not answered any of his messages. He and Akemi had been thrown together by this strange secret they shared, but he was grateful to share it with *her*, someone who was brave and smart and easy to be around, who made him feel brave and smart as well. They just . . . fit. That was it. Like he and Ashok had fit.

She was looking at him with a worried expression, and he realized he hadn't answered what she'd said. He looked her right in the face.

"Yeah," he said. "I didn't have anyone this year, either. So— I'm sorry you had to move here, but I'm glad too."

She smiled her big, impossible-not-to-smile-back-at smile. For a second, he thought she was about to hug him, but she leaned down to hug Morpheus instead.

✴

In bed that night, Ben pored over *The Book of Keys* with a flashlight, as if he might notice something new, until his eyes grew so heavy he couldn't keep them open any longer. Leo had both dogs in his room now, having promised that he'd get up and take Poubelle out in the night. He'd set the alarm for two a.m.

Ben put the book on his night table and turned off the flashlight. A shadow moved in the corner of his room. He flicked the flashlight back on and sat up, heart pounding. The shadow went still. Clutching the flashlight, heart in his throat, he crept over to look at it. It was just a clothes hanger. *But it moved*, his brain insisted. And I didn't leave a hanger there, thought Ben. He crouched down, shining the light over the coat hanger, inch by inch. It was a regular hanger, made of thick green plastic, but it gave off a faint smell of rotten meat. Then the beam of his flashlight hit a half inch of . . . *something* . . . at the base of the hanger. A bit that was not plastic, but coiling and white. Seething. He peered at it more closely. It looked like *maggots*. They were squirming across the half inch of missing hanger. He tasted bile; his mind reeled. It took him a moment to make the next step in his mind: *Not a clothes hanger.*

He dove back to his bed and pulled the silver briefcase Damon had given them out from under it, flinging it open. When he turned, the clothes hanger was cartwheeling right at him. He grabbed it out of the air, and then it wasn't a clothes hanger at all anymore. It was a translucent *thing*, about a foot long. Its body was segmented like an insect's, and at the end of a swiveling neck it had a shrunken, monstrous, eyeless head, with rows and rows of teeth that seemed to keep going down its throat—of which he had a full view, since it was waving its mouth right in his face. The thing let out an airless shriek, writhing in his hands. His own scream got stuck in his throat. Six clawed hands grabbed at his pajamas. The creature was pulsing, and it seemed to be *growing*, getting stronger, the head reaching for him, teeth snapping as he held it as far away from him as he could. *They feed on fear*, Damon had said. But there was no way to stay calm; he was in a full-fledged panic. He tried to jam the thing into the briefcase. The case burst open again before he could get it completely shut. The creature sprang out, grabbing his pajamas again; the head reared back and then struck, quick as lightning, biting his shoulder. He heard himself scream as he tried to get it off him. It was definitely getting bigger—it was half his size now, a bluish-purplish light flickering through its translucent body. It wrestled him down, its head rearing back again.

A snarl came from behind them, and then Poubelle had the Sneak's long neck in her jaws. She yanked it off Ben and shook it violently. Morpheus was in the doorway, hackles up.

Ben scrambled for the briefcase again.

"Drop it, Poubelle!" he gasped.

Poubelle dropped the creature, which had shrunk slightly,

straight into the briefcase, and Ben slammed the lid shut as fast as he could. He twisted the knob. Electric-blue light flashed around the join of the case.

He knelt over the closed briefcase, his breath coming out in gasping half sobs. He was shaking all over. He didn't want to open the briefcase again, but he was just as scared to leave it closed. Morpheus was next to him now. The old dog whined and licked his face. Poubelle was standing alert, tail in the air, ears pricked.

"So . . . Agatha didn't house-train you, but she trained you to attack Sneaks?" he asked. He patted Poubelle's head. "You saved me, buddy."

Poubelle wagged her tail.

"Okay, ready?" whispered Ben. His fingers were trembling. Slowly, carefully, he opened the case an inch and peeked in with his flashlight.

There was the green plastic clothes hanger. He opened the lid wider. The hanger didn't move. Morpheus sniffed it. There was no maggoty half inch, no rotten-meat smell. It was green plastic all the way around. It was like Damon had said—the briefcase had sent the Sneak back into the gap, and left behind the object the Sneak had been inhabiting. Still, how to be sure? Ben picked the hanger up, and heart galloping, he snapped it in half over his knee. It was green plastic all the way through. Even so, he was never going to be able to sleep while it was in his room.

"What's going on?" Leo was in the doorway in his pajamas, half-awake. "Did you yell?"

"Bad dream. I'm going to take Poubelle out to pee," said Ben, his voice shaking. "Why don't you turn off your alarm and go to bed?"

"Okay." Leo stumbled back to his own room. Ben took the broken clothes hanger down the hall and through the kitchen, Morpheus and Poubelle at his heels. He opened the back door as quietly as possible. The yard was dark and silent. Morpheus went out and peed on a dandelion patch, and Poubelle followed. Ben went to the side of the house in his bare feet, shoved the clothes hanger deep into the garbage bin, and then went inside with the dogs.

He got a glass of water from the kitchen to keep at his bedside. Damon had said water would paralyze the Sneaks. Then he crept into the bathroom at the end of the hall, next to his parents' room. His dad kept a white-noise machine running in their room at night, because Lily snored and the white noise drowned her out. Ben wasn't sure if he was glad or not that they hadn't heard him.

By the too-bright glare of the bathroom light, he examined the bite on his shoulder in the mirror. There were two perfect concentric circles of tooth marks, the larger one maybe three inches in diameter, and the smaller one just inside it. The skin was broken, and blood smeared his chest. When he washed off the blood, he could see faint scratches of a third circle inside the second. Those layers of teeth. He shuddered, put antibiotic cream on the cuts—who knew what kind of bacteria interdimensional monsters harbored?—and searched for Band-Aids but couldn't find any. It wasn't bleeding too much anymore, anyway.

Morpheus and Poubelle were waiting for him in the hall, alert. They followed him back into his room, which he searched thoroughly, but there was nothing else obviously Sneak-like. The dogs were at the foot of his bed when he turned the light out. He lay awake for a long time, heart slamming against his rib cage, clutching his flashlight against his chest. He felt like he'd barely slept at all when he woke to his alarm and twenty messages from Ashok, who'd been on a weekend trip to Lyon and not allowed to bring his phone.

✳

Ashok: It wanted the book, I bet.

Ben: What?

Ashok: The clothes hanger! The Sneak! It wanted *The Book of Keys* because it has the secret map of the multiverse in it. Why else would it be in your bedroom?

Ben: Multiverse?

Ashok: That's what scientists call it—the idea of many universes. The multiverse. I've been reading about it.

Ben: But how did the Sneak know I have the book?

Ashok: That guy Simon saw you had it at the square. If he's working with Sneaks, he could have told them. But it's bad news that they've figured out where you live.

You have to hide that stuff somewhere good, and you have to tell Ms. Pryce.

Ben: She'll think we're crazy.

Ashok: No, she won't! She's the one throwing water on Sneaks and hiding them. She knows what's going on.

Ben: You're right.

Ashok: You have to tell her. This is getting too dangerous. A clothes hanger tried to kill you!

Ben: Okay. I'll talk to her.

Ashok: Promise me, Ben. We don't know what might be coming after you next. You need her help.

Ben: I promise. What's crazy is that I think Agatha trained her poodle to recognize Sneaks and attack them.

Ashok: Then keep that poodle close!

MONDAY, OCTOBER 1

SNEAKS
AT SCHOOL

23

Ben spotted Charlotte plodding through the school parking lot. He locked his bike and ran to catch up with her.

"Guess what happened last night?" he whispered.

He told her about the clothes-hanger attack and showed her the photo he'd taken with his phone of the bite mark on his shoulder, the two concentric circles. There was some purple bruising around the broken skin now. He wished he'd managed to get a photo of the Sneak itself. When he'd finished telling Charlotte everything, her eyes were shining and her face was bright with excitement, like when Damon had come down the tree. It made her look almost like a different person.

"The Sneaks *must* be after *The Book of Keys*," she said. "Or maybe they want the vocoro. Or both."

"I've been sending pictures of the book to Ashok," he told her. "He thinks it's a map . . . of interdimensional travel or something. It might be in code."

"If it's a code, can he break it?" asked Charlotte. "Ashok is good at stuff like that."

Even though Ben and Charlotte Moss had barely spoken to each other in all the years they'd been at school together, there

135

was a strange familiarity from growing up in the same place, he thought. Of course Charlotte knew that about Ashok. There were things he didn't know how to explain to Akemi—like why it was really better not to cross Jessica Masterson—that Charlotte just *knew*.

Akemi coasted up next to them on her bike.

"Hey, guys!" she called.

"Tell her," said Charlotte.

Unlike Charlotte, Akemi reacted with queasy horror.

"This is bad!" she said. "How do the Sneaks know where you live?"

"Maybe they're following us around." Charlotte looked suspiciously at the ground. There was a bottle cap lying nearby, and she nudged it with her toe.

"Did you tell her about Simon following us yesterday?" asked Akemi.

Ben shook his head, and Akemi told Charlotte about their weekend adventure—finding Poubelle in the park on Friday, and Simon following them on Sunday. Charlotte listened but didn't say anything, her expression going distant again. The first bell rang, and they hurried to their classroom.

"The letter from Agatha's nephew *said* he was being followed, but it didn't say if he meant by humans or by Sneaks," Akemi whispered as they hovered around Ben's desk.

"You never showed me the letter," said Charlotte, sounding vaguely accusatory.

Ben glanced over at Danny Farkas, who had a pencil in

each nostril and was making seal noises to entertain Jake and Lekan at the back of the class. Ben didn't want to be seen *passing a note* to Charlotte Moss—he'd never live it down—but he slid the letter out of his backpack and handed it to her.

"Peter Gael," she said, skimming it quickly. "Weird. You guys didn't mention that part."

The letter began with his name: *As you can see, you were right! Peter Gael—or somebody else—did make a copy of* The Book of Keys.

"What's weird about it?" Ben asked.

"I wonder if he has some connection to Gael House," said Charlotte.

Akemi and Ben stared at her blankly.

"That old heritage house right behind Agatha's place," she said.

For a moment, Ben was speechless. "I forgot that was the name," he said at last.

"We should look him up," said Charlotte.

"Look him up how?" said Ben.

"The *in-ter-net*," Charlotte deadpanned, like he was an idiot. "We can do it during library hour."

✳

Within minutes of getting on one of the computers in the library, Charlotte had found Peter Gael, a professor of astronomy and a prominent member of the Livingston community in the early nineteenth century. He'd designed and built Gael House himself in 1825.

"There must be some connection, if he made *The Book of Keys* as well," said Charlotte. "Maybe all those descriptions of rooms in the book are actually rooms in the house."

She clicked through to an old photograph of Gael House.

"That place can't have a hundred rooms in it," said Ben, looking at the picture. "It isn't that big. Plus, not all the places in the book are rooms. There's, like, ponds and theaters and stuff."

"Why don't we use the house for the monument in our town history project?" suggested Akemi. "We only have a week to finish. That way we can find out more about Peter Gael at the same time. Two birds, one stone."

"Gael House?" said Ms. Pryce quietly. She was standing right behind them. They all jumped. Charlotte closed the page.

"For our project, we were thinking," said Akemi.

Ms. Pryce's mouth was a thin line. "I see."

"Do you know how Agatha Bent is doing?" asked Ben.

"She's still unconscious," said Ms. Pryce. "If you want to write a card, I'll take it over this afternoon."

"Can we come with you?" asked Akemi.

Ms. Pryce frowned. A long pause stretched unbearably, and then she said, "Did something happen when you visited Ms. Bent?"

Ben took a deep breath. Akemi and Charlotte were looking at him with panicked expressions.

"Nothing happened," said Charlotte, before he could answer.

Ben's head was spinning. Ashok was right—he had been attacked by a monster, it was getting too real, too much, too scary. He had to trust *someone*. He needed a grown-up.

"But we wanted to ask you about some . . . stuff," he said.

He glanced around at the rest of the class, chatting and working on their projects. This was almost certainly not the right time or place. Charlotte was glaring daggers at him.

Ms. Pryce's expression didn't change, but Ben had the feeling she was very alert.

"Come and see me after school," she said.

24

"We don't know if we can trust her!" Charlotte hissed as soon as they left the library.

"We have to tell someone," Ben said. "I'm the one who got attacked, okay?"

"What if she's working for the wrong side?" said Charlotte desperately. "And even if she *isn't*, if she's part of the Gateway Society or whatever, she's just going to take the briefcase and the book and everything, and then . . . it'll be over."

They filed into their homeroom.

"Ben's right. We *have* to tell her," said Akemi in a low voice. "This is dangerous, Charlotte! Don't you get it?"

"I *know*," said Charlotte. She looked like she might cry. "But what if we can figure out the book? What if it's actually possible to travel to another universe?"

Ben looked at her in amazement. "Are you kidding me?"

"Did you see that map the Locksmith had? We've found out about something *huge*, and if we tell Pryce, there's just no way she's going to let us—"

"No! Talking!" barked Ms. Kennedy.

Charlotte's expression went blank again, and they took their seats. Ben was a little shaken by her intensity, but Ashok was right. Ms. Pryce knew something. She could help.

He slid his phone out of his pocket and surreptitiously texted his mom another reminder to take Poubelle outside. She didn't respond.

✳

Charlotte was quiet at lunch. They had gym final period. Ms. Pond divided them into teams for dodgeball, which was always a vicious display of dominant social status. Charlotte was out first, and sat on the bench with her rice-pudding face for the rest of the class. Jessica Masterson was furiously intent on getting Akemi out, without much luck. Ben knew he shouldn't, but he fired a ball straight into her knees while she was aiming—again—for Akemi, and the glare she gave him made his stomach flip over. Akemi shot him a grateful grin, and then Danny Farkas's ball hit him right in the head.

When it was over, Ms. Pond told them to tidy up the blue and orange mesh pinnies they'd been wearing, separating them into two boxes. Ben trudged over to one of the orange pinnies, which someone had left lying on the floor off to the side of the gym. As he got closer, he noticed a strip of greenish sludge next to it.

"Gross! What is that?" yelled Danny Farkas, who had reached the pinny first. "Benji, is that your snot?"

Cackling at his own wit, he looked up at Ben. A tiny squirt of green sludge landed on the toe of Danny Farkas's shoe. It was coming from the pinny.

Ben ignored Danny Farkas and bent over the pinny.

"Gro-o-o-s-s!" yelled Danny again. "Benji is snotting every-where!"

There was a pair of tiny blue lips—not even an inch wide—at the neck of the pinny. They puckered and shot out another squirt of slime.

Not a pinny, thought Ben. He felt immediately light-headed.

The silver briefcase was in his homeroom classroom, right across the hall. He grabbed the pinny and shouldered past Danny Farkas. The pinny twisted in his grasp. He bunched it into a ball.

"Akemi," he whispered, hurrying toward her. "Do you have any water?"

She shook her head, eyes widening.

He looked to see if Ms. Pond was watching, but she was arguing with Jae Park about something. He ducked out of the gym into the hall. The pinny was trying to wriggle out of his hand. Its edges turned translucent. A pale clawed hand shot out of the balled-up fabric in his fist, grabbing at his chin. He doused the thing in the water fountain, spraying water all over it. The pinny went limp, and the translucent arm it had grown flopped loosely over the side of the fountain. He left it there and dashed into the classroom. He grabbed his backpack off its hook and fumbled the briefcase out. The pinny was starting to stir in the damp fountain by the time he got back. He opened the briefcase and threw the half pinny, half something else inside it. He twisted the knob just as Ms. Pond said, behind him, "*What* are you doing, Mr. Harp?"

His stomach went icy, and he straightened up.

"Nothing."

Behind Ms. Pond, Danny Farkas looked gleeful and Akemi looked horrified.

"Give me that." The gym teacher reached for the briefcase. Ben held on to it stubbornly. Ms. Pond yanked it out of his hands and unlatched it. The soggy pinny—now just a pinny—fell out.

She picked it up between her thumb and forefinger and looked at him with narrowed eyes.

"So," she said. "You're stealing school property."

Danny Farkas was doubled over with silent laughter behind her. Ben had no idea what to say.

"I told him to put it in there . . . as . . . a joke," said Akemi desperately. "It was my idea."

It was pretty feeble, but Ben appreciated her trying to help.

"I fail to see the humor," said Ms. Pond. "Line up, everybody! Except Miss Hanamura and Mr. Harp. You're going to see the principal."

25

Mr. Susskind delivered a speech on honor and honesty. It sounded like the kind of thing a computer program might assemble out of key words and movie quotations. His teeth gleamed. His head shone. His chest was even puffier than usual. He stashed the briefcase under his desk and told them they would serve a detention with Ms. Pond and could retrieve the briefcase after their detention.

Ms. Pond had them sweep the bleachers and polish the floor for forty minutes. After that, they had to endure a ten-minute lecture on theft. When they returned to the principal's office, Mrs. Demetriou told them that Mr. Susskind had already left.

"Can you just get my case out of his office?" asked Ben desperately. Suppose there was another Sneak in his bedroom tonight? What would he do? "It's really important. Mr. Susskind was *supposed* to give it back to me today."

"Sorry," she said, not looking sorry in the slightest. "His office is locked. You'll have to get it tomorrow."

They went up to the library, but it was nearly four o'clock and the doors were locked. Ms. Pryce's car was no longer in the parking lot. Of course she wouldn't have waited; how would she know they were still at school so late? Charlotte was gone too. Dejectedly, they left the building.

✻

When Ben got home, Leo was in the backyard with Morpheus and Poubelle. He was setting tiny soldier figurines in formations in the bushes. The soldiers were battling giant plastic bugs—neon spiders and scorpions and big red ants the size of Leo's thumb.

"The soldiers stand no chance against the giant insects of Azalea," muttered Leo.

"Azalea?" said Ben.

"Guess what?" Leo beamed up at him. "Poubelle didn't even pee in the house! She was whining at the back door when I came home and she ran right out to pee!"

"Poubelle!" said Ben, patting the dog. "Great job."

Morpheus was sitting by the steps and gave him a mournful look.

"I know—you've been doing a great job your whole life," said Ben.

Their mom was blaring Bach sonatas from the basement, and Ben could see his dad in the kitchen, moving around like a tornado.

"Dad's home?" he said.

"He's making Cincinnati chili," said Leo. "For Mom. So she can just eat it for three days straight, until she has her meeting with EnVision."

"Are we allowed to eat it too?" asked Ben, his mouth watering. His dad made excellent Cincinnati chili.

Leo shrugged. "Did you notice Poubelle's name tag is weird?" he said.

"What do you mean, weird?"

"It's like a locket, but I can't open it. I tried."

Ben knelt before the poodle to examine her tags. There was the thin metal rabies tag, and a silver heart that said *Poubelle* on it in looping cursive letters. The heart was a quarter-inch thick, with a seam along its edge.

"Sometimes tags are just like that," he said, trying to keep his voice casual, but his heart had started to race.

"I'm having a problem," said Leo.

"What kind of problem?" Ben asked, sliding the name tag off the collar and putting it in his pocket. Poubelle licked his face.

"A friend problem," said Leo.

"You mean with Christina?" asked Ben, desperate to get inside and examine the tag in private.

"Yeah. Christina and Mikey and Taryn and Gabriel. We all play together at recess, usually."

"I have to go do something, Leo. Let's talk about it later."

"But I need your advice. It's about another kid."

"Later, okay? I promise."

"Whatever," grumbled Leo. He made a striped spider knock five soldiers off a branch.

✳

In his bedroom, Ben opened the smallest blade on his pocketknife and slid the tip of it into the seam on the name tag. The tag popped open. There was a slip of paper tightly folded up inside it. Fingers trembling, he unfolded it. The handwriting was the same as the writing in the letter to Agatha from her nephew, Colin. It said:

> *Checkmate in one → St. Petersburg → Persephone →*
> *Marie Antoinette → Hydra → Blue Riddle → Target VII*
>
> *Target XIV → Green Riddle → Perseus →*
> *Napoleon → Idun → Tokyo → Check with black queen*

Ben fumbled his phone out of his pocket and took a picture to send to Ashok.

✳

Ashok: It might be a key to the code, or a route. I'll work on it.

Ben: Thanks. Agatha's nephew said in the letter that he'd sent her directions and she should hide them. If that's what this is, she hid them really well!

Ashok: What are you going to do if another Sneak gets in your room tonight? How can you secure it overnight without the briefcase?

Ben: I could get a metal toolbox from the basement—my mom has some strong ones—but the Sneak that looked like Ms. Kennedy's watch tunneled right through a car door. Damon said they can get through solids easily.

Ashok: What if you filled the box with water? Would the Sneak stay paralyzed if it was in water?

Ben: I don't know. Maybe. That's a good idea.

Ashok: Here's what you do. Fill your biggest water gun and keep it right next to you, so you can protect yourself. Fill a strong toolbox with water and get a bungee cord to keep it shut. If you do catch a Sneak, you blast it, secure it in the box, and put the box in the basement freezer. Then refill your water gun and get another box, so you're ready if it escapes or if it happens again.

Ben: Solid plan. I wish you were here.

Ashok: So do I. How much does Malcolm know about all of this?

Ben: What? Why would Malcolm know anything?

Ashok: You said he was your partner for the town history project. And once or twice you said "we," so I thought maybe you were doing all this stuff with him.

Ben: No, Malcolm doesn't know anything.

Ashok: Better to keep it that way. That guy has a big mouth.

Ben: Yeah.

TUESDAY, OCTOBER 2

THE RETURN OF
MS. KENNEDY'S
WRISTWATCH

26

Poubelle had spent thirty minutes barking and growling at something in the yard in the middle of the night, so Ben was under-slept and uneasy Tuesday morning. He felt sure it had been a Sneak lurking around the house.

Akemi met him at the bike racks, her face panicked.

"Come quick!" she said, before he had a chance to tell her about the paper hidden in Poubelle's tag.

He ran after her, around the side of the school, to where the garbage bins were. Charlotte was crouched next to one of the bins.

"Is it still there?" asked Akemi.

Charlotte nodded.

"It's the watch," Akemi told him.

Ben got down on his hands and knees and looked under the garbage bin. Something was moving in the shadows back there. He wished he'd brought his water soaker. He got his water bottle out of the side pouch of his backpack and unscrewed the lid.

"We don't have the briefcase," whispered Akemi.

"We can paralyze it with a splash, and put it in the bottle with water inside. Then we'll go get the briefcase," he said.

Ben got on his belly and wriggled under the bin, inching toward the watch, which became more obviously a watch the closer he got. It stayed still at first, and then, when it was almost within reach, it reared up on its back strap, the front strap pointing at him. A row of tiny needle-sharp teeth glinted along the buckle. He reached for it with one arm, coming at it from the left. He'd expected it to run away, moving right, and he had the other arm ready with the water bottle, but instead it ran straight into his left hand and bit him viciously on the thumb. He howled, and threw water at it, but it dodged and shot out from under the garbage bin.

Charlotte pounced on it, moving faster than he'd ever seen her move, scooping it up in her jacket.

"Put it in here!" said Ben. The water bottle was still half full. She dropped the wriggling watch inside, and he screwed the cap on tight. There was a feeble splash, and then nothing. Ben crammed the bottle into the bottom of his backpack.

"We shouldn't keep *The Book of Keys* and the vocoro in the same bag as the Sneak," said Akemi. "Give them to me."

Ben felt strangely proprietary, but there was no reason the book belonged to him any more than to Akemi, and she was right about separating it from the Sneak, so he took it out, along with the copper wheel, and she put both items in her backpack.

"What are those weirdos *doing?*" said Jessica Masterson,

sauntering by with Jake and Lekan. "Crawling around under the trash. Maybe they found a really cute rat!"

Her eyes darted to Ben and then away again.

He ignored her; he was way too freaked out to think about Jessica Masterson. He ran straight into the school, to the main office, with Akemi and Charlotte right behind him. They came to a halt before Mrs. Demetriou's desk just as the bell rang.

"Is Mr. Susskind here?" asked Ben.

Mrs. Demetriou looked offended. "What's wrong?"

"I need my briefcase," he said.

Mr. Susskind appeared in the doorway of his office, all gleam and puff.

"My briefcase!" panted Ben. "Please!"

"*After* school, Ben," he said patiently. "As I said. Ha-ha-ha."

"That was *yesterday*, and you weren't even here after school yesterday!" cried Ben. "I really need it!"

"You don't need it during the school day. Ahem," said Mr. Susskind. "Integrity! Respect! A position of . . . ahem . . . ha-ha-ha. *Young man*, I think we need to have a little chat about this new *attitude* of yours. Come back after school. You can have your case then."

Ben looked helplessly at Akemi.

"Get to class, all of you!" said Mr. Susskind, his face turning suddenly thunderous, like someone had flicked a switch. "The bell! Timeliness! Punctuality! Ha-*ha*-ha!"

✳

They slunk in late. Ms. Kennedy rapped out sharply, "Miss Hanamura, Miss Moss, and *Mis*-ter Harp, all tardy."

"Oooh," said Danny Farkas, making kissing faces with his two hands.

Ben hung his backpack on its hook at the back of the classroom.

"Stop acting like you're in kindergarten," Akemi snapped at Danny over her shoulder.

"*Miss* Hanamura, that is quite enough!" cried Ms. Kennedy. "Coming in late *and* disrupting the class! Clearly, you don't know how things *work* at Livingston Middle School, but this behavior is not acceptable."

"But . . ." Akemi started to point at Danny Farkas and then gave up, a sullen expression on her face.

"Any more out of you, and it will be detention," said Ms. Kennedy. "*Open* your journals, please. We're going to do some contemplative writing about *peace* on *earth*."

They were fifteen minutes into contemplative writing when Ben heard it: a low grinding sound from the back of the class. He tried to ignore it, but it was gradually getting louder. He looked over at Akemi. She was staring at his backpack, wide-eyed with horror.

"What is that noise?" demanded Ms. Kennedy. Her watery eyes fixed on Ben—probably because he had gone very pale.

"That bag is *moving!*" cried Jessica Masterson. "Did Ratgirl bring another *animal* to school?"

Indeed, Ben's backpack was shifting about on its hook now. There was water dripping out of the bottom of it.

"*Whose bag is that?*" screeched Ms. Kennedy.

After a pause, during which the backpack dislodged itself from its hook and fell on the floor, Ben rose slowly to his feet.

"Mine," he said hollowly.

"*What* have you got in that bag, *Ben*-jamin Harp?"

"I'll . . . go check . . . ," he said.

Would he be accused of stealing her watch? Or would the fact that it was moving distract everybody from the fact that it was in his backpack? It was punching against the backpack like a tiny fist now.

Ben forced his limbs to walk over to the backpack. The whole scene felt unreal. Before he could reach the zipper, the watch punched right through the backpack, ripping a hole in it. Ms. Kennedy was behind him. The watch shot out of the bag, flew over his shoulder, and struck Ms. Kennedy in the face, breaking her glasses. She shrieked, and staggered backward. The watch zipped across the classroom, through the air, bouncing madly from wall to wall, and shot out the open door, into the hall.

27

"*Auuuugh!*" Ms. Kennedy was pulling tissues out of her sleeves. Her nose was bleeding, her broken glasses askew.

"What was that?" hollered Briony Moore, scrambling onto her desk.

"Rat!" shouted Jessica Masterson.

"That was *not* a rat!" yelled Danny Farkas. "You *freak!*" This was directed at Ben.

"I think it was a *lizard*," said Charlotte Moss loudly.

"I definitely saw scales," agreed Jae Park. "Did you bring a lizard to school, Harp?"

"That was no lizard, it was *flying!*" yelled Lekan Bassey. "It was a *bat!*"

Ben shook his head and said in an unsteady voice, "I don't know what it was. I didn't put an animal in my bag." That part was true, at least. He didn't think Sneaks qualified as animals. "It must have just . . . crawled in there."

He took out his water bottle. There was a hole in it, like the hole in Ms. Pryce's car door. From the end of the hall— where the library was—came the sound of glass shattering. He caught Akemi's horrified gaze.

Ms. Kennedy was distracted by her bloody nose. Ben ran out into the hall. Akemi and Charlotte followed him. One of the windows on the double doors that led to the library was smashed. Ben pushed open the doors, trying to avoid the glass as best he could. Ms. Pryce was under one of the computer tables.

"Got you!" she cried, and stood up. She froze when she saw them in the doorway. The buckle of Ms. Kennedy's watch, hanging free from her fist, swung up and bit her on the side of the hand. She gasped and nearly dropped the watch before grabbing it with her other hand.

"Get me a . . . container," she said, gesturing with an elbow at her desk. "Quickly."

"It can bust out of anything," said Akemi.

"We need the briefcase," said Ben. "Just keep hold of it."

"I'll get water," said Akemi, running to the water fountain in the hall.

Ben sprinted down the stairs, swerved left, and burst into the main office. Mrs. Demetriou glowered at him.

"Is Mr. Susskind here?" he gasped, heading right for the principal's door.

"Ben Harp, *what* has gotten into you lately?" cried Mrs. Demetriou as he slipped past her desk and banged on the principal's door.

Mr. Susskind swung it open, chest puffing, teeth shining in a half grin, half grimace.

"Ms. Pryce needs the briefcase *now!*" Ben shouted. "It's

actually hers, you can ask her, she asked me to bring it to her *right now,* she needs it *right away.*"

He saw the briefcase in the corner of the office.

"*I* will take it to her, ha-ha-*ha,*" said Mr. Susskind. "Ahem. Ben Harp. Sixth grade. Where are you supposed to *be* right now?"

"Library!" said Ben frantically. "Helping Ms. Pryce."

Mr. Susskind picked up the briefcase and strode past him, up the stairs, to the library. He crunched over the broken glass on the floor as if he didn't even notice it. Ms. Pryce's canary-yellow sweater was soaking wet—Akemi had clearly just hurled water all over her—and the watch was limp in her fist. Not for long, Ben knew. Charlotte was standing against the wall, chewing a fingernail and looking unhappy.

"I brought your briefcase back!" Ben yelled. "I mean, Mr. Susskind has it!"

Ms. Pryce put her fist with the no-longer-struggling watch at her side.

"This is *yours,* Ms. Pryce?" said Mr. Susskind, still hanging on to the briefcase.

Ben pleaded with his eyes.

"We just borrowed it for our project," he repeated. "But you said you needed it right away, *right?*"

Ms. Pryce looked from him to Mr. Susskind and said coolly, "Yes, that's right."

Mr. Susskind put it on her desk and said to Ben, Akemi, and Charlotte: "You three, *in* my office, right now. Ahem."

"Mr. Susskind, I need their help cleaning up here," said Ms. Pryce. "I'll send them down to you when we're done."

He looked taken aback. "Ms. Pryce," he began, his expression glazing over, like he was trying to compute how to handle insubordination.

Ms. Pryce turned the same withering, wide-eyed look on him that she turned on misbehaving students. It seemed to have the same effect. His chest puffed, but he shut his mouth on whatever he'd been about to say.

"It will only be a moment. Thank you," said Ms. Pryce in her best *Don't you dare argue with me* voice.

Mr. Susskind spun around and strode back out, crunching over the broken glass again.

The end of the watch was starting to twitch. Ben could see the bite mark on Ms. Pryce's hand where it had got her.

"Quick," he said, grabbing the briefcase off her desk and opening it. "Put it in here."

Ms. Pryce did so. Ben slammed the case shut, twisted the knob. The blue light flashed along the join. He took a deep breath and opened it again. There was Ms. Kennedy's watch: no more teeth on the buckle, not moving around, just a regular— if waterlogged and no longer functioning—watch.

The phone on the library wall began to ring. Ms. Pryce went to answer it. When she was done, she turned to look at them.

"Apparently, you three ran out of Ms. Kennedy's class, and there is a flying lizard on the loose in the school," she said dryly. "Ms. Kennedy wants you to report to Mr. Susskind's office."

159

They looked at each other disconsolately.

"You should return Ms. Kennedy's watch—subtly, if you can," she added, handing it to Ben. She put the briefcase under her desk. "Please come and see me *immediately* after school. All three of you."

28

Mr. Susskind paced back and forth in his office, lecturing them—more or less, but it wasn't easy to follow the thread—about respect for teachers and wildlife. There was a brief, vehement tangent about climate change that veered abruptly into the importance of caring for school property.

At lunch, Ben finally had a chance to show Akemi and Charlotte the paper he'd found inside Poubelle's name tag.

"That was a smart hiding spot," said Akemi admiringly, unwrapping her sandwich. "No way was Poubelle letting Simon get near her! She *hates* him!"

"And then he ditched Poubelle in the park with no idea that she had something he was looking for," added Ben.

"Something we *think* he might be looking for," put in Charlotte. "We still don't know. But I bet this could help us figure out the book."

"That was smart, saying you thought the watch was a

lizard," said Akemi to Charlotte. "Everybody latched on to that."

"Thanks," said Charlotte. "It just makes me think how under no *circumstances* should an animal, *terrestrial* or *aquatic*, be kept in a backpack, ha-ha-ha, a sweatshirt, or anywhere on *school property!*"

It was such a flawless impression of Mr. Susskind that Ben and Akemi both cracked up. Charlotte looked pleased and a little startled. Her cheeks pinked, and she turned her attention to her cup of noodles.

Ben checked his phone under the table hopefully. Still nothing from Ashok.

✱

After school, they had detention with Ms. Kennedy. Akemi tried to tell their homeroom teacher that she had basketball practice, but Ms. Kennedy was unmoved. They had to organize the book bins and sharpen boxes full of pencils. Ben managed to slip Ms. Kennedy's ruined watch onto a corner of her desk, under a folder, while she was in the restroom.

When the detention was over, the three of them trooped over to the library. This time, the lights were on and the doors unlocked. There was cardboard over the broken window and the glass had been swept up. Ms. Pryce had waited for them.

"I still don't think we should just tell her everything," said Charlotte sadly.

"I'm telling her," said Ben.

Ms. Pryce locked the double doors of the library behind them, ushered them to a table, and sat down across from them, hands folded before her. There was a Band-Aid on her hand where the watch buckle had snapped at her.

"Explain," she said crisply.

They looked at each other. Where to begin? Ben had questions of his own.

"So . . . you know about Sneaks?" he said.

She let out a breath, removed her glasses, and rubbed the bridge of her nose. She looked startlingly young without the glasses. She put them back on and said, "Yes. I should never have included Agatha Bent in the town history project. I thought you'd meet her in public and you could tell me a little about her health, and that would be it. Her carer had turned me away and blocked my calls. I just wanted to know if she was all right. But I never intended for you to get mixed up in . . . all of this."

"All of *what*, exactly?" asked Ben.

She gave him a long look. "Tell me what happened at her house," she said. "Then I'll explain."

"There was a package by her porch, in the rain," began Akemi, and the whole story poured out—the Morse code tapping, *The Book of Keys* and the vocoro, how they had seen the watch crawling around, Damon coming down from the tree and giving them the briefcase, the clothes hanger in Ben's room, the pinny in gym class. Ben was nearly dizzy with relief. Ms. Pryce listened calmly and seriously, but when they got to the part about the Sneak in his bedroom attacking him, she lifted a perfectly manicured hand to her heart in horror.

"I am so sorry," she said, when at last they were done, and her voice quavered very slightly on the word *sorry*. "I *never* imagined something like this would happen. I wish you had come to me sooner, but I can understand why you didn't. How is the . . . bite?"

"Healing," he said. "Just looks like a bunch of little scabs."

She closed her eyes and took a deep breath. When she opened her eyes again, she returned to her crisp, school-librarian voice: "Where are *The Book of Keys* and the vocoro now?"

Ben was about to tell her they were in Akemi's backpack, but Charlotte replied: "At Ben's house."

He stared at her. She looked back at him, her eyes very intense.

"I would like to come and collect them, if I may," said Ms. Pryce.

"Your parents will think that's weird," said Charlotte to Ben. "They're so protective and always asking questions about school and stuff. How would you explain it?"

She was still giving him that crazy stare, and he didn't know what to say. He glanced at Akemi.

"I'll speak to your parents," began Ms. Pryce.

"Maybe I can bring it all tomorrow," said Ben, stalling for time.

Ms. Pryce nodded slowly. "All right. I'm going to give you my cell phone number. You can call me at any time—even in the middle of the night—if something happens."

He handed her his phone so she could put her number in his contacts.

"Can I keep the briefcase tonight, just in case?" he asked.

"Of course," she said. "That's best right now."

"So, you're part of the Gateway Society?" asked Charlotte, leaning forward.

Ms. Pryce looked right at Charlotte, and then she said, "I will be here at seven-thirty tomorrow morning. Please bring the briefcase, *The Book of Keys*, and the vocoro. I will answer all your questions then. Or as many of them as I can."

They got to their feet, dismissed and disappointed. Ms. Pryce added, "I hope I don't need to tell you that it is better if you don't repeat any of this to anyone else? I don't like to encourage children to keep secrets from their parents, but . . ."

"We won't tell," said Ben quickly.

She nodded. "Thank you."

"What about Agatha Bent?" asked Akemi.

"The longer she's in a coma, the worse the odds," said Ms. Pryce.

29

Ben and Akemi unlocked their bikes and walked Charlotte to the bus stop on Finch Street.

"Why did you tell her we didn't have the stuff?" he asked Charlotte, even though he knew why.

"Because she'll take it. I was right," said Charlotte. "And she'll shut us out."

"She said she would explain things," said Akemi. "I thought you wanted to know more! Ms. Pryce is probably our best chance at understanding what's going on."

Charlotte seemed to be giving this serious consideration.

Ben knew how she felt, even though he was mostly relieved at the idea of handing everything over to Ms. Pryce. Now that he knew there were other universes and alien creatures crawling around, pretending to be watches and clothes hangers, how was he supposed to go back to normal, living as if he *didn't* know this?

"We'll have to give her the book and stuff tomorrow," he said. "Hopefully she'll explain everything then."

Charlotte sat down at the bus stop and took the white bow barrettes out of her coat pocket, pinning her hair back ferociously and speaking between clenched teeth. "You two just make all the decisions. After school. On the weekend. Together. But you didn't even know about Gael House. You didn't even guess the vocoro was like a combination lock. You wouldn't have figured *anything* out without my help."

"I know," said Ben, startled. He'd watched Charlotte being picked on for years, but he'd never actually seen her mad or upset.

"We're not trying to leave you out," said Akemi in a small voice.

But they *had* left her out, without really meaning to. It had just been natural to invite Akemi in when they were walking home the same way. Charlotte had been at chess club on Friday when they exchanged phone numbers, but he hadn't tried hard to track her down on the weekend, or asked her to wait for them when he and Akemi had detention on Monday. Trying to explain it would only make it worse, he thought.

Akemi couldn't seem to help herself, though. "You told me your uncle is really strict, and I just thought . . . you probably wouldn't be allowed to go downtown on the weekend. You were always saying you were late and you were going to be in trouble."

Charlotte said nothing.

"Uncle?" said Ben, confused. "I thought you lived with your grandmother."

"She had a stroke this summer," said Charlotte stonily. "She's in a rehab place now. I had to go stay with my aunt and uncle in Pennington, and now they're saying I should live with them, even when my grandmother gets better. They say she's too old to take care of me. But really they just like having me around to babysit their bratty little kids."

As far as Ben knew, Charlotte had lived with her grandmother since she was a baby. He hadn't heard about the stroke. She didn't have friends at school, so maybe nobody knew about it. He wasn't sure what to say.

"So . . . what's it like living with your aunt and uncle?" he asked finally.

Charlotte looked at him for a long second, and then she ground out between her teeth: "I. Hate. Them."

"That really sucks," said Akemi, her voice soft, inviting more. But Charlotte didn't say anything else.

They waited in awkward silence, Charlotte staring across the street with her rice-pudding face, the huge white bows pulling her hair back so tightly that the skin on her forehead looked stretched, until her bus came. Ben hurriedly wrote his number down on a piece of paper from his homework folder and gave it to her.

"I'm not allowed to use the phone," she said dully, but she folded it up and put it in her pocket. Ben and Akemi waved helplessly as she got on the bus and took her seat. She didn't look at them.

"She told you about her uncle?" said Ben as the bus pulled away.

"I didn't know about her grandmother," said Akemi

miserably. "I asked her the other day why she put those barrettes on when she got on the bus, and she said her uncle made her wear them."

They rode their bikes up Finch Street, stopping in front of Gael House, which loomed in its decrepitude among all the newer houses, with yellow DANGER tape around the fence and boards hammered over the front door.

"Maybe I should keep *The Book of Keys* and the vocoro tonight," said Akemi.

Ben thought of Poubelle barking at something in the yard last night. It probably *was* better if he didn't have the book at his house.

"Do you want the briefcase too?" he asked. "Just in case?"

"You keep it," she said. "The Sneaks know where you live. You might need it."

They got back on their bikes. Ben wanted to invite Akemi over, but he felt strange about it after Charlotte's outburst, and she seemed to feel the same. They parted ways at the corner of his street.

"Call me if anything happens!" she said.

"I will," he promised, and pedaled fast toward home.

30

Aaron Harp had taken the day off work so he could keep Lily supplied with snacks and drinks as she worked in the basement. He was doing the crossword, with Poubelle at his feet, when Ben came in.

"Did you take Poubelle out?" asked Ben. He didn't smell pee.

"This dog is smart," said Aaron Harp. "She yips when she wants to go out. She goes a *lot*. Tiny bladder, I guess."

"Yeah. Thanks, Dad."

Leo was eating Doritos in the kitchen. Ben reached into the bag, but Leo yanked it away angrily.

"What's your problem?" said Ben, startled.

"You," grumbled Leo. "And other problems that you don't even care about."

"What are you talking about?"

Leo hardly ever got mad like this. Ben stared at him. Leo looked up, and his eyes glazed with tears.

"You're too busy to ever play with me or even talk to me now," he said. "I need your help, but you always say you can't listen to me and you go off to your room or with your phone or whatever."

Ben was about to snap back, but the complaint was too familiar. He remembered feeling that way himself. His parents moved in a kind of self-absorbed whirlwind around him, and for as long as he could remember, he had felt alone in the eye of the storm—an ignored point of stillness. He'd mostly given up trying to ask them things or tell them things. It was true, he *had* been putting Leo off lately, wrapped up in his own stuff.

His phone pinged. He knew it was probably Ashok, but he stopped himself from checking immediately.

"There's just a lot going on right now," he began, and then cringed. He really did sound like his parents. "So, what's the problem you were telling me about the other day?"

"I have too many friends," sighed Leo.

Ben felt his annoyance return. "Yeah, that sounds like a really big problem," he said sarcastically.

"It is if they gang up," said Leo. "I'm only one person."

"Your friends are ganging up on you?" That was a shock.

"Not on me," said Leo. He spoke very fast, like he was afraid he'd lose Ben's attention at any moment. "Another kid. He came to our school this year. His name's Jordan. He wanted to play with us, and I said okay, but the others said no. And they *really hate* him. He peed his pants at school once because he was scared to ask where the bathroom was, and now they call him 'the Pee-pee Kid.' And I hate it. But if I tell them to stop, they get mad and say that if I want to be friends with him, then I can't be friends with them. But it made me really

170

sad how he was always playing by himself. So on Friday I just said I was going to play with him, and I did, and now none of them will speak to me, not even Christina!"

Tears were pouring down Leo's face.

"Whoa," said Ben. He was about to say "Why didn't you tell me before?" but then remembered that Leo had been trying to tell him all week. "That sucks."

"I know," said Leo. "Christina is my best friend, and now she doesn't look at me, even. And Jordan is nice, but I miss my other friends."

"Maybe they'll get over it?" said Ben. "Did you try talking to them?"

"They just walk away when I try to talk to them!" wailed Leo. "Mikey said if I stop playing with Jordan, they'll be friends with me again, and I sort of want to, except then Jordan will have nobody and they're still mean to him."

"You're doing the right thing, sticking up for Jordan," said Ben. "You can't let your friends get away with being jerks."

"I know," said Leo forlornly.

Ben's phone pinged again. It took all his willpower not to take it out of his pocket. Leo shoveled the last of the Dorito crumbs into his mouth.

"You can answer your phone," he said, with a tragic expression. His lips were stained orange from the Doritos. He looked like a sad clown.

"I'll answer it later," said Ben. "Want to take the dogs to the ravine with me?"

Leo wiped his mouth on his arm, leaving orange Dorito streaks across his sleeve, and nodded tearfully.

✳

Ashok: You've captured three Sneaks now! You're turning into a pro.

Ben: I'm pretty far from a pro still.

Ashok: Well, I spent the whole afternoon matching that list you sent with instructions in *The Book of Keys,* and it's definitely a route. The first thing in the list is "Checkmate in one," right? And on the first page of the book, it describes a peaceful room with a chessboard and gives a bunch of chess move options. "Checkmate in one" takes you to the Coordinates Room. And the next thing on the list after "Checkmate in one" is "St. Petersburg," right? That's one of the options in the Coordinates Room, and it takes you to a place called "Mythic Feasts."

The next word is "Persephone." In the Mythic Feasts place, if you "weigh Persephone's choice," that takes you to the Dressing Room, and choosing "Marie Antoinette" takes you to the Constellation Room. If you choose "Hydra" there, you go to the Riddle Room, and if you answer "the Blue Riddle," it takes you to the Target Room.

The last thing in the list is "Target VII," which takes you to the Staircase. But I couldn't find a staircase in the book. I'll keep working on it. The next group of words sort of matches up with the first line but going backward—like, same themes, not the same words—so it should take you back to the start from wherever you end up.

Ben: But we still don't know what any of the clues mean! A route to where? From where? How do you choose "Marie Antoinette," and how does that take you anywhere else?

Ashok: No idea. If it's in code, it's way too complicated for me to figure it out.

Ben: Anyway, tomorrow I'm done. I won't have the briefcase or the book or anything anymore.

Ashok: You're doing the right thing, telling Pryce. This is too much for you to handle on your own.

Ben: . . . I'm not actually on my own.

Ashok: You mean you told Malcolm? Dude! Malcolm is so unreliable!

Ben: Not Malcolm. I'm not doing the town history project with Malcolm. I don't know why I said that.

Ashok: ?

Ben: There's this new girl, Akemi. I didn't have a partner, so I got put in a group with her and Charlotte Moss. They've been part of the whole thing.

Ashok: Why didn't you tell me that in the first place?

Ben: I don't know.

Ashok: Wait. Do you have a crush on the new girl? I thought we told each other everything.

Ben: It isn't like that. We're friends. Anyway, Charlotte didn't want to tell Pryce anything, and she's acting really weird.

Ashok: Charlotte Moss has always been weird.

Ben: She's different than she seems, once you get to know her. But today she told us her grandmother had a stroke and she lives with her uncle and aunt and she said she hates them.

Ashok: Is her grandmother okay?

Ben: I'm not sure. She said she's in rehab.

Ashok: That sucks. Poor Charlotte.

Ben: I know. I don't know what to do.

Ashok: Tell Pryce about it. There's a social worker at school too. If Charlotte's having problems, they might be able to help.

Ben: But what do I say? She seems sad? She doesn't like her uncle? I don't really know anything.

Ashok: Just say you think she might not be doing okay. Seriously, it's their job to help with stuff like that.

Ben: Okay.

Ashok: So . . . what's the new girl like?

WEDNESDAY, OCTOBER 3

EATER OF WORLDS

31

They were all three waiting outside the school at seven-thirty in the morning when Ms. Pryce pulled up. Charlotte was in full rice-pudding-face mode, but didn't bring up their tense conversation from the day before. This time, Ben had his water soaker as well as the briefcase stuffed in his backpack, which he'd patched with a thick layer of duct tape where the Sneak had ripped a hole in it.

Ms. Pryce was dressed in a lime-green pencil skirt and matching heels and a brown faux-leather jacket zipped up over her blouse, with her bulky bag over her shoulder.

"Good morning," she said, as if it were an entirely normal thing for them to be meeting this early. They followed her into the school and up to the library. She shut the doors behind them and gestured to the same table they'd sat at yesterday.

"No Sneak attacks last night, I assume?" she asked.

Ben shook his head.

"May I see *The Book of Keys?*"

Akemi took it out of her backpack and handed it to her while Charlotte scowled.

"I also found this . . . hidden inside Agatha Bent's dog's

name tag," said Ben, passing her the slip of paper. "We think it's some kind of directions. It's connected to the book."

Ms. Pryce examined the list of words, read the letter from Colin Bent, and then opened the book. She paused a long time over the poem on the first page before flipping quickly through the other pages.

"I understand that this past week must have been very confusing and frightening, and I hold myself responsible," she said at last. "I never imagined this scenario . . . but I feel that I should have. As much as possible, I need you now to put it out of your minds. It's not something that you should be involved in."

"You said you would explain!" cried Akemi.

"We're *already* involved," added Ben. "We know stuff, and we've captured Sneaks, and I've been hurt. If we're going to keep secrets for you, we deserve to know what's going on. It isn't fair to tell us to keep quiet *and* try to keep us out of this."

Ms. Pryce studied them. "It *is* unfair," she agreed. "But having so foolishly put you in harm's way, I am trying to do whatever I can to keep you safe."

Charlotte was giving him an *I told you so* look.

"Just explaining things isn't going to put us in danger!" insisted Ben.

"If I tell you a little bit . . . about the multiverse, the history of the gap . . . will that help you to put this matter aside?" she asked.

They all three nodded vigorously.

"Very well," she began. "This is an oversimplification, of course, but imagine different universes—perhaps with distinct physical laws—as beads on a thread. The thread linking all our universes together is a kind of tunnel or road passing through them, although in reality it is not so orderly as beads on a single thread. The Gateway Society refers to this tunnel as a "transdimensional wormhole." Think of the gap as the hole in the bead that the thread runs through—a space within the universe and between universes that is not part of the multiverse itself. The entryway to the gap in *our* universe happens to be located right here in Livingston."

Charlotte laughed. They all stared at her.

"Sorry," she said. "That's just super weird. I mean . . . *Livingston*. Nothing ever happens here."

"As the multiverse expanded, these gaps within and around the universes widened as well," continued Ms. Pryce. "The borders thinned. In order to maintain the integrity of each distinct universe—to prevent them from bleeding into each other and collapsing the boundaries of reality as we know it—beings that we call 'Cartographers,' capable of traveling the tunnel between universes and traversing the gaps, closed the widening gaps with flexible seals. The seals had to be flexible in order to withstand the stretching of time and space, which makes them slightly porous, allowing smaller energies and creatures to occasionally slip through. And there is always a way to *open* the seals. They are like locked doors between universes that can be unlocked with the right key."

She paused and looked at the book again, a frown flickering across her face.

"So that's what Damon is?" asked Akemi. "A Cartographer?"

"I believe you contacted a Locksmith," said Ms. Pryce. "Think of the Cartographers as upper management—the planners and designers—and the Locksmiths as those who implement the plans practically."

"No wonder he seemed so busy," said Charlotte. "Can *people* go on this road between universes? Has anybody ever gone to another universe?"

"I don't think so," said Ms. Pryce, taken aback.

"But you don't know for sure?" Charlotte pressed her.

Ben thought of her saying, "I wish I could go to Paris. I wish I could go anywhere."

"What about Sneaks?" he asked. "Damon said they evolve in the gaps. But what *are* they? And what do they want?"

"Sneaks—or 'Malsprites,' as they were originally named—are creatures belonging to no specific universe. They are a life-form that evolves out of the energy of the gap. There may be many kinds of life-forms in the gap that we don't know about, but the predatory Sneaks feed on fear and are drawn to our world, which offers quite a feast. There have been Sneaks slipping through the gap since the beginning of time, no doubt—but the arrival of Morvox at the door to our universe raised the stakes."

"Damon mentioned Morvox—right?" said Ben to the

other two. "He said . . . if Sneaks were coming back here, it was for Morvox. Or something."

Charlotte and Akemi nodded.

"Our first knowledge of Morvox came in the early nineteenth century," said Ms. Pryce. "At that time, the Gateway Society was mostly a loose organization of adventurers, hunting and capturing Sneaks, under the leadership of an astronomer at Livingston University."

"Peter Gael," said Charlotte.

"Yes," said Ms. Pryce. "Together with a Locksmith, he designed a maze—a trap—to place *over* the seal, so that even Sneaks that slipped through the seal would be stuck, kept from the world."

"Gael House," said Charlotte.

Ben looked at her. She was putting all this together a lot faster than he was.

"I must ask you not to go near the house," said Ms. Pryce. "It could be incredibly dangerous. It was built in response to . . . a crisis of sorts. Sneaks of small energies have always been able to slip through the seal, and while they sometimes caused trouble, it was nothing terribly serious. They get classed as Level Ones or Level Twos. Sometimes a Sneak already in the world will evolve as far as a Level Three—they can borrow animal forms and are capable of complex planning—but even they are basically manageable. In 1823, a different sort of Sneak came through. He was able to evolve and devolve at will. He shrank himself down in order to come through the gap, but he was able to return to his full power, his immense intelligence and capability, once in the world. He does not need to borrow an object or animal as a disguise—he can *imitate* whatever form he chooses, even human form, though that is incredibly difficult, as the variations on human are so vast and he must still have a physical flaw, like all Sneaks, that distinguishes him from the true form he is imitating. This Sneak has been classed as a Level Four—the only one on record. His aim was to open the seal and allow through a creature of tremendous energies—something that had evolved far beyond a mere Malsprite."

"Morvox," whispered Charlotte.

Ms. Pryce nodded. "Morvox. Fortunately, Peter Gael and his daughter—that gets left out of the history, you know: the important role his daughter played—were able to track down and imprison this Sneak before he could complete his task."

"Wait, is that Sneak—the Level-Four Sneak—called 'Sabrin'?" asked Ben. "In the letter Agatha's nephew wrote, he talks about someone called Sabrin, who escaped a few months ago from some prison in the Aleutian Islands."

"That's right—Sabrin," said Ms. Pryce grimly. "The Gateway Society claims to have everything under control. Gael House has acted as a very successful trap over the seal for almost two hundred years now. Any Sneaks that slip through the seal get stuck in Gael House and no longer make it out into the world. The Sneaks in the world *now* are Sneaks that came through before the house was built. However, if they are returning to Livingston, gathering around the gap, it suggests some instability . . . something *happening*. The fact that they know about *The Book of Keys* . . ." She broke off, a pinched expression on her face. "But the Gateway Society is responsible for managing the house, the seal, the gap, and all Sneak activity. They are monitoring the situation. It is certainly not something you ought to get mixed up in."

"So, Agatha is part of that society? And her nephew?" asked Akemi.

"Yes. Agatha is a direct descendant of Peter Gael, and her role in the Gateway Society is that of Liaison to the Locksmith," said Ms. Pryce. "She is Peter Gael's great-great-great-granddaughter, I believe, and has been involved with the Gateway Society from a young age. She is also the official owner of Gael House."

"What about you?" asked Ben.

Ms. Pryce adjusted her glasses. "I am an employee of the Gateway Society, but I have minor clearance only. I was sent here as an observer. My job is only to monitor Sneak activity in town and report it. Agatha is the official Liaison."

"She really doesn't seem like a spy in an organization involved with aliens," marveled Akemi.

"As a librarian, I must remind you never to judge a book by its cover," said Ms. Pryce with a faint smile. "Now, I've told you what I can. . . ."

"So, did you report the watch and stuff to the Gateway

Society?" interrupted Charlotte. "And everything we told you yesterday?"

"Yes. I've been assured that everything is under control. These are minor Sneaks, they say, and nothing to be overly concerned about." Her expression was stiff when she said this, and her knuckles tightened on *The Book of Keys*.

"But Sabrin isn't a minor Sneak," said Ben. "If he's escaped . . . and Sneaks are here trying to get the book . . . doesn't it sound like . . ."

". . . they want to open the seal and let Morvox into the world, like they tried to do before?" Charlotte finished. "What *is* Morvox, exactly?"

"Morvox . . . ," said Ms. Pryce heavily. "All Sneaks feed on fear. Morvox is . . . hungrier than the average Sneak. Morvox requires chaos. It is nicknamed 'Eater of Worlds' because it breaks into vulnerable universes to wreak terror and devastation, feeding upon the panic and fear, and leaving worlds in ruins before moving on. Morvox has had an interest in *our* planet for some time."

"Whoa," said Charlotte softly.

"So where is Sabrin now?" asked Akemi.

"I don't have clearance for that kind of information," said Ms. Pryce. "As I said, Sabrin *can* take human form, but there would still be something wrong, something not quite human about him, if he did."

Ben felt his chest tighten.

"What about Mr. Susskind?" He said it before he could stop himself.

Ms. Pryce looked startled.

"There's something really weird about the way he . . . smiles. And acts," said Ben sheepishly.

Ms. Pryce's mouth twitched, like she was trying not to laugh.

"A person may be eccentric without being a Sneak. To the best of my knowledge, Mr. Susskind simply has an . . . unusual communication style," she said. "I do *not* believe him to be a Sneak!"

"Simon's feet don't touch the ground," blurted out Charlotte.

They all stared at her.

"You didn't notice that?" she said.

Ben thought of how Simon had seemed to enter the room noiselessly, his distinctive, gliding walk, and the frantic way Poubelle had barked at him. The dog had calmed down so much, away from Agatha's house.

"Agatha's carer?" said Ms. Pryce faintly. "His feet . . . don't touch the ground?"

"He walks in the air. About an inch over the ground."

There was a drawn-out, horrified silence, and then Akemi yelled, "*When were you going to mention that?*"

Charlotte shrugged guiltily.

"If that's true . . . ," said Ms. Pryce. Her voice trembled slightly. She was normally so calm and self-assured; her obvious fear alarmed Ben more than anything else had so far. "Charlotte, are you quite sure?"

Charlotte nodded.

"Thank you, all three of you," said Ms. Pryce, standing up. "I must ask you to go now."

"You're going to contact Damon, aren't you?" said Akemi excitedly.

Ms. Pryce didn't answer.

"You can't just shut us out now," cried Ben.

"You're too young," she said.

"But *Damon* isn't dangerous," said Ben, though he had no real way of knowing if this was true. He grabbed the vocoro from the table and spun it. "I'll show you how to do it!"

"Wait! Not here," began Ms. Pryce, but she was too late.

The numbers were etched in his memory, and he spun the wheel quickly: XVI–LV–XI.

32

There was a bang from the supply closet. Blue light flickered around the edges.

"In there!" cried Akemi, running over and flinging the door open.

Damon stepped out and slammed the closet door behind

him quickly. He looked exactly the same as before—neat suit, combed sandy hair—but distinctly irritated this time.

"You again?" he said, glaring at Akemi and Ben. "I did say only in an *emergency*, didn't I?"

Then his eyes fell on Ms. Pryce. He straightened up a little. "Ah," he said. "Hello."

"I'm Lenore Pryce," she said, holding out her hand.

He shook it and smiled winningly, as if he hadn't just been snapping at them. "Delighted to make your acquaintance. Call me Damon. So glad to see that there *is* a human of full maturity handling things here. I was most surprised to be called upon by, ah, young humans . . . children . . . the other day."

"That was a mistake," said Ms. Pryce.

Something banged inside the closet. Damon gave the door a swift backward kick, then smiled at Ms. Pryce again.

"It was *my* mistake," continued Ms. Pryce. "However, I'm concerned that the Gateway Society either does not recognize the seriousness of what is happening here or does not care. There have been two Sneaks in the school, presumably keeping tabs on me, and one in this boy's home, and we have reason to believe that Sabrin himself may be here at the gap. I think they are looking for Peter Gael's *Book of Keys*, and I think I know why. I have just looked at the book myself. I am very concerned to see that it seems to provide both a map of the maze and a *recipe* of sorts for opening the seal."

Damon looked startled. "May I see?"

Ms. Pryce handed him *The Book of Keys*. He looked

through it, his expression shifting from surprise to horror. "My understanding was that the Gateway Society destroyed *The Book of Keys* more than a hundred years ago, agreeing that it was too dangerous!"

"There was a copy," said Ms. Pryce grimly. "It seems to have been passed down in the Gael family, briefly lost, and now found again. If Sabrin is loose . . . It seems to me that he and the Sneaks acting under his direction are searching for *The Book of Keys* in order to open the seal and release Morvox."

"Hmm. The design of the maze is quite ingenious, I'll grant him that. This planet has only been in my jurisdiction for roughly a century, and the previous Locksmith, who worked with Gael, is known to be somewhat . . . well, eccentric, I suppose. The method they concocted for opening the seal is frankly rather off-putting."

" 'The blood of the young, the flesh of the old,' " began Ms. Pryce.

"Yes. Gruesome, really. But as long as the book is safe . . ."

"Agatha Bent is in the hospital right now, and missing the tip of her little finger," said Ms. Pryce.

Akemi gasped. Damon stared at Ms. Pryce, speechless, for a moment.

"Well . . . coincidence . . . ?" he suggested.

"I hope so," said Ms. Pryce. "But the fact that she entrusted the book to these children in the first place suggests she was frightened and knew she was in danger."

"Simon looked at the book," said Ben. "The package was

open in his bag. So he could have read the poem on the first page. If that's the ... uh ... recipe for opening the seal."

"And he wiped up my cut," said Charlotte with a funny gleam in her eye.

"What?"

"Remember? I distracted him by saying I needed a Band-Aid? When I peeled off my scab? He cleaned it up for me. With a cotton ball. He put it in a baggie instead of the garbage. I thought that was weird."

" 'The blood of the young,' " murmured Ms. Pryce.

"Oh, dear," said Damon. "Who is Simon?"

"I'm afraid that he may be Sabrin," said Ms. Pryce. "He began working as a carer for Agatha after she was hit by a car—and I am beginning to suspect that was not an accident at all. The driver was never caught. Simon took over Agatha's care. He refused my calls, denied me any contact with her. Charlotte here claims that his feet do not touch the ground. He walks ... an inch in the air."

"Have you mentioned this to the Gateway Society?" asked Damon. "They are your first point of contact, you know. Not that I mind being called in the *slightest* ... charmed to make your acquaintance, truly."

Ben and Akemi exchanged a look.

"I will inform them, but the men stationed here have put me off at every turn, and I have no means of contacting anyone higher up," replied Ms. Pryce. "They do not seem to understand the seriousness of the situation."

"If Sabrin is here at the gap and gathering the materials to open the seal, then this universe could fall to Morvox very quickly indeed," said Damon. "Once Morvox is unleashed . . . Well, it would be better to deal with this *before* that happens, obviously. Dear me, it is such a busy time in the multiverse. But you were quite right to contact me. I'll go to the Cartographers at once."

"The Cartographers?" said Ms. Pryce, with something like awe.

"I can't interfere without authorization," said Damon. "But I'll make my report immediately. No doubt authorization will be swift. Then I'll return to take care of this matter and re-make the seal, if necessary."

"Thank you," said Ms. Pryce, looking immensely relieved.

He beamed at her. "Thank *you*. It has been a pleasure. If only it had been under better circumstances. In the meantime, if there is *anything* I can do, any new information, do please contact me immediately, whatever it is, however small it might seem. Even a question you might think of . . . No trouble at all."

Akemi goggled her eyes at Ben. He shrugged in return.

"Thank you," said Ms. Pryce again.

"Perhaps I can check in with you again this evening," Damon added hopefully.

"I'd be grateful," said Ms. Pryce.

He shook Ms. Pryce's hand very heartily. Then he opened the door of the supply closet, which was now a smoking ruin. "Oh, dear, I *am* sorry about the mess. It's just, there's this revolution at the edge of an overinflated universe, and . . . Well, never mind. Lately something always gets through with me."

He sighed. Two armored metallic arms shot out of the closet toward him. Damon stepped straight into the arms, closing the door behind him. There was a crash, and blue light flared around the door. The door trembled.

"Do you think he's all right?" asked Ms. Pryce nervously.

Akemi opened the door a crack. Nothing. No sound. She pulled it wide. Everything inside was burned and tattered, but Damon and the creature, whatever it was, were gone.

33

Ms. Pryce put the list from Poubelle's name tag inside *The Book of Keys*, which she shoved into her already-bulky bag. She slipped the vocoro into the pocket of her faux-leather jacket.

"You three had better get to class," she told them, glancing at the clock. "Damon has put *my* mind at ease, certainly. The Livingston branch of the Gateway Society, I think I can tell you, is run by a rather pompous group of men who, from everything I've seen, have no idea what they're doing and are mostly caught up in the thrilling importance of being in on a secret. The Cartographers and Locksmiths, however, are another order of being altogether. They maintain balance in the multiverse; that is their job. Damon will certainly be able to deal with Sabrin. You did the right thing, bringing this to me. Now, difficult as it may seem, it is time to get back to your ordinary lives!"

"What about our project?" asked Akemi. "The interview with Agatha?"

"I'll give you a new subject," said Ms. Pryce. She rifled through a box of index cards on her desk and pulled one out. "Here. Harold Cane lives in the Livingston Nursing Home. You can call the staff to set up a visiting time. And you really *must* stay away from Gael House until this is resolved, so you'll need to choose a different monument. Might I recommend the public library? It's a wonderful old building with lots of history. You only have a few more days. The project is due next Monday, so you'd better get to work."

"Can we get an extension?" asked Ben. "Since our first subject got hurt and we've been, uh, battling interdimensional monsters?"

"Not *monsters*," said Ms. Pryce. "I suppose . . . aliens of a kind. And no, no extensions. You still have plenty of time to work on this, and it will be good to focus on schoolwork right now. It's a matter of being organized."

They went out feeling very glum. Ben wanted to ask Ms. Pryce if he could keep the briefcase, but he didn't. Just like that, their strange adventure was finished. He *did* feel better knowing that some big important powerful *somethings* were going to protect the world from some other big scary powerful *something*, but it was deflating and difficult to know as much as they did and not be in any way involved.

✱

Ben was putting his clarinet away in the band locker in the hallway after music class when Jessica Masterson came and stood in front of him, hands on her hips.

"Uh, hi," he said, startled.

"*Uh, hi*," she mimicked back nastily.

"Okay, well, nice talking to you." He turned away.

"Stop right there, Ben Harp," she hissed.

He didn't really know why he stopped, when she was clearly acting psycho, but he did. He turned around and looked into her eyes. He didn't like looking at her, because it was like looking at two different people. One was the snotty, beautiful sixth-grade queen Jessica Masterson, but her dark eyes and perfect features were superimposed over the face of the little girl he'd spent so many happy hours with when he was younger, and he couldn't just erase all those memories.

"So, it seems like actually you have no problem being friends with girls," she said icily. "Or maybe you and Akemi are *more* than just friends."

Why did people always do that? This was exactly why it was hard to be friends with girls. Everyone acted so weird about it. He vividly remembered his anger and embarrassment in kindergarten when adults had cooingly referred to Jessica as his girlfriend.

"We're friends," he said. "So what?"

"So nothing," she said, tossing her hair. "I just *happen* to remember you saying that boys and girls couldn't *be* best friends."

Ben was too bewildered to be angry. "I didn't say that," he said. "What are you talking about?"

Jessica Masterson had barely spoken to him in years, and suddenly she was ranting at him in the hallway. What was going on?

She leaned closer to him, so her face was just inches from his, which was extremely unsettling, and said: "You and I were *best* friends, and then *you* told *me* that boys and girls couldn't *be* best friends, and you went off with Ashok and never talked to me again."

Ben was overcome with the terrible urge to burst out laughing, except that Jessica Masterson looked furious.

"Are you making a joke?" he asked. "That was in first grade, and I'm pretty sure I never said that."

She actually stamped her foot. "Yes. You. *Did.*"

Ben couldn't remember exactly how they'd drifted apart. He remembered that Ashok had come to their school and they'd become friends. And he distinctly remembered one dreary recess with Jessica and Audrey and Briony, where Jessica was assigning everybody superpowers and Audrey had decided to be a unicorn and Briony wanted to be a fairy and

Jessica was a ninja-hamster and he, Ben, just wanted to go on the swings. But mostly, in his memory, there was the time when he and Jessica were inseparable, and then the time when he and Ashok were inseparable and Jessica had gone off with the girls. *Had* he said something inane about boys and girls not being friends? He couldn't really remember what had gone through his mind back then.

"I don't remember that. But you were playing with other kids too," he said carefully—still a little worried that she was messing with him and that Briony and Audrey were about to jump out laughing. "And, you know, we were six."

"Whatever," she snapped, turning away.

He didn't know what possessed him to say it, but he said, "Leo was talking about you the other day. He was remembering how we used to be surgery-hamsters and pretend to operate on him."

She stood still with her back to him, but she said, "Leo was so cute."

"He's still pretty cute," said Ben. "He's having friend problems at school."

"What kind of problems?" she asked, turning to face him again, her eyes narrowing.

So he told her about Leo's problem with Christina and the others, and the new kid, Jordan, just because he was relieved that she'd stopped yelling at him. She folded her arms across her chest and didn't say anything. He trailed off.

"Little kids sure can be jerks," she said bitingly.

"Yeah. So . . . I didn't know you were mad about, uh, that," he said. "I thought that we just, like, made friends with other people."

"We did," she said. "But then you *never talked to me again*."

"We're talking right now!" he protested, realizing as he said it that it sounded stupid. "I mean . . . do you want to hang out sometime, or . . . ?"

"Of *course* not," she snapped at him. "We're *completely* different people now, and I don't miss you anymore, Ben Harp. I just thought your new-best-friend choice was kind of *interesting*, after your reason for ditching me in first grade."

"Uh, okay," he said.

Briony and Audrey emerged from the girls' washroom and spotted them.

"Hey, Jessi," said Briony, obviously confused to find her talking to Ben.

Jessica Masterson spun around and stalked off. Briony and Audrey fell into step on either side of her. Ben exhaled. Charlotte Moss was right across the hall, trumpet case in her hand. Their eyes met, and she gave him her spooky grin.

"That was *almost* the weirdest thing that's happened this week," she said, and he snorted in spite of himself.

34

In the parking lot after school, Akemi invited them to her place, but Charlotte said she had to go home.

"Are you sure?" said Akemi. "I mean, I really want you to come. *We* want you to come. Right, Ben?"

"Of course," said Ben, thinking Akemi was laying it on a bit thick.

Charlotte rolled her eyes. "I'm not *fragile*, you know."

Akemi looked confused. "I know. I didn't say that."

Charlotte slowly took the white bow barrettes out of her pocket and pinned back her hair. She looked more rice-pudding-ish than ever.

"Charlotte," said Akemi, almost pleadingly. "We need to talk."

"Okay," said Charlotte.

"I was thinking we could talk at my place."

"We can talk here. I'll be in huge trouble if I'm late again."

"Okay." Akemi took a deep breath. "Why didn't you tell us about Simon?"

Charlotte's expression didn't change, and her voice was neutral: "Why didn't you tell me you were doing stuff on the weekend? Why do we wait for you after basketball, but you don't wait for me after chess club?"

"I'm sorry about that, but it isn't the same thing," said Akemi.

Charlotte shrugged.

"When did you notice that he wasn't ... normal?" asked Ben.

"When he gave me the Band-Aid," she said. "I was going up the stairs behind him." She sighed, shoulders slumping suddenly. "He was nice to me. I didn't want him to get in trouble until I figured out what was going on."

"He's not a nice person," said Ben. "He ditched Agatha's dog in the park!"

"He's not a person at all," pointed out Akemi. "And trying to end the world is a little bit worse than abandoning a dog."

Ben didn't think there was *anything* worse than abandoning a dog, but he could see Akemi's point.

"Okay. I get it, I'm sorry," said Charlotte, not sounding particularly sorry. "I better go."

They walked her to the bus stop, discussing everything Ms. Pryce and Damon had said, but the tension remained. Ben and Akemi waited with Charlotte for her bus, then rode their bikes to Akemi's condo. She let them in with the key around her neck.

He followed her into her bedroom, where she set a ramp down to the floor and opened the doors of the rat cage. The rats came scampering out of their hammocks and hidey-houses.

"Why do they need to come out?" said Ben.

"It's good for them," said Akemi. "You wouldn't want to live your whole life in a cage, would you? They're litter-trained, and this room is pretty rat-proofed, but I have to put my books away or they chew on the spines."

The rats came prancing down the ramp in a row and onto the carpet, sniffing at Ben's toes. One of them took the end of his sock in its teeth and tugged.

"Hey!" He pulled his foot away, and all three rats scattered and vanished.

"Oops," he said.

Akemi laughed and made a *psss-psss-psss* sound with her mouth. The rats came running straight back to her from their hidden corners of the room. She sat down and gave them each a Cheerio from a tin labeled "Rat Snacks." They settled on her lap, holding the Cheerios in their witchy little hands and gnawing at them contentedly.

"Do you remember the rest of the stuff from the poem at the beginning of *The Book of Keys?*" she asked. "Ms. Pryce said it was like a recipe to open the seal. 'Flesh of the old'—gross— 'blood of the young'—gross—and there were two more."

" 'Breath of the servant' and 'tears of the bold,' " said Ben. He'd read it so many times, trying to puzzle out its meaning, that he had the whole thing memorized. He'd thought it was a code, but it seemed to be literal.

"What is the 'servant' supposed to be? *Whose* servant?"

"Maybe anybody who serves somebody else?"

"I still can't believe Charlotte didn't mention that Simon

was *not human*—like, tiny detail there!" said Akemi, stroking one of the rats with her index finger. "I think she had a crush on him. But how messed up is that?"

"I know," said Ben.

"She's crazy smart," said Akemi. "I don't just mean the chess thing or her math scores. I mean . . . she notices stuff. She thinks fast." She frowned. "I'm worried about her."

"Because she said she hates living with her uncle and aunt?"

"Well, that, yeah. But I mean I'm worried that she didn't tell us about Simon sooner. He was definitely following us that day we met up downtown. Charlotte put us in danger, not telling us. It just makes me think there's something really . . . off."

"She's always been kind of an oddball," said Ben. "I mean, I've known her since kindergarten."

"You've known she *exists*. That's not the same as knowing her. You didn't even know her grandmother had a stroke and she moved."

He thought of the strange ease of being with Charlotte in the library while Akemi was at basketball practice. They had talked, kind of, but mostly just did homework in companionable silence. She wasn't chatty like Akemi. And neither was he, really. Even if they were becoming friends, Charlotte Moss was still a mystery to him. He'd missed whatever was going on with her, just like Jessica Masterson had said. Just like he'd missed what was going on with *Jessica Masterson*, who had apparently been feeling rejected by *him* for years.

"Tomorrow, let's talk to Pryce," he said, thinking of what Ashok had said. "About Charlotte, I mean. Maybe she can help."

"How can she *help*? If Charlotte's uncle is awful, there's nothing Ms. Pryce can do about it."

"But maybe a grown-up should know what's going on with her."

"You're probably right." Akemi huffed out a breath. "Ugh. I guess we should start working on our new project. Harold Cane."

"Let's start it tomorrow," said Ben, suddenly exhausted.

Akemi grinned at him. "Okay. Do you want to make cardboard mazes for the rats?"

He grinned back. "Sure."

✳

Later, bicycling home, he spotted Ms. Pryce in the window of a little bistro on Autumn Street. He was about to wave, and then realized she was at a table with *Damon*. He nearly fell off his bike, but he regained his balance and rode by quickly. They were too engrossed in each other to notice him. He wished Akemi had her own phone and he could text her.

✳

Ben was in bed, rereading Ashok's messages, when Leo knocked on the door. He came in and sat on the floor next to the bed.

"Any ideas about my problem?" he asked, picking at the carpet.

Ben glanced around the room, hand drifting over to the water soaker next to him, hoping there weren't any lurking Sneaks that might attack Leo. Poubelle was calm at the foot of the bed, snuggled up against Morpheus, so that must mean the room was Sneak-free.

"Uh, not really," he said. "Christina and the others are still being stubborn?"

Leo nodded sadly.

"So, do you play with Jordan every day now?"

"Yeah. They said I can't play with them unless I tell Jordan I don't want to be his friend," said Leo. "But I can't say that. I *do* want to be his friend, but also it's so mean, and he doesn't have other friends."

"You're a good person, Leo," said Ben. He sighed. "Jessica Masterson told me today that I dumped her in first grade and told her boys and girls can't be best friends. I don't remember any of that."

"Do you think it's true?"

"I don't know. Maybe I did say something dumb one day, because I didn't like her new friends and I wanted to play with Ashok, and sometimes people called her my girlfriend and I didn't like that. But I don't remember saying it."

"That must have made her really sad, if you did," said Leo.

"I know. But she never told me she was upset at the time.

If she'd said something to me . . . I don't know, I think it would have made a difference. I just wonder if there's a way to get your friends to think about the way they're acting."

"But *how?*" said Leo. "They won't talk to me! When I try to talk to them, Christina just says, 'You know the choices,' and she walks away, and they all follow her!"

"Wow," said Ben. "She sounds like a piece of work."

"I still love her, though!" said Leo tragically.

"Okay, okay. We'll come up with something," said Ben. "I'll keep thinking about it."

"Why do you have a water soaker in bed with you?"

"Um . . . it just helps me sleep."

"That's weird."

"Yeah."

✳

Ashok: This is a lot.

Ben: I know.

Ashok: There are really multiple universes. There's a TUNNEL between multiple universes. There is a world-eating THING that wants to EAT OUR WORLD. The part I really can't get over, though, is that Jessica Masterson is mad at you about something you said in first grade.

Ben: Very funny.

Ashok: I'm not kidding. But by telling Ms. Pryce and

summoning that Damon guy to stop Sabrin, you guys might have saved the entire world. That's big.

Ben: I hadn't thought of that. We deserve ice cream.

Ashok: You deserve SO MUCH ice cream. I tried to help from afar, so I deserve ice cream too.

Ben: Ice cream for everyone! Do you think I would really have told Jessica Masterson that boys and girls can't be best friends? I feel bad if I did.

Ashok: Who knows? YOU WERE SIX!

Ben: I always thought we just drifted apart. What if I actually ditched her?

Ashok: You ditching Jessica Masterson is a pretty hilarious idea.

Ben: I'm serious. She was my best friend before you. What if I was a jerk to her?

Ashok: She's returned the favor by being a jerk to everybody she doesn't deem worthy for the last few years! You're not the jerk, Ben. Can we talk about multiverses again?

Ben: Yeah. Multiverses.

THURSDAY, OCTOBER 4

MORVOX'S ARMY

35

The Fetcher landed on Ben's stomach and rolled up his chest as he lay spread-eagled on his bed. Its single-eye lens swiveled, and it stuck a note in his face. He unfolded the scrap of paper. It said: *Wake up, Sleepyhead!* He rolled over to look at the clock. 7:45 a.m. He'd slept right through his alarm. He scrambled out of bed and tripped over the still-full water soaker that had fallen off his night table. He shoved it into his backpack, dressed hurriedly, helped Morpheus off the bed, and ran down the hall to the kitchen, the Fetcher rolling cheerfully behind him and Morpheus following more slowly.

Poubelle was already in the kitchen, eating breakfast. Ben was impressed—Leo must have let her out and fed her. In a role reversal, his father looked completely unkempt—and a little sweaty—still in his robe, hair on end, while Lily Quist was wearing an outfit Ben would never even have imagined she owned: a knee-length skirt with a blazer. Her hair was in an almost-neat bun, and she was wearing lipstick. She smiled—a wide, panicky smile.

"Um . . . ," he said.

"EnVision! Today!" yelled his dad, knocking over his mug

of coffee and then diving to clean up the mess. "She'll do breat! I mean, great!"

"Good luck, Mom," said Leo, hugging her tightly around the middle.

"Yeah," said Ben, feeling guilty that he'd forgotten. "Good luck."

His mom whistled sharply four times. The new and improved Fetcher rolled toward her and leaped into her purse.

"Wish me luck!" she said.

"We just did," said Leo.

"Good luck," said Ben again. He grabbed a muffin out of the freezer and tossed it in the microwave. He was going to have to eat breakfast on the go.

✽

Ms. Pryce was not at school. There was a substitute in the library, a bony woman with a shiny black bob and beige lipstick that made her lips blend into her face in an alarming way. Ben, Akemi, and Charlotte sat at their table during library hour, their work packet open before them, but they couldn't focus on the town history project.

"Where do you think she is?" asked Akemi nervously.

"She probably took the day off because she's busy," said Charlotte. "Maybe she had to meet with the Gateway Society people."

"But what if Simon really *is* Sabrin and he found out *she* has the book?" said Akemi.

Ben felt nervous about this too, even though it was hard to imagine Simon—Sabrin—*anyone* going up against Ms. Pryce.

"Let's ask at the office after school," he said.

✳

"Don't know," said Mrs. Demetriou with a sniff when they went down to the office to ask about Ms. Pryce. "I've been calling her all day. She didn't call in sick, didn't show up."

"Aren't you worried?" said Akemi. "What if she got in a car accident?"

Mr. Susskind came lurching out of his office.

"You three again?" he said, ratcheting out his mechanical grin. "What are you up to now?"

"We're wondering where Ms. Pryce is," said Ben nervously. He glanced at Mr. Susskind's feet, but they were firmly planted on the ground. He couldn't see anything obviously not-human about him, other than his behavior.

"None of your *beeswax*, I'd say!" boomed Mr. Susskind. "Are you improving your *attitude*, Benjamin Harp?"

"Um . . . I think so?"

Mr. Susskind stroked his chin like a villain in a cartoon and stared at them. Mrs. Demetriou was shuffling papers around on her desk, pretending not to listen.

"Okay, well, thanks," said Akemi, backing out of the office. Ben and Charlotte followed her.

"We should check on her," said Akemi once they were in the hall. "Something might have happened."

"She gave me her number, remember?" said Ben, getting out his phone. He tried calling. It rang and rang, then went to voicemail: "You've reached Lenore Pryce. I'm unable to take your call at the moment. Please leave your name and number, and I'll get back to you."

"This is bad," said Ben, hanging up.

"We don't know where she lives, either," said Akemi.

"We can look her up," said Charlotte. "It's not hard."

They followed Charlotte to the library, where the substitute was packing up and didn't look at all happy to see them.

"We just need to look something up for our project," said Ben.

She gave them a beige-lipped scowl.

Charlotte managed to find Ms. Pryce's home address from a real estate website in under three minutes.

"She bought this place just last year—see?" said Charlotte.

"You're like a superspy," said Akemi admiringly, and Charlotte beamed. "Let's go see if she's home."

"Don't you have basketball practice?" said Ben. It was Thursday.

"This is more important," she replied.

✳

Charlotte didn't have a bike, so they walked to Ms. Pryce's address, a two-story brick condominium downtown, near the square. Ms. Pryce's apartment was on the second floor. They found her name on the panel of doorbells, *L. Pryce*, but nobody answered when they rang.

"Let's look around back," said Akemi. Charlotte and Ben followed her along the side of the building, to a little garden with a pavilion and chairs. They looked up at Ms. Pryce's second-floor balcony, which was riotous with flowers and pots of herbs.

"We could climb up there," said Akemi. "Easy."

"What if she's home sick?" said Ben. "We can't just climb in her window and say, 'Hey, how are you?'"

"If she was sick, she would have called the school," said Akemi.

Ben dragged over a picnic table and put a chair on top, so Akemi could climb up to the balcony and scramble over the railing.

"Come up here!" she called down to them, her voice panicky. The chair on the table was not very steady, but Ben and then Charlotte climbed up after her. The balcony sliding door was ajar, and the apartment was a mess—like Agatha Bent's house after Simon ransacked it.

"I don't think Ms. Pryce is that messy," whispered Akemi.

Ben pulled the sliding door wider and called, "Ms. Pryce?"

"All shall be well, all shall be well, all manner of thing shall be well!" came Ms. Pryce's voice from the next room, bright and singsongy.

They stared at each other in horror.

"Ms. Pryce? Is that you?" called Ben again.

Ms. Pryce started singing something in Spanish.

"I don't think that's her," said Charlotte, looking spooked.

They stepped inside the apartment. Ben felt like a criminal, but he was scared for Ms. Pryce too. He took his water soaker out of his backpack.

"Smart," said Akemi, and somehow that made him feel a little tougher.

The sofa cushions had been pulled up. She had an old-fashioned record player, and records were strewn around the room, along with books and knickknacks. A big planter had been tipped over, and Ben righted it. There was a door ajar where the singing was coming from. Ben pushed it open, water soaker at the ready. It was a small room with a desk by a window. A mynah bird was singing in a cage. It fell silent and stared at them with bright black eyes.

"It's been a long day, Penny," said the bird in a world-weary voice that sounded just like Ms. Pryce's.

Ben was so relieved that he laughed out loud, and then something landed on his back.

"Sneak!" screamed Akemi, clobbering him with her backpack. Whatever it was leaped onto his shoulder and then onto Charlotte. It was a blur of movement. Ben squirted it with the water soaker, hitting it squarely with a jet of water. It fell to the ground, and he grabbed it. It was a little figurine of a ballet dancer with darting red eyes.

"The briefcase!" said Akemi. "It's here!"

She had found the briefcase under the table in the main room, open. Whoever had ransacked this place hadn't known what it was. Ben threw the figurine inside, shut the case, and twisted the knob. They knelt panting over the briefcase as the electric-blue light flashed along the join.

"Thank goodness you brought the water gun," said Akemi.

He opened the briefcase and took the figurine out again, its eyes ordinary ceramic now.

"There's her bag," said Charlotte. "The one she put *The Book of Keys* in."

A laptop, wallet, makeup bag, paperback novel, cell phone, and notepad were on the floor, making a trail to the satchel, which was half behind the curtains. Charlotte turned it upside down, but it was empty—*The Book of Keys* was gone.

"Someone took it," said Akemi hollowly.

"But where's *Ms. Pryce?*" said Ben. "Did they take her too?"

They looked in the bedroom, the kitchen, the bathroom. Those rooms were still tidy. Whoever had been here had found what they were looking for in the main room and hadn't stuck around to look for anything else.

"What are we going to do?" said Akemi helplessly. "We can't even call Damon without the vocoro."

"Wait!" said Ben. "She put the vocoro in her jacket pocket, remember?"

He ran to the closet by the front door and flung it open. The brown faux-leather jacket was hanging there. He felt in the pocket, and his chest expanded with relief as his hand closed on the little wheel.

"Here it is!" he cried.

He held it out triumphantly. At the same moment, a squirrel hopped into the room from the balcony, opened its mouth, and spat a thin thread of flame in their direction.

36

"Sneak!" screamed Akemi.

Ben shot the squirrel with the water soaker, and it went limp. Before they could get it into the briefcase, four more squirrels came leaping into the room from the balcony.

"Run!" He grabbed the briefcase and flung open the front door. The three of them barreled down the hallway, fire-breathing squirrels in pursuit. Something hot singed the back of his leg, and he heard Charlotte yelping. They raced down the stairs and burst out onto Fairfield Avenue.

"Keep going!" cried Akemi. "To the square—it'll be crowded!"

They ran to Elm Street and turned right, in front of the library, running straight into Danny Farkas on his bike.

"*Hey-y-y*, it's Benji and his girlfriends!" said Danny, his face lighting up with malice.

"Get lost, Danny," said Ben, darting past him. But Danny turned his bike around and followed them.

"Where are you guys going?" he called. "Can I come? Like a double date? I'll take Ratgirl. Does she bite, though?"

"No, but she punches," said Akemi, rounding on him and clocking him right in the face. Ben was so startled and delighted by this development that he froze on the spot. Danny hollered, falling off his bike, then bounced upright and tackled Akemi to the ground.

"Hey, you kids, quit fighting!" yelled an elderly man at the bus stop across the street.

Ben and Charlotte pulled Danny off Akemi. She sprang up looking furious.

"Akemi, we have to get out of here!" said Ben.

"I'm *sick* of this jerk!" she shouted.

"You punch like a rat!" taunted Danny, whose lip was bleeding.

Ben tried to pull Akemi away from Danny, and then his heart seemed to stop in his chest. There was a raccoon on the sidewalk, trotting fast straight toward them—but not an ordinary raccoon. A raccoon with horns, he thought at first, through the haze of his terror. But as the creature got closer, he saw that they weren't actually horns—they were like the swirling prongs of an electric drill, metal twisting round and round, each coming to a fearsome point. The drill-headed raccoon lowered its head and charged.

Ben shot it with the water gun, but his first blast had no

effect. The second blast slowed it slightly, making the creature stumble. Ben scrambled backward up the steps of the library, out of its path. It took a few more blasts—all the water he had left—before the thing flopped over. Ben threw open the briefcase.

"What the heck?" said Danny, peering at the raccoon, and then he loosed a blood-curdling scream. A large white cat had appeared out of nowhere and pounced on his back. Its claws and teeth glittered red, like rubies.

Ben dropped the empty water soaker and hauled the cat off Danny, leaving Akemi to stuff the immobile raccoon in the briefcase. The cat twisted in his grasp, transforming, and he was holding a true-form Sneak, a pulsing purplish translucent thing, its face full of teeth flying right at him. Panicking, he threw it as far as he could. It bounced off the steps of the public library and bounded right back at them. Danny screamed again, covering his head with his arms. Charlotte swung her backpack, knocking the creature sideways.

A woman was running down the steps of the library toward them now, and the old man at the bus stop was crossing the street. The Sneak got Danny by the leg of his jeans. Danny was howling blue murder. Charlotte pulled it off, but it slipped out of her hands, hurtled over the head of the woman who'd just reached the bottom of the library steps, and took off.

"Are you kids all right?" asked the woman who had come out of the library.

"Did you see that?" the old man shouted at the woman. "A stray cat just attacked these kids! *And* a raccoon! Rabies, d'you think? You need to get the rabies shots, young man."

Danny was examining his shredded jean leg; his shoulders were shaking with sobs.

"It didn't get you too bad," said Ben. "Just scratched your neck up."

Danny's pale eyes locked on his.

"What the heck was that?" he rasped.

Ben looked at Akemi.

"Cat," she said, clearly not feeling very sorry for Danny Farkas. She was holding the briefcase tightly to her chest.

"I want to go home," he said, shuddering and wiping his face. Ben had a sudden flash of Danny in kindergarten with a perpetually snotty nose.

"We'll walk you there," he said. Akemi gave him an incredulous look, but Danny nodded shakily.

"Are you kids sure you're all right?" asked the woman. "Where did that cat *go?*"

"Weird-looking cat, don't you think?" said the man.

"We'll be fine," said Ben. There was really no way to explain, after all. They left the two grown-ups puzzling over what they'd seen and talking themselves out of it.

37

They walked a sniffling Danny toward the train tracks, almost entirely in silence. At one point, Charlotte said coldly, "Stop crying," which seemed harsh to Ben, but then again, she had just pulled an alien monster off Danny's leg after he'd bullied her for years, so maybe she was entitled.

Danny was quiet after that, and he went into his house without a word of thanks, banging the door shut behind him.

Ben examined the burn holes in his jeans. Charlotte had a big blister on the back of her calf.

"Now what?" asked Akemi. "Ms. Pryce is missing. Sneaks are *everywhere*. It's like Morvox has an army of them. They have the book and the directions. This is bad."

"We'll contact Damon," said Ben. "I'm pretty sure this qualifies as an emergency. The river's near here. It should be quiet. And if we get attacked again, we can jump in the water."

It was a five-minute walk from Danny's house to the river, where tugboats plied the water. Akemi knelt down to open the briefcase, and a dazed raccoon stumbled out onto the clay riverbank and slunk away quickly. Damon had been right: even Sneaks that looked too big for the briefcase fit inside it.

Ben took out the vocoro. Fingers shaking slightly, he twisted the wheel: XVI–LV–XI.

A crack and a bang came from beneath them. A hole blew out of the ground, sending chunks of clay and pebbles flying. Damon scrambled out of it, brushing bits of clay off his suit.

"You *again?*" he said. Something roared from inside the hole. Damon took a palm-sized disk out of his pocket and fired a beam of bright vapor at it. The roaring stopped and turned into an annoyed squeak.

"Where is Lenore?" Damon asked, looking around the riverbank hopefully.

"She's gone," said Akemi. "And *The Book of Keys* is gone, and there are Sneaks all over her apartment and all over town. They look like animals. That means Level Threes, right?"

"What do you mean, Lenore is *gone?*"

"She didn't come to school today, and she isn't at her apartment, and the place is trashed!" cried Ben. "You said you were going to take care of this!"

It came out more petulant than he'd intended.

"I requested authorization to remake the seal," said Damon. "The thing is . . . this isn't a particularly high-priority planet. It's so damaged already, and resources are urgently required for the protection of other universes at the moment, making it a bit tricky. . . ."

" 'Damaged'?" said Akemi. "What happened? The Sneaks *already* damaged the planet?"

"No, no, by . . . well, by *you* people. You know—plunder

of the earth, environmental disaster, war, prejudice, violence, cruelty, and so on. It's a mess. A low-tier world, as far as the Cartographers are concerned. What's worth protecting?"

"'Low-tier'?" Akemi's voice got shrill. "There are . . . there are a lot of good things here too!"

"Oh, absolutely," said Damon hurriedly. "I don't mean to offend you. I just mean that from a wider, multidimensional perspective, it's not a top-priority world. There's already so much chaos and fear and such that, really, would letting Morvox take it make such a difference? The Cartographers feel that might be preferable to Morvox turning its attention elsewhere. Of course, I can see that from *your* perspective . . ." He trailed off.

Charlotte had been peering eagerly into the hole in the ground that Damon had come out of, but now she looked up and said, "That's a fair point, I guess."

"So, nobody is coming to help?" asked Ben, trying to keep his voice from shaking.

"I will make my case to the Cartographers again," said Damon. "Obviously, Sabrin has managed to lure quite a number of Sneaks back here. Most of them left the gap behind centuries ago, put as much distance as possible between themselves and the highest concentration of Gateway Society Sneak-hunters. If they're braving this town again, they must be very sure of themselves. I wish that I could do more, but . . . without authorization, you see . . . I could lose my job."

"Okay, forget it. We'll just let the world end, then," said

Akemi furiously. "We wouldn't want you to lose your *job*. No problem."

Damon looked very unhappy.

"I *want* to help, truly. This isn't simple, you know. I'm responsible for a great many universes, a great many gaps and seals, and there are bigger problems out there, frankly, than Morvox eating *this* world. I can't play favorites or bend the rules. The goal is broad multiverse stability...." He stopped, as if he were barely paying attention to his own words. "Lenore contacted me yesterday afternoon to let me know that Agatha Bent had woken up. That's good news, at least. We ended up speaking about so many things, at length—about time, and space, and duty. It was a wonderful conversation. We talked late into the evening." He got a dreamy look on his face, and then anxiety swept it away again. "Lenore is very capable. Where would she have gone? I can't think.... Do you suppose Malsprites *took* her?"

"Yes!" Akemi shouted.

"But what on earth *for*?" he muttered. "Tracking a human ... it can be done. I need to apply for authorization...."

Akemi threw up her hands in frustration, but Ben had stopped listening. *Agatha Bent was awake.*

38

After Damon had disappeared back into the hole in the river-bank, promising to push through authorization to track Ms. Pryce, Ben, Akemi, and Charlotte took the bus to the hospital. Akemi borrowed Ben's phone to call her father. She told him that she was working on a project with Ben and would stay at his house for dinner.

"Do you need to call anyone to say you'll be late?" Ben asked Charlotte.

She shrugged, so he put his phone back in his pocket.

At the main desk, they asked for Agatha Bent.

"Visiting hours are over at five-thirty," the man at reception told them, after checking the approved-visitors list. Agatha Bent must have been told about their call, because their names were there. "You don't have long."

A nurse took them up to the third floor. Agatha Bent was sitting up in a hospital bed, with a gruesome row of stitches over one eye and an IV attached to her arm. There was a tall glass of water and a vase full of flowers on her side table, and three men in the room with her, standing around the bed. Something about them made Ben think of police officers.

"These children came to visit you, Ms. Bent!" chirped the nurse.

The three men turned in unison to look at the door and scowled, but Agatha threw out her arms in delight and said, "Ben! Akemi! Charlotte! How *good* of you to come!"

"Hi, Ms. Bent," said Akemi.

Ben said, "Poubelle is at my house, just so you know. We're taking care of her till you get better."

She raised a hand to her heart, and he saw the bandaged finger. *Flesh of the old.* He shuddered.

"*Thank you,*" she breathed. As soon as the nurse was gone, she said: "And . . . *The Book of Keys?*"

"They took it," said Ben. "The list of clues your nephew sent was with it, and Ms. Pryce is missing too."

Agatha swore under her breath.

"Agatha!" cried one of the men indignantly. "Who *are* these . . . *children?*"

He said "children" as if he were describing something stuck to the bottom of his shoe.

"Ben, Akemi, and Charlotte, from Livingston Middle School," said Agatha. "I had to turn to them for help. . . . I was desperate. I had realized by then that my carer was, in fact, Sabrin in human form. He was keeping me from all contact with the outside world. I was his prisoner! Poor Poubelle was absolutely frantic. Children, these men are Gavin Wentworth III"—she waved her hand at the giant red-bearded man who had spoken—"Gregory Mac"—her hand danced in the direction of an older, white-haired fellow with dramatic jowls—"and Alexander Hooptree!"—the hand danced toward a thin man who looked ready to explode with outrage. "Agents from the Gateway Society."

Ben couldn't keep the names straight, and immediately began to think of the three men as Red Beard, Jowls, and Anger Management.

"Where!" shouted Anger Management, pointing at the briefcase in Akemi's hand. "Did *she*! Get *that*?"

It was as if he had to break his sentences into small parts to keep himself from dissolving with fury.

"From the Locksmith," said Akemi, lifting her chin.

"Give it to me," said Red Beard sternly. "This is outrageous."

Akemi looked at Ben. Ben looked at Agatha. Agatha sighed.

Akemi said, "You can ask the Locksmith for one yourself."

"We *have* one, you ridiculous little brat!" snapped Jowls.

Anger Management looked at him admiringly.

"We're trying to help," said Ben. "We actually caught a bunch of Sneaks."

"Agatha! What! Why!" screeched Anger Management. "This is! *Highly classified information!*"

"We asked the Locksmith to find Ms. Pryce," said Ben to Agatha in a rush. "But he needs to get authorization, and if Sabrin has *The Book of Keys* . . . he's going to open the seal, right?"

Agatha sank back on her cushions. Her eyes were blazing with intensity.

"You've certainly learned a lot in just a few days." She sounded impressed. "Lenore called me last night and told me what you've been up to. I'm *so* grateful to you for taking in dear Poubelle. But now we must make sure Sabrin doesn't succeed in his task."

"The maze is *impenetrable*; the lock is *secure*," said Red Beard. "If anyone goes into the house, they will simply get lost in there! It does you no good at all to work yourself up this way."

Agatha gave him a steely look. "You are underestimating Sabrin."

"He has the book and the clues, so he basically has a *map*," said Akemi. "And he must have looked in the book and seen how to open the seal before we took it from Agatha's house, because he started collecting the stuff he would need. Blood of the young, flesh of the old . . ."

Charlotte touched a hand to her elbow, where she'd picked the scab. She was looking curiously at the three Gateway Society men.

"*The Book of Keys* is a *myth*," said Jowls irritably. "Wentworth, what are we going to do about these children?"

"They'll need to come back to HQ for processing," said Red Beard.

"Don't be silly," said Agatha. "They've kept the secret so far. Imagine explaining to their families why you need to detain them! Besides, Sabrin is on the loose and in possession of *The Book of Keys*, which, I assure you, is *not* a myth at all. I think you have other priorities at the moment. Please remember, gentlemen, that I am the Liaison, and your superior officer."

"You are not at your *best*, if I may say so, Agatha," said Red Beard. "We have no evidence that your carer is Sabrin, as you claim. I rather think the blow to your head has confused you."

"He *pushed me down the stairs*," snapped Agatha. "I believe he intended to kill me. It's pure chance that the mail carrier saw me on the floor through the window and called an ambulance."

"A violent man," said Jowls. "Occam's razor: the simplest explanation is most likely the correct one."

"As if! You don't *think*! We know *how*! To do! Our *jobs*!" sputtered Anger Management.

Charlotte was staring very hard at Jowls's chest. Ben followed her gaze and did a double take. Jowls's wallet was peeking out of his jacket pocket. And the wallet had eyes. On stalks. The eyes swiveled, and then the wallet ducked back down inside Jowls's pocket. Charlotte gasped, and gave Ben a panicky look.

"Not! An Argument! I care to! Have!" Anger Management was sputtering.

"You don't seem to *realize*—" Agatha was saying at the same time.

Ben inched over to the side table and picked up the glass of water. The wallet peeked out of Jowls's pocket again, eyes

226

wiggling on its stalks, and this time Ben hurled the water from the glass directly at it. The wallet flopped limply back into the pocket.

"*Aaah!*" Jowls screamed, soaked. "Disrespectful little—"

"Your wallet has eyes," said Charlotte flatly.

They all fell silent. Jowls fumbled his wallet out of his pocket. The eyes dangled limply from the seam. He stared at it for a long moment, and then the eyeballs sprang to attention again. The wallet leaped out of his hands and scuttled across Agatha's bed. Agatha grabbed the vase of flowers off the table next to her and dumped water and tulips all over the wallet, which fell still again.

"Briefcase," Red Beard said to Akemi, looming over her, and this time she gave it to him. He opened it and put the wallet inside, fastening it again with a little fumbling. When he reopened the briefcase, Jowls took out his wallet, looking it over grimly.

"They're sending spies after us," said Red Beard.

"Well spotted, Charlotte, Ben," said Agatha pointedly. Her breathing was getting raspy, and a sheen of sweat had appeared on her forehead. "When my nephew arrives . . . Colin . . . he'll know what to do. . . ."

"Are you okay?" asked Akemi.

"I'm rather . . . tired," said Agatha. "My head . . ."

"We should go," muttered Charlotte.

Red Beard straightened up, but Agatha raised one hand and said, "Let them go."

"Search them first," said Red Beard.

"Are you kidding?" said Ben. "We just helped you!"

Agatha had collapsed back against her pillows. The three men crowded around Ben and Akemi and Charlotte, who handed over their backpacks, not sure what else to do. Anger Management found the vocoro in Ben's backpack and held it up triumphantly.

"Aha!" he crowed, as if he'd just found evidence of a crime. "*Aha!*"

"Damon *gave* it to us," said Akemi.

"That will be all," said Red Beard sternly, still hanging on to the briefcase. "Can't you see that Agatha needs to rest? This is too much for her right now!"

She really didn't look well.

"Okay, but . . . are you going to *do* anything? About Sabrin?" asked Ben.

"Young man, we have this situation completely under control," said Red Beard. "Go home. Not a word of this to anybody. We will be speaking to the three of you at some point in the future."

Agatha's eyes were drooping closed.

They went back outside and stood by the hospital doors, looking at each other uncertainly. The sky was dimming.

"You can both come over for supper if you want," said Ben. "My parents will probably order pizza."

"I have to get back," said Charlotte. "My uncle . . ."

"We could come up with a good excuse for you," started Ben, but Charlotte just shook her head.

They walked to the bus stop. Charlotte took her white bow barrettes out of her pocket and pinned back her hair with more than her usual ferocity. Ben and Akemi looked at each other.

"Charlotte . . . how much trouble are you going to be in?" asked Akemi hesitantly.

Charlotte shrugged. "It doesn't matter," she said. "I'll never get it right anyway."

"Never get *what* right?" asked Akemi.

"Being however they want me to be," said Charlotte. She sounded almost cheerful suddenly. "Like at school—I've known forever that I couldn't get it right. That I'd never be however you're supposed to be so other kids will be nice to you. There's really no point trying. It's the same with my uncle and aunt. I'm just all wrong, everywhere."

"You're not all wrong," said Akemi. She shot Ben a desperate look.

"Yeah," he said. "You're not."

Charlotte laughed, which was unsettling, and Ben didn't know what else to say.

"I can't believe those idiots get to know all these secrets about the multiverse and *we* aren't supposed to know anything," she said as the bus to Pennington arrived.

Ben and Akemi waited for the bus back to school to get

their bikes. The parking lot was empty, and the building looked strange in the near dark. Ben felt like he'd swallowed a stone.

"Do you think Pryce is okay?" he said.

"I don't know," said Akemi. "We told Damon, and we told the Gateway Society. What else can we do?"

Ben called Ms. Pryce's number again, but there was still no answer. Her brisk voice on the answering service made him feel queasy. The world was coming undone, and with Ms. Pryce missing, the vocoro taken, and Agatha still clearly unwell, he didn't know where to turn for help.

39

The dogs rushed over to greet them as soon as they came in the back door—Morpheus with his arthritic shuffle, Poubelle bouncing like a puppy. Leo peeked around the corner, into the kitchen, eyes wide.

"Bad news," he whispered.

Ben's heart jolted. He hurried to the living room, where his dad was sitting next to his mom on the sofa. They looked like someone had died.

"What happened?" Ben asked, fear rising in him fast. Perhaps the seal had opened, it had already started. What would the end of the world *look* like? What would the first signs be?

"*Nothing* happened," said his mother, her voice thick, like she'd been crying. She stood up and strode past him, shoving the Fetcher into his jacket pocket. "Here. You can have it, since it's basically just a clever toy. Turn it into something for *kids*. Well, you're a kid. Have fun."

She brushed right past Akemi and headed down the stairs into the basement. Akemi stared at Ben.

"The meeting . . . ," said his dad. He looked pale and miserable. "EnVision . . . uh . . . failed to see the potential of the Fetcher."

"Oh," said Ben in a small voice. He'd forgotten all about his mom's meeting with EnVision.

His dad got up as well. "Hi there, um . . . hello . . ." Forgetting Akemi's name, he left the sentence dangling and followed Lily down to the basement.

"I should just go," said Akemi.

"Your dad thinks you're having dinner here," said Ben, not wanting her to leave.

The doorbell rang. He went into the front hall, looked through the peephole, and froze.

"Who is it?" asked Leo.

"Uh . . . Jessica Masterson," said Ben, not quite believing it.

"Okay, that is *definitely* my cue to leave," said Akemi, grabbing her backpack.

"Akemi, wait!" said Ben.

"No way! I'll see you tomorrow. Call me if you hear from Damon or Pryce."

She bolted out the back door. The doorbell rang again. Ben took a deep breath. The world might be about to end, and Jessica Masterson was the last person he wanted to deal with right now, but she'd probably heard his voice through the door. He opened it.

"I need to talk to Leo," she said.

✳

It was strange having Jessica Masterson in his house after five years. Morpheus and Poubelle came over to greet her, and she exclaimed in distress over how slowly Morpheus was moving, kneeling to pat him while he licked her chin. She gave Leo a hug, and then whipped out a notebook.

"I'm going to help you with your problem at school," she told Leo.

"You are?" he said, looking up at her adoringly, like she was his fairy godmother.

Ben was finding the whole scene so strange that he excused himself to make sandwiches, since it didn't seem like there would be anything else for dinner. He made one for Jessica too, feeling it would be too pointedly rude not to. He sliced the cheese and tomatoes in a kind of daze.

When he went back into the living room, the dogs were lying at Jessica's feet, and Jessica and Leo were huddled over a page he'd written.

"It's really good," said Leo, his face glowing.

"What's really good?" asked Ben, putting down the plate of sandwiches. Poubelle got up to sniff at them and Morpheus whuffed sternly at her. She sat meekly back at his side.

"Look what Jessica helped me write," said Leo, handing the piece of paper to Ben, covered in Leo's neatest print. "It's a letter to Christina. She says Christina is the leader and the others will do whatever she does, so I need to focus on her."

Jessica and Christina were more than a little alike, thought Ben, glancing at her. You never knew if you were going to get the good version or the evil version. Did that make Jessica exactly the right person to help Leo with his problem or exactly the wrong person? She looked very pleased with herself. There was something so incongruous about seeing her on their worn-out sofa, looking impossibly beautiful, her lace headband keeping her hair back. She had her ice skates in a bag next to her, and he remembered all those hours spent watching her practice at the rink when they were little, how she'd taught him to glide along the ice. He hadn't been skating in years.

He took the letter from Leo and read it.

Dear Christina,

I miss you. I think we have a great friendship and I'm sad that you want to throw it away. I want to be friends again, but I am not okay with being mean to Jordan.

This is my idea: please give Jordan a chance for one week. If you still don't want to be

233

friends with him or with me after one week, then that is your choice, but please don't be mean to him. You were never a mean person before.

If our parents say it's okay, we should all go to the middle school basketball game on Monday and we can go to the team party at Perera's Pizza after. We could make signs together this weekend to cheer on the team.

I really hope you decide to be friends again.

Sincerely,
Leo

"It's a good letter," said Ben, impressed in spite of himself. It even had a plug for his school's first basketball game.

"Sometimes you just need to find the right way to say something so that the person will really understand," said Jessica smugly. "That's why a letter is a good idea. You can think about exactly what to say and exactly how to say it. And they don't have to react right away to a letter, so there's time for it to sink in."

"I think it'll work," said Leo. "If she gives Jordan a chance, she'll see he's really funny."

"What if she still doesn't want to be friends with him?" asked Ben.

"Maybe she'll decide not to be so mean, at least," said Leo. "I could take turns playing with them."

Ben wanted to hug his brother, or break down crying. He wished he could show Leo to Damon as evidence of what was worth saving in the world. What would happen to Leo and his parents if Morvox got loose? He felt sick to his stomach.

Jessica stood up, slinging her ice skates over her shoulder. She looked around.

"Your place is exactly the same," she said. "It even smells the same."

Ben wasn't sure if this was meant to be insulting or if she was actually feeling nostalgic. Her voice was neutral. She walked to the front door, and Ben followed her.

"Thanks for helping Leo," he said, opening the door.

She turned her too-direct, dark-eyed gaze on him.

"You and Akemi and Charlotte," she said. "Running around everywhere together and whispering. It's so weird. What's Ashok going to think about this new group of yours when he comes back?"

Ben shrugged. He thought of how she'd confronted them on the square over the weekend, and what she'd said about Charlotte.

"Last weekend, why did you say Charlotte was losing it?" he asked.

"Isn't it obvious?" she said. "She has this *look*. I mean—remember when you tripped on the front steps of the library when we were four and got that big cut on your forehead and scraped your hands up? For a few seconds, you just had this weird, blank look on your face, staring at your bloody hands, before you started screaming your head off. That's how Charlotte looks, but, like, *all the time.*"

Ben thought of her rice-pudding face.

"Plus, her uncle must be totally bonkers, making her wear those old-lady clothes," Jessica added.

For a moment, Ben was too startled to speak. Then he said, "*You* know about her uncle?"

"My dad knows her grandmother," said Jessica. "He visits her sometimes. He told me Charlotte's uncle is really strict about how girls and women should dress. It was bad enough when her grandmother was buying her clothes. Anyway, when someone starts dressing completely different, it *means* something."

"So, what does it mean?" Ben asked.

"*I* don't know. She's not *my* friend!" She gave him an assessing look and then said, "I feel like you don't notice much. About people."

Ben wondered if that was true. He'd had no idea what was going on with Charlotte—or with Jessica Masterson, for that matter. He'd forgotten about his mom's big meeting at EnVision. And here was Jessica, helping Leo, taking on his problem, when it should have been Ben helping his brother.

"I was thinking about what you said yesterday," he said, and paused, trying to figure out how to continue.

Apparently, Jessica Masterson had been mad at him for *years* without saying anything. It was sort of like the way he was angry with his parents—not in a big, explosive way, just this low hum of anger that had been brewing in the background for a really long time. He knew it was pointless being angry with them. He knew they couldn't change who they were, and they couldn't change the things they had already done and not done. But he wished they would say to him, just once, *Wow, Ben, we really asked a lot from you. We're so sorry. We should have paid more attention to you.* He couldn't change anything in the past, either, but it wasn't too late to say sorry.

Jessica raised her eyebrows and waited.

"You know . . . about when we were in first grade," said Ben haltingly. "And what I said."

"When you told me boys and girls couldn't be best friends and never talked to me again?" she said coldly.

"Um, yeah," he said. "So, anyway, I don't remember saying it . . . but I believe you. I mean, I really could have said something that dumb, and I'm really sorry. We had so much fun together when we were little. I wish I hadn't done that. I wish I could go back and change it."

Something in her expression seemed to collapse for a moment, making her look, briefly, quite un-Jessica-Masterson-like.

"I wrote you a lot of letters, but I never gave you any of them," she said. She sounded sad.

"I wish you had," he said, although he wasn't sure he wished that at all.

Then she tossed her hair and said in her normal voice, "Well—apology accepted."

They looked at each other. Ben didn't know what else to say. He hoped she would say something, but she didn't, so after an awkward pause he said, "Thanks for coming by. And for helping Leo. It was nice seeing you."

Weirdly, this was almost true. She flashed him a sudden smile so radiant it left him a little stunned, and she went bouncing off, skates over her shoulder, long dark hair swishing down her back like she was in a shampoo commercial. He didn't know how to reconcile this version of Jessica Masterson with the nasty school-version of Jessica Masterson and the imaginative little girl he used to love playing with. They felt like three entirely distinct Jessica Mastersons, and he was too tired to think about it anymore. He shut the door and leaned on it.

"She's the *best*, right?" said Leo happily. "Are you friends again now?"

"I don't know," said Ben.

He needed to talk to Ashok.

✱

Ashok: You're telling me this might be the end of the world as we know it.

Ben: I don't know. I have no idea what happens if Morvox gets out. "Eater of Worlds" doesn't sound very good, though.

Ashok: It really doesn't. How can we stop it?

Ben: We just have to hope the Gateway Society isn't as useless as they seem. Or that Ms. Pryce is doing something to stop it, and that's why she disappeared. Or that Damon works fast.

Ashok: That sounds like a lot of hoping.

Ben: I don't know what else to do! I keep checking the news to see if anything's happened.

Ashok: I know. Me too. I can't sleep.

Ben: I probably won't sleep either.

Ashok: So I guess we were right, in a way. The book is a map, but it's a map through a maze, and the list of clues must be directions to the seal . . . and back again, I guess.

Ben: I still think it has to be in code. Gael House isn't big enough for a hundred different rooms, and not all of the descriptions *are* rooms. Plus, how would each room lead to twelve or more other rooms with clues like talking to ducks in Spanish? Maybe Sabrin won't be able to figure it out.

Ashok: Maybe. But we don't know how things work in the house. If Peter Gael built it with the help of a Locksmith, it doesn't have to follow the rules of our world. I mean, you've seen a sports pinny turning into a monster and squirrels spitting fire. . . . Who knows what it's like in there.

Ben: I wish we could do something.

Ashok: Hopefully Pryce is on it. Just call me if anything happens.

Ben: What good will that do? You're so far away.

Ashok: I know. But if the world ends, I want to talk to you first.

FRIDAY, OCTOBER 5

GAEL HOUSE

40

Ben woke to the ping of his phone. His clock said 7:15 a.m. He fumbled his phone off the night table and stared at the text. It was from Ms. Pryce:

Meet me at Gael House. 9 a.m. All three of you.

Adrenaline jolted him wide awake. He leaped out of bed and yanked on a pair of jeans, Morpheus and Poubelle scrambling up in unison, excited by his hurry. He texted Ms. Pryce back:

We'll be there. Are you okay?

But there was no reply.

His mother was at the kitchen table in her pajamas. She had hollows under her eyes. His dad was next to her, worried and solicitous. Leo was finishing his oatmeal in silence.

They didn't know. None of them knew. And he couldn't tell them. It would be impossible to explain.

He let the dogs out and fed them, forced down some cereal, brushed his teeth. His parents hadn't moved, and they weren't talking. The silence was unsettling. Leo had his backpack on and was hovering in the entrance to the kitchen, looking anxious.

"Bye, Mom," said Ben. "Bye, Dad."

No reply. He went over and wrapped his arms around his mother.

"I'm sorry it didn't work out with the Fetcher," he said. "It's a *really* amazing invention."

He felt her shoulders shake a little, and he squeezed harder.

"Thanks, hon," she said, her voice a little hoarse. "Onward and upward, I guess, right?"

"Yeah," he said. He hugged his dad as well, who looked surprised but hugged him back.

"Bye," he said again. And then Leo burst into tears and hugged his parents, and they were all hugging in a big awkward mass at the end of the table. His mother started laughing.

"You guys," she said. "I should stop being so dramatic, right?"

"Right," wept Leo, and they all laughed again. Ben's laugh was forced, though. His parents drove him crazy, but they were his parents, and he didn't know what was going to happen to any of them now.

He dropped Leo at the elementary school and gave him an awkward half hug as well, because he couldn't help himself.

"Good luck today," he said.

"Thanks," said Leo, clutching his letter to Christina like a talisman. "I hope you have good luck too."

Ben couldn't tell his brother how much they were all going to need it, so he just waved as Leo headed into the building, then got back on his bike.

*

He waited outside the middle school, his stomach in knots, watching for Akemi and Charlotte. Jessica Masterson glanced at him on her way in, like she wanted to say something. He waved, trying to look friendly. She smiled, and he was relieved when she went by without speaking. Danny Farkas arrived, his lip scabby and his neck scratched, and went past with his head down, ignoring Ben. Malcolm Church and Ryan Yu yelled hi as they hurried into the school.

As soon as he saw Akemi on her new bike, the weight in his chest lifted, just a little. She coasted to a halt beside him.

"I got a message from Ms. Pryce this morning," he said, holding out his phone.

"Oh, thank goodness!" she cried, but the color drained from her face as she read the message.

"What do we do?" she whispered. "We have no briefcase, no vocoro. . . ."

"She's asking for our help, though," he said.

"But . . . ," she trailed off, and looked across the parking lot with him, where Charlotte Moss was trudging toward them.

*

At Murphy's ToyBox on the square, Ben bought three large water soakers, each with a two-liter chamber for water.

"Don't you kids have school today?" asked Mr. Murphy, side-eyeing them.

"Nope," said Ben blithely.

Mr. Murphy snorted. "Kind of chilly for a water fight," he said.

They filled the water soakers at the fountain in the square and walked north along Finch Street, stopping in front of Gael House. The gate, with its yellow tape and DANGER signs, was lying on the sidewalk, ripped off its hinges. They all stared at the front door. The wooden boards that were normally nailed across it had been torn aside and lay in splinters across the porch and the lawn.

"What did *that?*" said Ben, shivering.

They stood in shocked silence for a moment, and then Akemi said, "She's not even here. Are we going to get in trouble for missing school?"

It was nine a.m. Ben tried calling Ms. Pryce, but there was no answer.

"Maybe she's inside," suggested Charlotte. "*Somebody* is inside."

Ben stepped over the gate and the broken boards. Charlotte and Akemi followed him up onto the porch. The front door was open a crack.

"She *told* us to meet her here," he said, uncertain.

"Let's go in," whispered Charlotte, her eyes wide.

He pushed open the door.

41

They stepped into a narrow foyer. There was a dirty mat on the floor, an empty umbrella stand, and another door directly in front of them. Cobwebs clustered in the corners. Ben raised his water soaker. Akemi did the same. Charlotte grasped the knob and opened the door.

Ben was braced for something scary, but instead, they entered a clean, book-lined room with comfortable chairs and a table in the center. On the table was an old-fashioned, very beautiful chess set, the pieces carved from marble and jade. It looked as if a game was in process. There was another door on the opposite side of the room.

"The Chess Room," said Ben. "That's the first page of *The Book of Keys*. If the list I found in Poubelle's name tag is meant to be a route, the first clue is 'Checkmate in one.'" He looked at Charlotte. "I think we need you for this one."

She approached the board and studied it.

"Where does the other door go?" wondered Akemi. She crossed the room and opened it.

A roar filled their ears, and a sucking blackness from the other side of the door pulled at them. There was *nothing* beyond that door—nothing at all. Ben found himself stumbling straight toward the rectangular void and flailed for something to hold on to. Charlotte fell to her knees, grabbing the leg of the chess table, and Akemi was clinging to the door, working her way behind it.

"Close it! Close it!" shouted Ben. He was going to be sucked right into whatever that was. He dropped to the ground, trying to clutch at the carpet, but the gravitational tug of the doorway dragged him along the floor.

"I'm . . . *trying*," Akemi grunted. She managed to brace herself between the wall and the door, and slammed it closed again with her legs. Immediately the pull was gone. She sank to the ground, trembling.

"What was *that*?" squeaked Charlotte.

"I have no idea," said Ben.

Slowly all three of them got to their feet again.

"Are you okay?" he asked Akemi.

"We can't go out that way," she said, with a shaky laugh. "Obviously."

"We have to follow the directions in the book," said Ben.

"But we don't *have* the book anymore!" said Akemi. "There are a hundred rooms, according to *The Book of Keys*, and anywhere between twelve and twenty different ways they connect, which means thousands of possibilities, and we don't have the book or the list to tell us how to get from one room to another anymore. This place is a maze—that's what Ms. Pryce said. What if we get lost?"

"Ben has pictures of the whole book on his phone," said Charlotte before Ben could say it.

Ben looked at her in surprise. "How did you know?"

"Your recent photo thumbnails, when you showed us the picture of the vocoro and the one of your Sneak bite—it was all just pages from the book. And you *told* me you were sending pictures to Ashok."

Akemi was right: Charlotte noticed everything.

"Yeah, I have the whole book on my phone," he said. "And the list, which I'm pretty sure tells us the order of rooms we're supposed to take to get to the seal. Look." He showed them the picture:

Checkmate in one → St. Petersburg → Persephone →
Marie Antoinette → Hydra → Blue Riddle → Target VII

Target XIV → Green Riddle → Perseus →
Napoleon → Idun → Tokyo → Check with black queen

"Do we *want* to go to the seal?" asked Akemi.

"I don't know," said Ben. "But I'm guessing that's where Ms. Pryce is—to close it or keep it closed or something."

"If she's not answering her phone anymore, it could be because something bad happened," said Akemi.

"I see checkmate in one," said Charlotte. Her hand was on the black knight. "Should I move?"

"I don't know," said Ben nervously.

"We can't just leave and go back to school, though, right?" said Akemi. "I mean, if Ms. Pryce is in trouble . . ."

Ben took a deep breath. "Move," he said.

Charlotte made the move.

They all braced for something to happen.

Nothing happened.

"Maybe . . . Let's try the door again," said Ben. He put his phone back in his jacket pocket, and readied his water soaker. He went to the door, heart pounding, and opened it an inch. No roar, no sucking darkness. He opened it a little wider and peered into the next room.

The floor was stone, and etched with a map of the world. A blue feathered arrow stood on its tip on the floor, feathery end pointing straight up. Set into the opposite wall was a vertical row of nine wheels, surrounded by carved numbers from zero through nine, with a single dot at the top, and another horizontal row of identical wheels. A blue arrow on each wheel pointed to the dot at the top.

"Weird," he said, trying to work up the courage to step inside. Charlotte helped him out by giving him a shove from behind.

He walked over to the blue arrow on the floor. It was perfectly balanced on its tip, resting right where Livingston should be on the map of the world.

"So . . . the next clue on the list is St. Petersburg, right?" said Akemi. "Isn't that in Russia? Do we just move the arrow there?"

Ben reached down to pick up the arrow, but he couldn't budge it. He tugged. "I think it's stuck."

Suddenly the arrow began to move, zigging and zagging south.

"Look!" said Charlotte. She was spinning the wheels on the far wall.

"*Coordinates*," said Ben. "We have to put in the coordinates for St. Petersburg, I think!" He searched through the photos on his phone until he found the Coordinates Room, and read out the instructions: " 'A large room with a map of the world on the floor and coordinates on the walls. For the forest of Dunsinane: Seoul. For the Candy Shoppe: London. For the Butterfly Pavilion: Lima. For the Haunted Barn: Berlin. For Mythic Feasts: St. Petersburg.' There it is!"

"Uh, anybody know the coordinates for St. Petersburg off the top of their head?" said Akemi sarcastically.

"We can just keep spinning until we get it," said Charlotte. The arrow was dipping toward Antarctica now.

"Wait, I'll look it up," said Ben.

"I guess this maze was a little harder in the days before cell phones and Google," said Akemi.

"Latitude 59.934280, longitude 30.335098," said Ben, reading the coordinates off his phone. "Okay, so the dot at the top must be the period. Maybe the horizontal line of wheels is for latitude, and the vertical one is longitude?"

Charlotte spun the first wheel to 5 and moved on to the

second, spinning it to 9. She rolled the third around to the period, and said, "Read it again."

She spun the wheels as he read out the numbers, and the little arrow zipped around until she was done, by which time it had landed firmly on St. Petersburg.

"But the only door is the one we just came in," pointed out Akemi. "There *isn't* another door."

"Yeah, but this place doesn't work like normal space does," said Charlotte, her face shining. "The changes we make here change what's on the *other* side of the door."

Akemi opened the door cautiously. The book-lined Chess Room was gone. In its place was a room the size of a gymnasium, with a pond set deep into the stone floor, and, at the center of the pond, a stone island, upon which lay a huge platter of fruit and a golden scale. There were stepping stones from the edge of the pond to the island.

"What's the next clue on the list?" asked Akemi.

"Persephone," said Ben, scrolling through the pictures on his phone. "Okay—the book says, 'Mythic Feasts abound at the center of the pond. For a feather bed, weigh the choice of Pyramus and Thisbe; for Tokyo, weigh the choice of Idun; for the Dressing Room, weigh Persephone's choice . . .' We want Persephone."

"What does it mean, 'weigh Persephone's choice'?" said Charlotte. "That doesn't even make sense."

"It does," said Ben, crossing the stepping stones to the fruit platter on the island. "It's from a Greek myth. Persephone is the goddess of spring. The god of death, Hades, kidnapped her and took her to the underworld, and while she was there, she ate six pomegranate seeds. Her mom, Demeter, got her back, but because she ate those six seeds, she has to spend six months of the year in the underworld, and that's why we have winter."

"What?" said Akemi. "That's bonkers!"

"I feel like we shouldn't eat anything in here," said Charlotte nervously.

"No, it says *weigh* her choice. I'm guessing that's what the scale is for," said Ben. "This is all starting to make sense. On the way back, one of the clues is Idun. She's a Norse goddess, and she guards golden apples. There's a golden apple here too."

"How do you *know* all this?" marveled Akemi.

"My dad is a classics professor," said Ben. "He told us all these stories when we were little. My parents never had normal books in the house."

He took six seeds out of the sliced pomegranate and placed them on the scale.

"Bet you that works," he said, and went skipping back across the stones. "Try the door again."

This time, the door took them into what looked like a theater dressing room, with three dressmaker's dummies, one child-sized and two adult-sized, against one of the walls. Costumes hung from racks and spilled from shelves all around the room, which was long and narrow, like a large hallway.

"We're almost halfway!" said Ben. "This is easier than I thought. The next clue is . . . Marie Antoinette."

They frowned at each other.

"Do we dress up one of the dummies?" suggested Akemi.

"Maybe," said Ben. "So I guess we find a Marie Antoinette costume?"

"Look up a picture of her," said Charlotte.

Ben googled Marie Antoinette and found a painting of a woman in a white gown with a white powdered wig piled high atop her head.

"There's a blond wig," said Charlotte, pointing to a wig that matched the picture, on top of a pile of teetering boxes. Ben jumped to grab it triumphantly.

The wig writhed in his hand and turned translucent; its toothy maw made a dive at his face. He reeled back, flinging it off and blasting it with his water soaker. The Sneak flopped to the ground, but now a red fluffy sweater was wrapping itself around his neck from behind. He grabbed it, flailing.

The whole Dressing Room seemed to have come alive. Charlotte was wrestling with a fur coat, and Akemi was shooting water at a feathered hat that kept dodging her and snapping the metal teeth along its brim. Ben managed to get the red sweater off him. He stomped on it as it tried to rear up again. It stopped being a sweater and became something resembling a purple-tinged octopus, waving pincered arms, its mouth making that awful, airless scream, circles of teeth all the way down its throat. He blasted it right in the face with the water soaker just as Charlotte and Akemi managed to subdue a pack of high-heeled shoes.

"We need to get out of here!" screamed Akemi. She flung open the door they'd come through, and Ben dove after her. Charlotte was right at his heels. They piled through the door and it slammed behind them.

They were in a long hallway—the floors, walls, and ceiling made of mirrors.

"Oops," said Akemi, breathing hard. "What did we do?"

"We can find our way back," panted Ben. "I'm pretty sure I remember a Hall of Mirrors in the book."

"But if the Dressing Room has been taken over by Sneaks, can we still use it?" asked Charlotte.

Ben hadn't thought of that. He reached in his pocket for his phone, and then Charlotte shouted: "*Sneak!*"

Something small and brown was scuttling fast across the mirrored floor right at them. Akemi blasted it with water, but it dodged and kept coming. She stomped on it. It made a crunching sound.

She lifted her foot.

"Eww," she said. "That was a cockroach, not a Sneak."

A pause, and then all three of them fell around laughing. Ben wasn't sure if it was relief or just terrified hysteria.

"Okay," he said, once they had calmed down. "Don't panic. We can figure this out."

"I just want you two to know, I can't imagine anyone I'd rather be lost in a supernatural maze with," said Akemi, still giggling a little.

Charlotte got a funny look on her face at that. "You

guys . . . ," she began, and then she stopped. Her eyes went wide, and all the color drained from her face.

"What is it?" said Ben. Then he spotted something in the mirrored glass behind Charlotte.

It was Leo.

He was tied to a post in a concrete room, a gag around his mouth, eyes wide and full of tears, pleading.

"Leo?" Ben's voice came out dry. He stepped toward him.

Something was coming at Leo from behind, a big shadowy shape Ben couldn't quite make out. Leo was twisting against the post now, his expression increasingly desperate.

"Leo!" Ben ran smack into the mirror and reeled backward, clutching his forehead. The scene changed. Ashok was lying on the floor of his old bedroom, ashen and still, eyes empty.

"Wait!" said Ben, unable to look away, his insides turned to ice. "It isn't real, right?"

He heard Akemi whimper, "*Mom?*"

Charlotte let out a hoarse scream and took off running down the hall.

"Charlotte!" Akemi raced after her.

"It isn't real, Charlotte!" called Ben—hoping desperately that this was true.

But what if Morvox had already escaped? What if the world outside was falling to chaos even as they blundered around in here? What if the splintered boards at the front door were not a sign of something breaking in but of something breaking *out*?

Charlotte flung open the mirrored door at the end of the hall and hurtled through it. Akemi was right behind her, reaching for her, grabbing her jacket. Ben chased after them, shouting: "Wait!"

The door slammed in his face. He yanked it open without thinking, so afraid to be left behind, alone. The roaring, sucking darkness reeled below him. He tried to scramble backward, tried to grab hold of something, but his hands found nothing, and the pull of the darkness had him. For one horrible moment he teetered at the edge of the void. He opened his mouth to scream, and the darkness flooded into him—into his mouth and nostrils and ears—the darkness poured through him, swirled inside him, and yanked him off the edge, into the nothingness.

42

It was a moment that seemed to last forever. There was no up or down, no air, no light, nothing at all. He landed on something soft—it made a creaking sound—and the world spun and righted itself. He choked and coughed out tendrils of darkness, and then he lay still, gasping for breath, eyes squeezed shut, only relieved to no longer be falling in that airless space.

Once he had a handle on breathing again, he opened his eyes. He was lying on a large double bed in an otherwise empty wood-paneled room with one door. On the pillow right next to him, staring into his face, was a brown toad the size of his fist.

Slowly, the toad's mouth stretched into a menacing, horribly human, toothy grin.

Ben screamed and rolled right off the bed, landing with a thud on the hardwood floor. He'd lost his water soaker. He'd lost Akemi and Charlotte. He fumbled frantically in the pockets of his jacket. He still had his phone, thank goodness—and something round and smooth. It was the Fetcher his mother had stuffed in his pocket last night, for all the good that would do him. Maybe if he threw it at the toad hard enough, the toad would go away.

The toad peered over the edge of the bed and croaked, "Yum, that was great. Can we do it again?"

Its voice was distorted, as if by radio static, and it spoke with a slight, unplaceable accent. Ben sat frozen by panic and indecision on the floor. He didn't know where he was. He didn't know where to go. He didn't know what this *thing* was. It must be a Sneak, but the Sneaks he'd met so far hadn't been exactly talkative. Except for Simon—Sabrin.

"Are you . . . Sabrin?" he asked, his voice quavering.

The toad scowled. "No. Do I *look* like Sabrin? Honestly."

Ben opened his mouth and then closed it again, unsure of what to say.

"That was a joke," said the toad. "Ha-ha. Obviously Sabrin can look however he wants. As can I."

The toad pulsed, once, twice, turned purplish and translucent and blobby, and then a misshapen man with no mouth was sitting cross-legged on the bed. Ben screamed again, scrabbling backward across the floor.

The mouthless man flickered, pulsed, and became a huge white possum with a cruel, narrow face.

"Human is difficult—I always get something badly wrong. I don't know how Sabrin does it, frankly. Exhausting. Stressful."

Ben had backed right up against the wall. He sat there, not yet trusting his knees enough to stand.

"Who are you?" he managed.

"Me?" The possum batted its eyelashes. "It's unpronounceable by human mouth. The Speaking Ducks gave me another name at one point—they said it was the most beautiful word in the English language, the language predominantly spoken in this area nowadays. They speak every human language— did you know that? But I wanted to learn English, and have a name—I was still an optimist back then—thought I'd find a way out. They named me Spatula."

"Spatula?" Ben stared at the possum.

"*Is* it a beautiful word?" asked the possum. "I don't know if the Speaking Ducks are the best judges of this sort of thing."

"Um," said Ben.

"Never mind," said Spatula. "There's no accounting for

taste. How did *you* get in here? Schoolboy prank gone awry? Took a dare you shouldn't have? Little lost lamb?"

"We're looking for our school librarian," said Ben cautiously. Whatever this thing was, it didn't seem immediately intent on tearing him limb from limb. A few days ago, he would have thought he was losing his mind if he found himself sitting and conversing with a giant possum, but his sense of the possible had dramatically expanded. "She sent me a message and said she was here."

"She? Meaning, a female human?"

"Yes. Have you seen her?"

"I haven't seen her," said Spatula. "But all the Sneaks in the house have been whispering about how Sabrin is back and brought a human with him. Sabrin thinks he's going to open up the seal. And far be it from me to underestimate Sabrin."

The large possum sat back on his haunches and stroked his whiskers.

"So . . . you know Sabrin?" asked Ben.

The possum gave him a sardonic look. "Everybody knows Sabrin. Morvox's favorite pet, once upon a time. It's been a very *long* time since he slipped through the seal and went out into the world. I remember him. 'The world is full of fearful humans,' he said. 'Ripe for chaos,' he said. 'We'll bring Morvox through . . . rule of terror . . . delicious,' he said. And then he was gone. None of us heard from him again—until now. I came through and thought *this* place was the world. Found it rather disappointing, until I learned better. I've been stuck here ever since. But now Sabrin is back. Claims to have a *map*, claims to have a plan."

"He does have a map," said Ben miserably.

"Hmm," said the possum, eyes gleaming. "You know, nobody ever saw fit to share a map with *me*. I've figured out a few things, of course, but not the way out. Not yet, anyway."

Ben's mind was racing. He needed help. He wasn't sure this creature was the help he needed, but he didn't have a lot of other options. "So, Morvox . . . ," he said, trying to make it sound as if this was a matter he had only a passing interest in. "Are you, um, working for Morvox as well?"

Spatula gave Ben as sarcastic a look as a possum possibly could.

"Do I look like an employee? I told you, I'm just stuck here. Morvox is on the *other* side of the seal—in the gap—and I'm here in this rotten maze—and your whole delicious disaster of a world full of frightened people is out *there*, but I can't get at it. I've been wasting away in here. Nobody to talk to— apologies if I'm a little chatty. And not a lot of fear to feed on, either. Can't tell you how much energy I'm getting from you just sitting there being terrified. Absolutely wonderful."

"Uh . . . great," said Ben.

"If Sabrin really does get Morvox out, I suppose the rest of us might get out of here too, but Its Majesty the Eater of Worlds will gobble up everything worth gobbling in your world, quick as anything. It will be a feast for a while, and then Morvox will move on, and it'll be follow behind or rot. I've never aspired to ride on someone else's coattails, if you know what I mean."

"Okay," said Ben, only half following this. "Maybe we could help each other."

"Maybe we could *help* each other?" said the possum. It pulsed, and grew several sizes larger. Its voice boomed. "I've satisfied my urge for conversation, thanks. Now I'm hungry, and do you know what I love? The taste of human *skin*. Enough chatting. Time to eat."

The possum pounced.

43

Ben dove under the bed, rolled out the other side, and ran for the door. He threw it open, bolted straight onto a frozen pond, and went flying, sliding on his belly halfway across the ice. He tried to scramble to his feet but immediately fell again. Above him was a starless darkness—he couldn't tell if it was the sky or a very high, unlit ceiling—and stone walls loomed at the edges of the pond, fading into the dark. A gnarled tree hung with ornaments stood at the center of the pond.

"Just kidding!" called the possum from the doorway. "Sorry! Couldn't help it! That was a *great* scare, gave me such a jolt of energy, fantastic, delicious!"

Ben crawled across the ice, away from the possum, toward a door on the opposite side of the pond. The possum appeared to be laughing.

"Come on—you don't want to go that way!" called Spatula. "The Speaking Ducks will talk your ear off! They say everything backwards at least half the time, and it's enough to drive you mad."

Ben stopped and sat on the ice, panting. He had his phone, so maybe he could still find his way to the seal, but if Sabrin had caught Ms. Pryce, he wasn't sure that showing up alone would do any good, and Charlotte and Akemi would never get out of here without the book. He had to find them.

"Let's make a deal," Ben called across the ice. "If you promise not to, um, eat me."

"Sneaks don't *eat* people, silly."

"I've been bitten before," said Ben.

"Biting, dear boy, is not the same thing as *eating*. Sneaks eat *fear*. Being bitten is surely quite frightening, and so the Sneak gets a nice snack *after* biting you. Explain how you could help *me*, other than giving a good fright now and then."

This was risky. But it was the only sliver of a chance Ben could see.

"You said if Morvox gets out, you'd just be riding its coattails, right?" he said. "I want to stop Sabrin. And I know the way out."

The possum came swiftly slithering across the ice toward him. It had settled on the size of a large dog.

"Fine, tell me more. But let's get out of here first. I'm cold. The Armory is more comfortable."

The possum skidded over to the tree, moved a golden sphere hanging from one branch to another, and then led Ben across the ice to the door on the other side of the pond. He opened it with one flexible paw.

"After you." He winked at Ben. There could be no way of knowing, until you experienced it, just how unsettling it was to be winked at by a giant talking possum. Heart thudding in his chest in a manner that he was sure must be energizing for Spatula, Ben went through the door into a lantern-lit hall filled with suits of armor, swords, crossbows, and spears all on display.

"Warmer," said Spatula, closing the door.

"How long have you been in this maze?" asked Ben, looking around at the weapons.

"According to the star charts in the Observatory Room, it has been almost two of your centuries," said Spatula. "I was just a wee unevolved thing when I first came through."

"So you've figured out all these ways from one room to another, but you've never found the way *out*, in almost two hundred years?" said Ben.

"You think it's so easy?" The possum stroked his whiskers, regarding Ben coolly. "But *you* know the way out, do you?"

"I have a map," said Ben.

"*Sabrin* has a map."

"I have one too."

"Then why are you lost?"

"I just . . . we got attacked and separated and . . ."

"You don't have a map."

"I do! Look, I'll show you."

Ben took his phone out of his pocket. He scrolled through the photos and showed a picture of one of the pages to Spatula, who stared at it keenly.

"Don't get any ideas about, um, taking it," said Ben, feeling churlish as he said it, but he couldn't help assuming that Spatula was probably thinking it. "I'm guessing you don't know how to use a phone. You need fingers to make it work. And you'd need my password and everything."

He clicked the phone off, so the screen went dark. Spatula gave him a long, hard look.

"All right," said Spatula. "Let's say we make some kind of deal. I help get you to the seal, then you get me out. But if Sabrin is at the seal, how are you going to stop him?"

"I'm not sure yet," said Ben. "I have to find my friends first."

"In a house with thousands of possibilities, we're supposed to go *find your friends.*" Spatula sniffed. "Well, fine. Let's ask Cassandra. She sees an awful lot of what happens within the house."

✳

Ben followed Spatula through a series of rooms—a brick kitchen with copper pots hanging everywhere, a lime-green room whose floor was all sand and seashells, an old-fashioned candy store that made his mouth water, an empty theater. Spatula lit candles, folded back carpets, moved trinkets around, gaining them access to one new room after another until they passed through a door that led into a stone tunnel. Down the tunnel, they emerged into a dimly lit cavern, though Ben couldn't discern the source of the light.

"I don't remember anything in the book about a cave," he said nervously.

"This house was built with materials from your world," said Spatula, "and also with energies from the gap—which means it evolves, just like we do. You could almost say we've grown up together, this house and I. Not *everything* is quite as the builders intended here. Too bad the house hasn't sprouted any extra exits. Now hush—there she is. Be polite."

"Where?" asked Ben, heart knocking hard against his ribs. He looked around. Spatula was pointing straight at the shadowy wall.

Two gigantic, wet brown eyes opened on the wall—so large Ben could have fit inside them. The spiky black lashes extended several feet. He took a step back. *"Oh,"* he whispered.

"Cassandra can see . . . all kinds of things," said Spatula. "Not the way out—or, if she does, she's not telling. But a lot of what's going on. A lot of what happened before. She's the one who told me all about Peter Gael, explained that I was in a trap and that the world lay just beyond this place." He cleared his throat and said loudly: "Hello, Cassie! This boy is looking for his teacher!"

"School librarian," said Ben.

There was a grinding sound somewhere deep in the rock, and a voice that sounded like rattling gravel said: "She's very . . . brave."

"Yeah," said Ben. "Do you know where she is?"

A slow blink of those enormous eyes—he felt the breeze from the eyelashes—and Cassandra ground out: "She left behind people she loved—for something she believed in. She has made . . . hard choices . . . for small reward."

"Oh, she's *noble*—how quaint!" said Spatula.

"And now she is at the seal, by the gap. She is trying to keep the universe intact."

"At the seal. Hmm, that could be good or bad for you," said Spatula.

"I'm looking for my friends too," said Ben. "Two girls. Their names are Charlotte and Akemi. If that, um, helps."

The scraping, gravelly voice came again: "Two bold girls, lost and afraid in a vast glass maze."

"Ooh, tricky," said Spatula. "A maze-within-a-maze sort of thing. But I can get us there. All right, well, thanks, Cass."

"Benjamin Harp," rasped Cassandra, and Ben froze. "You should . . . try to be . . . a good friend."

"Oh. Okay," he said.

Cassandra closed her eyes again, stone lids coming down, eyelashes disappearing into the shadows of the wall.

44

"The fastest way to the Glass Maze is through the abattoir, but last I heard, the Butchering Wraith was there, so we'd better find another way," said Spatula cheerfully as they left the cave.

Ben did not much want to cross the path of anything called "the Butchering Wraith." He was still shaken from his encounter with Cassandra.

"We're far from any good routes here. Let's try our luck, shall we?" said Spatula. He opened a door at the end of the tunnel. The howling, sucking blackness pulled them right through the doorway.

"No!" shouted Ben, trying to turn and run, but the void had him again, wrapped itself around him, spun through him, spun him around, until he landed on a red carpet in an elegant, old-fashioned parlor, spitting and coughing out the threads of darkness that had filled him. Spatula was next to him, exhaling a puff of black smoke with ease. He regarded Ben curiously.

"What are those?" Ben managed to say, struggling into a sitting position. He felt nauseous.

"What *those*?" asked Spatula dryly.

"I mean, when you open a door here, why does it sometimes lead to another room and sometimes you end up falling through space?"

"You wouldn't *fall* through *space*. No gravity—am I right?" chortled Spatula. "You should know this, Mr. *I have a map and you don't know how to use a phone because you need fingers.* Each room has a number of actions that function as keys to other rooms. But if none of those actions are performed, the void will drop you somewhere random. I've tried to figure out as many routes as I can. Boring way to spend the decades, I'll tell you—tweaking this, scratching that, moving an object and hoping it works. Never mind, I don't want to complain, but it's not been easy."

All at once, he became a wolf and barked loudly in Ben's face. Ben scrambled backward.

"Mmm, yum, thanks," said Spatula, settling back into a dog-sized possum, his tail coiled on the carpet like a giant snake.

"Do you have to look like . . . that?" asked Ben, gesturing at Spatula. "I mean, you could be anything, right?"

"Would you feel more impressive accompanied by a golden dragon or a tiger or something of that ilk?" asked Spatula sarcastically.

"Well, yeah," said Ben, getting up slowly.

The possum shrugged, a disarmingly human gesture. "We highly evolved Malsprites all have a form that feels most *comfortable*," he said. "A kind of natural, effortless form. This happens to be mine. No point getting vain about it. Now, from here . . . I'm not sure of the best route . . . Hmm. We might want to try another random jump."

"Please, no," said Ben shakily. "I'll check the map."

"Yes, good idea. Let's look at the *map.*" Spatula's eyes gleamed.

Ben flicked through the images on his phone until he found "ornate parlor with red carpet and figurines on mantel."

"So, it's all about moving these figures around," said Ben, going over to the mantel and looking at the row of little porcelain mice wearing army uniforms and wielding bayonets. "Uh . . . if the mouse pointing his bayonet at the sky moves one inch forward, we can go to the Chess Room. . . . We could start over from there, I guess. Or if I move the mouse with the blue coat, we go to the Winter Room. What's that?"

"Too cold," said Spatula.

"Um, moving this mouse with a sword an inch to the left will take us to the Wax Museum. . . ."

"Perfect!" declared Spatula. "It will scare you, *and* I know how to get to the Glass Maze from there. Come on!"

"Do you think it has to be exactly an inch?" asked Ben.

"Precision is key," said Spatula.

Ben called a ruler up on his phone and moved the mouse carefully an inch to the left. The door led them straight into a gymnasium-sized room full of wax figures. With slow-dawning horror, Ben realized they were all figures of people that he *knew.* His parents, his uncles and aunts, Mr. and Mrs. Dorian from next door, Mr. Perera from the pizza place and his teenage son Charles, kids from school, teachers. They were motionless, except for their wax lips, which moved in silent speech. Their eyes alone were not wax but real human eyes, pleading.

"This is creepy," said Ben, shivering. "They aren't real, right?"

"Depends what you mean by 'real,'" said Spatula.

"Okay, forget it," said Ben, trying not to look any of the figures in the eye. "Where to from here?"

"Let's just savor this room," said Spatula. "You were getting almost comfortable with me. Now you've got a nice current of high anxiety going."

"I don't know how much time we have," said Ben.

"Fine," grumbled Spatula. "From here, the Clock Room, and then the Glass Maze. Which I *happen* to be very good at. You have to shake your own hand. The wax figure of yourself, I mean."

The wax Ben was even wearing the same outfit as him— jeans, a T-shirt, the brown cargo jacket, small bulge in the pocket from the Fetcher. He had a worried look on his face. It was like looking in a slightly wrong mirror. There was a wax Morpheus next to him, wagging his tail in slow motion. Wax Ben extended his hand. His lips moved. He might have been saying "Good luck" or "Get lost"—it was hard to tell. Ben shook the cool, waxy hand.

"This is *so* creepy," he muttered.

"So tasty," agreed Spatula. "Come on."

The Clock Room was, unsurprisingly, full of clocks, all of them ticking away loudly and telling different times.

"Grandfather clock at the back there: open the face and change the time to ten o'clock," said Spatula in a bored voice.

Ben followed his directions, and they went through the same door by which they'd entered.

Black space, soundless and vast, lay beyond the door, and for a moment, Ben started to flee back among the clocks, before he realized this was not the same void that swallowed him and dropped him.

"Have a look," said Spatula, eyeing him mockingly. Ben crept to the edge of the room and looked out.

A glass maze was suspended in space, carrying on as far as the eye could see. A bridge, also glass, led from where they stood into the maze. He could just make out small figures in the distance, distorted by all the layers of glass between them.

"Akemi!" Ben shouted as loud as he could, but his voice got lost in the emptiness around the maze. She must have heard something, though, because a moment later he heard a faint cry in response.

"Amateurs," chortled Spatula. "Listen, I'd like to chase them a bit, okay? Give them a scare? You owe me that, after I helped you."

"They don't scare easy," said Ben. "You might find yourself getting soaked with water."

"Hmm," said Spatula. "I don't like the sound of that. All right, *you* tell them I'm harmless first, and then I'll make a really loud noise to startle them. That won't get me soaked, will it?"

"Maybe not," said Ben uncertainly.

Spatula bounded across the bridge and into the maze. Ben followed. He made the mistake of looking down through the glass floor at the wheeling galaxies in the blackness. His stomach lurched, threatening to empty itself. After that, he fixed his eyes straight ahead. The maze was made up of twisting, crisscrossing, identical-looking corridors. You could see through the walls to the adjacent corridors, but trying to find a clear route through it all was impossible. Spatula made his way confidently, however, and so Ben followed the tip of the possum's tail.

"Tell them to stop moving. They're making it more complicated," complained Spatula.

"Stay still—we're coming to you!" Ben hollered. His voice bounced around inside the glass corridor. He wasn't sure they could hear him. Every now and then he'd hear what sounded like a voice, and through the many layers of glass he could see the two figures moving, but they didn't seem to be getting closer. Something with a fiery tail shot beneath them—a comet?

And then suddenly they were all four in the same corridor, no glass between them.

"*Ben!*"

His name burst out of Akemi like a sob.

Spatula reared up on his hind legs and roared. Charlotte let out an ear-splitting shriek. Akemi blinked, like she couldn't believe what she was seeing.

"That was all right," said Spatula, mostly satisfied. "The black-haired one wasn't as scared as I expected."

"You look a bit . . . ratlike, actually," said Ben. "She likes rats."

"Humph," said Spatula.

"This is Spatula," Ben called, inching around the possum's big, hairy body. "He's helping me."

Akemi and Charlotte had stopped in their tracks several feet back, but now Akemi ran over and hugged him. She was still holding her water soaker, but Charlotte seemed to have lost hers. He hugged Akemi back. There were no words for how relieved he felt, so he just said, "Are you guys okay?"

"Yes," said Akemi. "I just . . . I didn't know if we'd ever see you again . . . or how we would get out."

"We thought we'd end up skeletons in here," said Charlotte. She'd gone rice-pudding-ish again. "We *saw* a skeleton."

"Oh, yes, people do find their way in here now and again; they get lost and stuck, and it's quite disgusting while they rot away. But then they leave a very interesting skeleton," said Spatula. "This is great, lots of lovely fear flowing."

"He's a Sneak," said Akemi, looking at the possum. "Isn't he? And if he can talk, he must be a Level Four—like Sabrin."

"Level *Four*," snorted Spatula. "That's very nice. How would you like it if I talked about you like you weren't there, and called you a Level-Three human because you don't seem very bright?"

"He's not one of the pro-Morvox Sneaks," said Ben quickly. "He's helping me."

"I'm the president and only member of the newly formed anti-Morvox faction, in fact," chortled Spatula.

"Let's get to the seal," said Ben. He glanced at Spatula. "Do you know the way from here?"

Spatula stroked his whiskers. "I do. But what *are* you going to do if you come across Sabrin?"

Akemi raised her water soaker. Spatula scoffed. "He's no ordinary Malsprite, you know. You could slow him down a bit, but you won't stop him with that."

"Ms. Pryce must have a plan," said Ben. "She asked us to come."

"Our deal stands, right?" said Spatula. "I get you to the seal, and you take me with you when you leave this place."

"Right," said Ben.

"Really?" said Akemi.

"It's better than the end of the world, isn't it?" said Ben.

Akemi and Spatula looked at each other, and she shrugged.

"She's awfully suspicious, isn't she?" said Spatula to Ben. "Well, come on."

They followed the possum through the maze. He really must have spent years working it out, thought Ben: the maze was huge and incredibly complicated. But Spatula seemed to know exactly where he was going. He led them out of the maze, through a door at the other end, into a room with nothing but a rusty old carousel in it. He twisted the horn of a unicorn on the carousel and took them through a door at the back. They entered a wood-paneled room with fifteen brightly painted cupboards on the walls.

"There's a riddle in each one," said Spatula. "A word problem, or what have you."

"The Riddle Room! 'Blue Riddle' is near the end of the list of clues," said Ben, opening the blue cupboard. Inside it lay a pile of tiles with letters on them, like Scrabble tiles but without the points. A voice came floating out of the cupboard, thin and reedy, making him jump.

"*What eight-letter word remains a word as you take letters away, one by one, right until there is only a single letter remaining?*"

"What?" said Ben.

"Hmm, a pickle," said Spatula.

" 'Pickle' doesn't have eight letters," said Akemi.

Spatula shot her a contemptuous look. "I mean, this riddle sends us to the Target Room, which is the shortest way. But it's difficult."

"That's what we want. We're back on track!" said Ben eagerly. "Remember, the last clues were 'Blue Riddle' and 'Target VII.'"

"But what's the answer?" said Charlotte. "We could spend forever thinking of eight-letter words and taking letters off them."

"It's 'starting,'" said Spatula.

They all looked at him.

"I've done this one," he said. "I had *time*. Spell it out with the tiles. Go on."

Ben found the letters and spelled out *starting*.

"Now take a letter away, one by one, until you're down to one letter. It has to still make a word whenever you take a letter away," said Spatula. "Go on."

"How do you even know how to read and write?" asked Akemi.

"Like I said," said Spatula. "I've had *time*."

"Take away the second *t*," said Charlotte. "Then it says 'staring.'"

Ben removed it. "Now what?"

"The *a*," said Akemi triumphantly. "'String'!"

"Oh yeah," said Ben, almost enjoying the puzzle now. "Then the *r*. We get 'sting.'"

"Take away the *t* to get 'sing,' and then the *g* to get 'sin,'" said Charlotte.

"Take away *s* to make 'in,' and take away *n* to make 'I'!" cried Akemi. "We did it!"

"Oh, well done," said Spatula, rolling his eyes. "I did the hard part for you."

They went back through the door, into a room with a numbered target board on the wall and a basket of darts at a red line drawn several feet back.

"This one is pretty obvious, I guess," said Ben. "We have to hit Target VII, right?"

"It's actually very difficult to hit it from behind the line," said Spatula. "We could be here for ages."

"Darts are easy," said Akemi. She stepped forward, took a dart out of the basket, and pegged it right into the little square that said VII.

"Huh," said Spatula. "Must be nice to have thumbs that you're used to."

"So that's it, right?" said Ben. "'Target VII' was the last clue!"

"Almost there," said Spatula.

He opened the door, and they faced a wooden staircase.

"The Staircase . . . ," said Ben. "This is where the clues end. Is the seal up there?"

"Yes," said Spatula. "But be careful—it's a trap. There are a few of them. 'Sneak-Eaters,' we call them. Gobble you right up—Malsprite or human—and spit you out into a black hole, or that's what the Malsprites believe, but no Malsprite has ever come back out to tell the tale. Just don't step on the fourteenth stair."

"A black hole?" said Ben. "Like, in space?"

"I'm no physicist. All I know is that nobody swallowed up by this staircase comes *back*. Anyway, you'll see, there's a crack on the fourteenth step. If you step on that crack, the stairs fold up, and then you're done for, Sneak or not. Anyone on the stairs at that time is done for. I've seen it close up, and it's pretty awful. Nasty Peter Gael. So make sure you skip over it."

Ben shuddered.

"Don't like these stairs," muttered Spatula, half to himself.

He went bounding up them first, with a long leap over the thirteenth, fourteenth, and fifteenth steps.

"Careful now!" he called after them, once he reached the top.

Ben, Akemi, and Charlotte came up the stairs in single file. The crack on the fourteenth step was just a hairline crack, barely visible, but you could see it if you knew to look for it. They stepped over it, one by one.

"Good, all right," said Spatula, relieved, when they reached the top.

"So now what?" asked Ben, looking at the door at the top of the stairs.

"Right through that door," said Spatula. "I got you here. Now I want the phone."

"I'm not giving you my *phone*," said Ben. "I said I'd help you get out . . ." He started to say "if we get out" but couldn't bring himself to say it.

"The odds of you getting out don't seem particularly high to me," said Spatula coldly, as if he'd heard Ben's thoughts.

"Come on," said Charlotte.

Akemi held up her water soaker, a determined look on her face. The chamber was three-quarters empty, but there were still a few good blasts left.

"Here goes," said Ben.

Spatula looked set to argue but then slunk back against the wall, as if he didn't want to see what happened next.

Ben opened the door.

The room was all white marble, with four pillars around a

well at the center. Ms. Pryce was bound to one of the far pillars by what looked like a stone cuff on her wrist. When she saw them, her eyes widened with horror.

"Ms. Pryce!" cried Ben.

Simon stepped out from behind one of the pillars. Ben looked immediately at his feet. Charlotte was right. He was floating just above the ground. His smile was warm and appreciative. He flashed his dimples and said, "You did it!"

Ben was about to reply when he realized Simon wasn't talking to all of them. He was talking to *Charlotte*. He turned to look at Charlotte. Her face was shining. She was breathless, triumphant.

"I did it," she said. "I brought them here. Just like you said."

45

Akemi raised her water soaker and fired at Simon. He leaped effortlessly into the air, over the stream of water, straight toward her. He moved so fast that Ben barely registered what was happening until Akemi hit a pillar with a thud and slid to the ground, stunned, the water soaker slipping out of her hands. Ben charged at Simon with no idea of what he was going to do, pummeling at him with his fists. Simon caught Ben's fists in his hands and lifted him into the air. He was strong—stronger than any person should be. Caught in his grip, Ben couldn't move at all; he dangled helplessly, swinging his legs. Simon carried him over to one of the pillars, drove his hand into the marble as if it were butter, and pulled out a stone cuff on a chain, which he clapped around Ben's left wrist. Ben yanked hard against the cuff, the other end of which was buried in the pillar, but he couldn't break free. Akemi was on her hands and knees now, reaching for her water soaker. Simon was at her side in a flash, a blur, kicking the water soaker beyond her grasp. He pulled a cuff out of the pillar next to her and fastened it around her wrist. Akemi fought him with all her might, but her flying fists didn't seem to bother Simon in the slightest. She might as well have been a moth batting around him.

Ms. Pryce was struggling with her own cuff, her face rigid and her glasses crooked, while Charlotte watched from the doorway with her blankest rice-pudding expression.

"Why?" Akemi shouted at her. "We're your *friends*!"

At this, Charlotte's face changed completely. Color rushed into her cheeks. Her eyes flashed.

"You're not my *friends*," she said. "You put *up* with me. You're *polite* to me. That's not friendship."

"That's not true!" sobbed Akemi. "I *liked* you!"

Something seemed to crumple in Charlotte's face. She looked at Simon.

"Note the past tense," he said to her smoothly. "You have no place here. That's the thing about your world: so many people with no place, nobody to care for them, nobody to take an *interest* in them. But all the multiverse lies just beyond the seal, waiting to be explored. Morvox can give you that power. Morvox will know your value, you remarkable girl! You gave him the world. *You* did that. This ruined place is only fit to be his feast."

"Charlotte." Ms. Pryce's voice came from across the room—that crisp librarian voice that commanded attention. They all paused and looked at her—even Simon. "I know what it's like to be alone and misunderstood. But you cannot imagine what you are unleashing—"

"Nonsense! Charlotte understands very well," said Simon cheerfully. "She certainly doesn't lack imagination."

"Why did you tell us to come here?" Akemi flung this at Ms. Pryce, who looked stunned.

Charlotte laughed, but it was an odd, broken sound. She pulled Ms. Pryce's phone from her pocket and held it up.

"I took it," she said. "When we were at her apartment. I sent that message to Ben this morning and then turned it off. You guys are so dumb." Her voice wavered a little on the word *dumb*. Her expression was defiant, but there was something else there, something Ben couldn't read.

"How *could* you?" Akemi shouted.

Charlotte's face closed up. She looked like rice pudding again. She turned away from them, toward Simon.

"We're ready to begin," said Simon to Charlotte. "Hold steady, my dear. Everything I promised you is about to come into being." He cast a satisfied look at the rest of them, cuffed to the pillars, and took a glass vial from his pocket. "I need strength to pull this off—a nice steady flow of fear to feed me—so keep it coming. Think about how the world as you know it is about to end, utter chaos unleashed, while Morvox spreads panic and destruction. Just *think* about it. There, that's excellent."

Simon's blond hair was getting brighter, its consistency changing. It looked less like hair and almost like filaments of light flowing out of his scalp. His blue eyes had turned an impossible electric color that filled the whites of his eyes as well. His face was lengthening, his arms and fingers too, and he was getting taller, longer, thinner. Translucent spikes burst out of his shoulders and down his spine.

We all have a form that feels most comfortable, Spatula had said. Simon's was terrifying. He didn't look like Simon at all anymore. This was Sabrin.

"The mouth of the seal," said Sabrin, in a high singsong voice that sent chills up Ben's spine, "is molded to hold . . . the blood of the young. That's *yours*, dear, and I must thank you for it."

Sabrin grinned at Charlotte. His teeth were diamonds now, sharp and glittering. Charlotte was staring at him like she was a starving puppy and he had a bone. He held the vial in his long, pale fingers, tipped it, and let a darkly stained cotton ball fall into the well.

There was a creaking, groaning sound from deep within the well. A shudder in the ground. It felt like the earth sighing.

"The flesh of the old," sang out Sabrin. He placed something grayish in the vial, bowed his head, closed his eyes, and then dropped that into the well too. The tip of Agatha Bent's finger, thought Ben, his mind racing.

"We have to stop it! We have to do something!" shouted Akemi, straining against the stone cuff that held her. Her face was mottled and tear-stained. Something deep in the well rumbled louder.

"The breath of the servant," said Sabrin. "That's me." He breathed into the vial and then tipped it again over the well.

The ground shook. Chunks of stone fell from the ceiling. The pillars began to crack. Ben's fear of what Sabrin was doing was replaced with an even more immediate panic that they would be buried alive. As if she were sleepwalking, Charlotte went to Sabrin's side and peered into the well.

"The seal is opening," he told her. "But it needs to be *wider* for Morvox to get through. Then you will travel the road between universes! You will see everything there is to see!"

An echoing roar came from the well, like the sound of a hurricane trapped in a tunnel.

"The last step: tears of the bold," sang Sabrin, and he grinned at them viciously. "Which is another reason I asked Charlotte to bring you, besides the extra-helpful fear. I had a feeling I wouldn't get tears out of *that* one." He gestured to Ms. Pryce dismissively. She was struggling hard against the stone cuff. The pillars were so cracked now that Ben thought they had a good chance of getting loose after all. But what would they do then? How would they stop this?

"*You* look like a crier," said Sabrin. He moved in a blur, and the next instant he was looming over Akemi. She gulped and tried to wipe her tears away, but Sabrin slapped her free hand aside and then hit her hard across the face. She let out a shout of pain, and Ben saw Charlotte flinch. There were tears on Akemi's cheeks, more spilling out of her eyes even as she squeezed them shut to hold them back. Sabrin caught a few of her tears in the vial.

"There," he crooned. "You'll be the first to witness Morvox's arrival in this universe. Your terror will be his little appetizer—a welcome gift—before he moves on to the rest of the world."

Ms. Pryce yanked herself free of the stone pillar as it crumbled. She went straight for Sabrin, swinging the chain attached to the stone cuff like a weapon. But Sabrin was too fast, too strong. He caught the chunk of marble at the end of the chain with one hand and flung Ms. Pryce across the room. She crumpled against the wall, by the door. Akemi screamed.

"You said . . . just their tears . . . ," said Charlotte in a high, panicky voice.

Sabrin did not bother to respond to this. Ben yanked at his own cuff, feeling the pillar around it weakening, the chain moving more freely inside the cracking rock.

"Get loose!" he shouted to Akemi. "Get the cuff loose!"

Sabrin threw back his head and laughed, all blue-fire eyes and diamond teeth, his tongue a terrible blood-red. He returned to the side of the well with the vial in his hand.

The cuff was loosening, but Ben knew it was no good. *It's over*, his brain told him. *You can't stop it. It's over for all of them. For Leo, Dad, Mom . . .*

Something in his brain flared.

Mom!

The Fetcher!

With his free hand, he took the Fetcher out of his jacket pocket, where his mom had put it just last night, and whistled once. The lens popped out, and the blue beam swiveled around the room. He aimed the beam so it fixed on the vial in Sabrin's hand. The beam flashed. Sabrin was towering over the well, triumphant, Charlotte at his side.

Ben flung the Fetcher in the air.

Sabrin tipped the vial.

Akemi's tears rolled down the glass sides.

The rock groaned beneath them, above them.

The Fetcher hurtled through the air, and a little prong with a pincered hand emerged from it. Akemi yanked her arm free of the pillar and ran to Ben, just as the Fetcher snatched the vial right out of Sabrin's hand. Its legs popped out as it landed, and it scurried fast across the cracking floor.

Sabrin let out a scream of fury. Together, Akemi and Ben tugged his cuff free of the pillar. The stone cuffs around their wrists disintegrated. The whole room seemed to be shifting, crumbling, marble turning to sand. Sabrin flashed after the Fetcher, which executed a marvelous dodge and leap and scuttled toward Ben, depositing the vial in his hand.

Ben hurled the vial at the cracking wall, and it shattered. But there was no moment of relief. Sabrin's long hands closed on his shoulders, squeezing so hard that he yelped in pain.

Sabrin's mouth was open, showing his diamond teeth, his blood-red tongue, and he was *screaming*—the sound was like a siren, utterly inhuman. Ben was sure he was about to be torn limb from limb, but then a jet of water caught Sabrin full in the face. Sabrin dropped Ben and then staggered a couple of steps back, his face distorted, still howling with fury. Ms. Pryce was back on her feet, and she had Akemi's water soaker in her hands. She fired another jet of water straight into Sabrin's eyes.

"Run!" she shouted at them. "I can only slow him down with this!"

She kept shooting water at Sabrin, who was shrinking ever so slightly, curling in on himself, his awful scream diminished.

Ben and Akemi ran for the door. Ben paused and looked back.

"Come *on*, Charlotte!" he cried.

Sabrin, shrunken and huddled, snapped an order at Charlotte over his shoulder: "Go to the opening—*now*—and shed your tears! It's not too late!"

Charlotte was frozen at the edge of the well, bits of rock and powder falling down around her, her face very white.

"You think they'll ever forgive you?" snarled Sabrin. "You've *betrayed* them. They *hate* you! Go!"

"Charlotte, no!" cried Ms. Pryce. She tried to fire another jet of water at Sabrin, but the water soaker was empty. Sabrin bared his diamond teeth at her.

Charlotte climbed over the lip of the well and disappeared into the darkness. And then the ceiling collapsed.

46

Sabrin was rising to his full height amid the shower of marble chunks, which bounced off him. The blue fire of his eyes made two burning holes in his white face. Ms. Pryce stood before him, breathing hard, the empty water soaker in her hand, while Ben and Akemi huddled in the doorway.

"Get Charlotte," said Ms. Pryce. "I'll hold him off."

Ben's mind was a whirl of panic, but he didn't think twice. He ran toward the well, and Akemi followed. It was half filled in with rubble from the collapse, making it easy to climb down. At the bottom, the well opened up into a tunnel. It was dark, except for a distant glow at the end of the tunnel—the deep orange of a sunset.

"Charlotte!" shouted Akemi, scrambling over the mounds of broken marble right behind him. "Come back!"

There was no reply.

The tunnel sloped downward at first, then leveled off and grew larger. Ben heard running water, and his next footstep made a splash. There was a pale stream running down the center of the tunnel all of a sudden, as if it had been there all along, although he knew it hadn't. As they went farther, they saw strange coral-like plants growing through cracks in the ground and on the sides of the tunnel—brilliant greens and pinks and yellows and blues. The plants gave off an eerie light, glowing in the dark. The roof of the tunnel was marbled with color as well, brilliant stalactites hanging down like other-worldly sculptures. Ben heard a rustling, whispering sound, a susurration, like groups of moths taking off all at once.

"Charlotte!" shouted Akemi again.

He spied something white in the stream and scooped it up. It was one of Charlotte's bow barrettes. His heart lurched, and he broke into a run. The fluttering susurration grew louder around him. He felt as if he were running in a dream, running away from something unspeakable, and he kept calling Charlotte's name, as if calling her had some power to change what had happened.

The orange sunset glow was getting brighter and larger at the end of the tunnel, and then he could see Charlotte silhouetted right before it, a shrinking hole at its center. He stopped running, and Akemi ran into him from behind.

"Oof!" she grunted, and then she saw Charlotte too.

The orange light was swirling like a whirlpool, round and

round, as if gathering force. Through the hole at its center, Ben saw a sepia-toned house that looked like Charlotte's grandmother's house, but everything was the wrong color. The grass and the sky and the clouds were orange, and the angles of the house were off, like an artist's skewed rendition of a house. Charlotte was hunched over in front of the hole, wiping her face with her sleeves. She was *crying*, he realized, but she wasn't giving her tears to the seal as Sabrin had commanded her to do. She was wiping them away. The hole in front of her was getting smaller by the second.

"Charlotte!" he called.

Bathed in the sunset glow, she looked at them over her shoulder. He thought that if he could say the right thing, he could get her to come back with them, but he didn't know what to say. The orange clouds beyond the seal were opening up, and behind them, behind the crooked imitation house, a bridge of colors so beautiful it made him gasp swept upward and into some impossible distance.

Charlotte's lips moved, she was saying *something*, but the whispering, rustling sound had risen to nearly a roar, drowning her out. It looked like "I'm sorry." She wiped her face one more time, turned away from them, and stepped toward that strange, wrong-angled house and the shining bridge beyond it.

"No!" shouted Akemi.

The bright orange whirlpool shut behind Charlotte, and she was gone.

Ben felt unsteady on his feet, like the walls were moving. No—the walls *were* moving.

"Akemi," he whispered.

The walls and the ground and the ceiling were swarming with luminescent little creatures as small as a fingernail, glowing with purple and silver and blue, almost like tiny jellyfish with undulating, threadlike legs. They were the source of the ever-louder susurration. Ben peered closer, his heart in his throat. One of the heads opened up into a tiny, toothy maw, emitting an airless shriek.

"Sneaks," he said, looking around in horror. "They're all . . . baby Sneaks."

Akemi drew in a sharp breath. The orange whirlpool pulsed, once, twice, and then poured down the tunnel toward them like lava. At the same moment, the Sneaklings, with a sound like a wave crashing to shore, came off the walls and swarmed them.

✷

Ben felt Akemi's hand closing around his arm, he felt her pulling him, he turned and ran back the way they'd come, but he couldn't see anything, the tunnel was alight with a lurid orange glow, and he could feel the tiny Sneaklings all over him, like insects. He ran blindly, trying to bat them off him, tripping once and landing face-first in the stream. Akemi yanked him up again, and then tripped over a chunk of marble. He pulled her up this time. They were almost back at the mouth of the well. The orange wave of light was right behind them. They scrambled up the rubble as fast as they could and out into the ruined room.

There was no sign of Ms. Pryce or Sabrin.

"Get them off, get them off!" Akemi was sobbing. She was tearing Sneaklings out of her hair, yanking off her jacket. Ben hopped around, trying to shed the little creatures, which scuttled away in the rubble. The orange wave rushed up the well but stopped at the lip of it, swirling there and then receding. The well was at an angle, the ground half broken marble and half sand, nothing but darkness pouring in through the holes in the ceiling. Something was happening just outside the door. There was the sound of a body hitting a wall.

Sneaklings hanging off his clothes, Ben ran out into the hall. Ms. Pryce was on the ground, and Sabrin was looming over her. Sabrin turned his terrible face toward them.

"Down the stairs!" said Akemi. They stumbled down the stairs, leaping over the fourteenth step and falling the rest of the way, collapsing in a heap at the bottom. Sabrin was gliding down the stairs already, an inch over the ground, so there was no hope he'd step on the fourteenth stair. A terrible growl was coming from his chest. Akemi had taken her shoe off.

"Get *up*, come *on*!" cried Ben, trying to pull her to her feet, realizing after the words were out what she was doing.

With flawless aim, she hurled her tennis shoe at the fourteenth stair. It hit the crack full-on.

Sabrin was near the middle of the stairs when the shoe hit the crack in the step. The stairs slammed shut like teeth. They heard Sabrin's high scream, suddenly cut off. For a moment, there was nothing but a blank wall in front of them. Then the stairs opened up again, the walls unfolding into their previous position. All was as it had been, but Sabrin was gone.

They sat in a loose-limbed huddle at the bottom of the stairs, breathing hard.

"Nice shot," whispered Ben.

47

Ben and Akemi climbed the stairs on shaking legs, carefully stepping over the fourteenth stair.

"Why did she help him? Why would she do that?" Akemi wept.

"We know why," said Ben. His voice didn't sound like his own at all.

Ms. Pryce was lying at the top of the stairs, breathing in sharp, painful gasps. Ben crouched at her side. When she looked up at them, her eyes were full of tears. Sabrin had been wrong about that.

"Did you get Charlotte?" she whispered.

Ben shook his head, but he couldn't speak.

"Can you move?" asked Akemi.

Ms. Pryce winced as she sat up, cradling her left arm awkwardly.

"That was absolutely *thrilling*," said someone behind them.

Ben spun around. Spatula, in enormous possum form, was sitting on his haunches and grinning widely. "Hate to break up this fabulous tempest of fear, in fact. But you *do* remember that deal we had?"

Ben couldn't shake the image of Charlotte stepping through that orange whirlpool, the light closing behind her. Had her barrette fallen out of her pocket, or had she tossed it away?

Where was she now?

"What's at the end of the tunnel?" he asked.

"The gap," said Spatula.

"I know. But . . . can a human survive there? I mean, is there . . . oxygen?"

Spatula looked thoughtful. "The gap has some properties of your world, especially close to the edges, where it offers a kind of reflection, but in other ways it is entirely different. I expect that *breathing* would be possible, but who knows? I don't think a human has ever gone into the gap before."

Ms. Pryce moaned. She looked like she was about to faint.

"We need to get Ms. Pryce to a hospital," said Akemi urgently.

"And we'd better hurry," added Spatula. "The house is full of Malsprites. With all this ruckus, I'm betting everyone is a little *jumpy*. Things could get ugly."

Ben struggled to focus. His mind was splintering in too many directions, snagging and tripping repeatedly over Charlotte's barrette, Charlotte's face, Charlotte betraying them, Charlotte going into the gap. But Ms. Pryce needed help.

"Okay. Let's go."

Something dusty rolled across the floor and stopped against his shoe. It was the Fetcher, holding a little shard of glass in its pincered hand, like an offering.

"Wow," said Ben. "Thanks."

He took the shard of glass out of the Fetcher's claw. The arm retracted, and Ben put the Fetcher back in his pocket.

✻

Ms. Pryce seemed to be having difficulty breathing. She couldn't use her left arm or leg. Together, he and Akemi managed to get her down the stairs, though he was terrified her dangling foot might hit the fourteenth stair. Spatula hurried ahead of them, so as not to be on the steps as they struggled down with Ms. Pryce between them.

It took a shaken Akemi three tries to hit Target XIV—the second dart going wide when a Sneakling crawled up out of her shirt collar and bit her on the earlobe.

"Ugh," said Spatula. "Babies."

Back in the Riddle Room, Ben opened the green cupboard. The cupboard said cheerfully: "*I am the beginning of the end, and the end of time and space. I am essential to creation, and I surround every place. What am I?"*

He and Akemi looked at Spatula.

"I don't know *all* of the riddles," said Spatula petulantly.

"The letter *e*," grunted Ms. Pryce, leaning against the wall.

"Oh!" said Akemi, brightening for a moment. "Neat."

Ben found the letter *e* tile and placed it in the middle of the cupboard. He didn't need to check the list of clues on his phone; he remembered it perfectly. The second line would be the return to the entrance: *Target XIV → Green Riddle → Perseus → Napoleon → Idun → Tokyo →* Check with black queen. He put aside the question of how they were going to manage the Chess Room without Charlotte. One step at a time. If he thought too much about any of it, he would fall apart, and he couldn't fall apart right now. From the Riddle Room, they passed into a large room with a star chart on the floor, and a shelf of glowing stones on one wall.

"This is the Constellation Room," said Ben.

Akemi helped Ms. Pryce to lean against the wall again, and asked: "So—we use those stones to make the constellation?"

"I guess so," said Ben, getting out his phone to look up *Perseus constellation.* "Twenty-one stars. Whoa."

"You see stars, do you, out in the world?" said Spatula, a little wistful. "Actual stars?"

"Yeah," said Akemi as they collected the shining stones in their hands.

"Here's Zeta Persei," said Ben, angling the star map on his phone and finding the constellation on the floor. He placed a shining stone on top of the star marking Zeta Persei. Akemi looked over his shoulder at the constellation map.

They moved quickly. Ms. Pryce leaned on the wall with her eyes closed, as if concentrating very hard on staying upright. Ben tried not to think of anything, to fix his mind on their immediate goals: *Get Out. Call an Ambulance. Get Home. Check on Leo.*

"Ugh, yuck!" squeaked Akemi, shaking another Sneakling out of her sleeve. "These things are so gross!"

Once the constellation was complete, they got Ms. Pryce between them again and made their unsteady way across the room to the door.

"It's the Dressing Room next," said Ben, hesitating. "Last time it was full of Sneaks."

"I'll deal with the Sneaks," drawled Spatula. "You get us out."

"The clue is Napoleon," Ben said to Akemi. "Any idea what a Napoleon costume looks like?"

"Look it up before we open the door," said Akemi.

With Ms. Pryce propped between them, they looked through portraits of Napoleon Bonaparte in a tight white suit, peacoat, and admiral's hat.

"Very handy," observed Spatula. "How does one go about getting one of these phones? I'm sure I could figure out how to use it without fingers."

Ms. Pryce swayed dangerously, and they caught hold of her

again. Ben could not think what advice to give Spatula about obtaining a phone.

Get Out. Call an Ambulance. Get Home. Check on Leo.

"Open the door," he said. "We're ready."

Spatula opened the door.

"Hat!" yelled Akemi, helping Ms. Pryce to lean against the wall and jumping for an admiral's hat on a high shelf. She put it on the dummy.

For a moment, looking around, Ben dared to hope the room was now Sneak-free. But then something like a pig with a wolf's head emerged from a rack of long coats and stalked toward them, growling. Several coats jumped off their racks and sashayed behind the creature, and a number of coat racks followed as well, like some nightmarish parade.

Ms. Pryce slid down the wall to the floor. Spatula sighed.

The pig-wolf creature lunged at Ben, who was frozen in front of a rack of period costumes. Spatula swelled up to twice his usual size and met the creature in midair.

"Ben, *hurry!*" cried Akemi.

It was difficult to concentrate while Spatula was rolling around with some demented, deformed beast, but Ben found a white suit that he hoped would serve. The coats jumped on him, one of them covering his head, but Akemi got it off him while he hurriedly fastened the shirt on the dressmaker's dummy. He was battered with coat racks as he tried to fix the trousers around the dummy's waist. A scarf coiled down from a shelf, hissing, a forked tongue flitting in and out of one of its seams. It wrapped itself around Ben's neck and tugged.

"*Gggghhh!*" He tried and failed to call for help. His vision narrowed and filled with gray blots. Akemi wrestled the Sneak off his neck and shoved something into his arms.

"Peacoat!" she shouted, still struggling with the scarf.

Ben slung the coat over the crooked white suit and adjusted the hat on the dummy's head. "Let's get out of here!"

Crabs the size of Ben's palm with whirling, kaleidoscopic eyes came scuttling out of shoeboxes. Akemi kicked them out of the way. Spatula had subdued the pig-wolf beast. Ms. Pryce, slumped next to the door, reached up and turned the knob.

Ben and Akemi grabbed her under the arms and dragged her into the next room, with various items of clothing and props in pursuit. Spatula leaped past them, into the Mythic Feasts room, with its enormous fruit platter on the island in the center of the pond.

"Into the water!" wheezed Ms. Pryce.

"Are you *joking?*" shrieked Spatula, hopping along the stones to the island.

Ben and Akemi pulled Ms. Pryce into the pond and propped her against the side so she wouldn't go under. The crabs scuttled around the edge of the pond, snapping their pincers. Ben and Akemi splashed water on them, making them go limp.

Spatula was on the island.

"What next?" he shouted to Ben.

"Idun!" cried Ben. "The golden apple! Put it on the scale!"

They were close. His head was swimming. *Get Out. Call an Ambulance. Get Home. Check on Leo.*

"*What?*" Spatula hadn't heard him.

A flock of screaming blue jays with metal spikes down their backs poured through the doorway into the room, followed by an old-fashioned telephone on bird feet, and several pairs of stockings, running as if they had legs inside. Whirling cloaks and dresses rushed in and surrounded the pond, clattering shoes and corsets and hairpieces mingling with surreal beasts. A dictionary came cartwheeling through the air and struck Akemi in the side, making her stumble, and then it fell into the water and went still. More and more Sneaks kept coming, an army of them, blocking any path out. Ben kept splashing water at them helplessly. The blue jays were circling overhead, diving at them.

"How are we going to get *out* of here?" wailed Akemi. They couldn't even see the door anymore.

There was a crash and a yelp of dismay from Spatula. The island had split open, scattering the fruit into the pond. Blue light played around the edges of the split. Damon crawled out of it and shouted, "Lenore!"

He looked exhausted and disheveled, and he was holding a tiny silver box the size of a box of matches.

Spatula hurtled away from Damon, leaping through the

air and landing on Ben's head, nearly knocking him over into the pond.

"You promised," growled Spatula, sliding off Ben's head and into his arms. The possum was very heavy, but he considerately shrank down to the size of a cat. "You said you'd get me *out* of here."

Damon opened up his little box. There was a whooshing sound, and Ben felt Spatula being pulled out of his arms. Spatula clung to him harder, snarling, digging his claws into Ben's jacket, and Ben instinctively hung on to Spatula, wrapping his arms tightly around the possum.

The other Sneaks were flying through the air. They shrank as they flew and disappeared into the box in Damon's hand—the blue jays, the telephone, the stockings, the costumes and crabs, all the creatures and objects that had surrounded them. Once all the Sneaks were gone, the room eerily quiet, Damon snapped the box shut, put it in his pocket, and came splashing through the pond to Ms. Pryce. He lifted her gently out of the water into his arms.

"You got . . . authorization," she breathed.

"No," he said. "I didn't. I came anyway. Let's get you out of here."

48

"Hold on to me," Damon commanded. "Both of you. This might be somewhat uncomfortable."

Weak with relief, Ben grabbed hold of Damon's suit jacket with one hand. Akemi held on to Damon's arm, and Spatula clutched Ben's front, trying to hide in his jacket, but Damon was too preoccupied with Ms. Pryce to pay any attention to the possum.

"I've contacted the Gateway Society," the Locksmith said tenderly to Ms. Pryce. "We'll go directly to the hospital. They'll meet us there."

The door swung open for them. This time, instead of another room or the horrible void, there was a blinding blue light, and wind.

"Hold on tight," said Damon. His voice seemed to be coming from nowhere and everywhere. Ben wasn't sure, afterward, if they stepped into the light or if the light swept over them, but everything in his mind went upside down and inside out. The blue brilliance seared his skin. He felt as if he might be spinning, and then the light was gone and they passed into darkness, but he still had the sensation of moving very fast.

Bright shining eyes stared at him from the dark and then vanished. He concentrated as hard as he could on holding on to Damon's suit and holding on to Spatula. *Don't let go. Don't let go. Don't let go.* They were back in the blue storm—it prickled across him like needles—and then everything went still and grayish and a bit smelly. The world fell into place in pieces, like a jigsaw puzzle being put together at high speed. They were in a heap in a bathroom stall. Ben let the hem of Damon's jacket slip from his hand. Damon had landed in a crouch, but he rose smoothly to his full height again and kicked open the door. Ben and Akemi scrambled to their feet and followed him out of the bathroom and into the waiting room at Livingston Hospital. Spatula was still clinging to Ben's front. Ben pulled his jacket around the possum as best he could.

"I'll take care of Lenore," said Damon. "Will you be all right? You can go home to your families?"

"I think so," said Ben. He didn't feel all right.

Damon nodded and strode to the front desk with Ms. Pryce in his arms. Ben and Akemi walked out the front doors on trembling legs and stood there in front of the hospital—both of them rather scratched and bruised, soaking wet from the pond, Akemi with just one shoe, and Ben still holding a possum. It was a bright afternoon, the street quiet, the leaves a riot of reds and yellows.

Spatula wriggled and leaped out of Ben's arms, landing on the sidewalk. He looked around, sniffing the air.

"So—*this* is the world?" he said, exultant. "The *actual* world?"

"Yeah," said Akemi, as if amazed by it herself. Ben knew how she felt. Everything normal looked so strange to him, as if he were seeing it with new eyes.

"What are you going to do?" Ben asked the possum.

"Oh, we'll see, we'll see!" said Spatula gleefully. Without so much as a goodbye, he folded up and took to the air, a dragonfly shooting away from them. Ben wondered anxiously what he'd just unleashed on the world, but he had other, bigger regrets than freeing Spatula.

"Now what?" said Akemi.

They stood there, shivering in the autumn breeze. A car screeched to a halt next to them. Red Beard, Jowls, and Anger Management climbed out, all three with matching, furious expressions on their faces.

"You kids," said Red Beard. "In the car. *Now.*"

✻

Ashok: Wow, those Gateway Society guys are pretty serious about keeping all this a secret.

Ben: It was crazy. They faked a whole bus accident to explain why we missed school! I mean, I don't think they crashed an actual bus, but they fudged all this paperwork, said we were knocked off our bikes, they even bashed my bike and helmet up, but at least they fixed the bike after. They called our families and said we were being checked for concussion at the hospital. One of them dressed like a doctor and talked to our parents when they came to pick us up. This organization is seriously far-reaching. It seems like they have connections everywhere.

Ashok: Which makes you wonder why they weren't in the house dealing with the world almost ending. Sounds like it was a close call for Pryce. She'll really be okay?

Ben: Yeah. Broken ankle, dislocated arm, and some broken ribs. She had a concussion too, but luckily it's mild. Nothing that won't heal, she said.

Ashok: And no sign of your buddy Spatula?

Ben: Nope. I don't know if I should be glad or worried about that.

Ashok: What about Charlotte?

Ben: Damon promised he would look for her. He said the edges of the gap should be kind of like a distorted reflection of the world. As in, there's oxygen and she can survive there, but she won't be able to go farther. I just wish I'd been a better friend.

Ashok: You can't blame yourself. You didn't know how messed up she was.

Ben: Yeah, I did, kind of. I think she felt like we weren't really her friends, and she had nothing to lose. I've known her all these years, but I didn't really *notice* her until the last couple of weeks, and I was still too late.

Even if the gap is survivable, she can't just . . . live there.

Ashok: But the Locksmith can go in the gap, right? So he can get her back?

Ben: I hope so. The Gateway Society guys are trying to cover that up too. The official story is that Charlotte ran away. They gave us this big talk about secrecy and said they'd be keeping an eye on us, which is creepy.

Ashok: No kidding. They can't do anything to you, though, can they?

Ben: Nope. Things are getting kind of shaken up in the Gateway Society. Those guys totally missed what was going on. Pryce says they were reprimanded by the "top brass," whoever that is, and she's being promoted. Agatha is still the Liaison, but Pryce is moving up the Gateway Society ladder! Those guys will be reporting to her now. So I think we're okay.

Ashok: Wow! Go, Pryce! She deserves it. Have your parents calmed down yet?

Ben: Not exactly. This whole thing snapped my mom out of her funk, though. She keeps saying how the only thing that matters is that we're all safe and together. She wants to take us bowling this weekend.

Ashok: Bowling?

Ben: I know, so random.

Ashok: Well, could be fun. Too bad you can't tell her that the Fetcher saved the world.

Ben: Right? But I said it was the coolest thing she'd ever made, and she got all teary.

Ashok: How is Poubelle doing? Still peeing everywhere?

Ben: Leo and I pretty much have her house-trained! Agatha is being released from the hospital in a few days, so Poubelle can go home, but she's going to hire me and Akemi as dog walkers!

Ashok: I can't believe how close Sabrin came to releasing Morvox.

Ben: Yeah. I keep looking around and just . . . feeling lucky. I never appreciated normal so much.

Ashok: Normal is pretty great.

GAME TIME

49

Danny Farkas didn't exactly thank them for saving him from an alien, but on Monday morning, as they sat down for homeroom, he said to Ben, "Where's Charlotte?"

It was the first time he had ever heard Danny Farkas call Charlotte by her name. Ben shrugged, his heart sinking. Her empty seat lurked accusingly in his peripheral vision. He'd hoped beyond hope she might be here.

Ms. Pryce *was* back at school, with a boot on her leg and her arm in a sling, but otherwise entirely herself. Ben and Akemi had cobbled together a quick project over the weekend, interviewing an extremely chatty Harold Cane in the nursing home and typing up a paragraph about the history of the public library, mostly copied from the library website.

"She can't really blame us for doing a bad job," Akemi reasoned as they handed it in that morning. "I mean, we *did* save the world."

✱

They went to the library after school. Ms. Pryce and Damon were behind her desk, deep in conversation. She looked up guiltily when they appeared, and then relaxed when she saw it was them.

"Any news?" asked Ben.

Damon and Ms. Pryce exchanged a look. He cleared his throat. "Charlotte is . . . alive," he said. "And Morvox has turned its attention elsewhere, for now, since the seal failed to open."

Ben felt nearly dizzy with relief.

"So, did you bring her *back?*" Akemi pressed.

"It's complicated," said Damon. "After the near disaster, I did manage to push through authorization to remake the seal. I created a temporary pathway for Charlotte—meaning *only* she can pass through it, back into the world. However . . . there are rules I can't disobey, even if I tried. I can't simply drag her through it. She has to *want* to come back."

"I've been speaking with the school social worker about her situation, and I believe her grandmother will soon be able to go home and that we can make a strong case that Charlotte is better off living with her than with her aunt and uncle," said Ms. Pryce. "After all, her grandmother is the one who raised Charlotte since she was a baby."

She sighed and added, "Charlotte needs to feel there is something in the world worth returning for. She knows by now that she cannot travel beyond the very edge of the gap— not without a Locksmith. But it may be that she is afraid to come back. She betrayed us in a terrible way. She may think that we cannot forgive her." She looked hard at Ben, and then at Akemi. "*Can* you forgive her?"

"Yes," they both said immediately, and Ms. Pryce's expression softened.

"Can we *talk* to her?" said Akemi.

"They could send a message, couldn't they?" said Ms. Pryce to Damon, who was looking at the two of them almost fondly.

"Certainly," he said.

Ben thought of Jessica Masterson helping Leo with his letter to Christina. *Sometimes you just need to find the right way to say something so that the person will really understand.* He hadn't said any of the right things to Charlotte, but maybe it wasn't too late.

"We could write her a letter," he said.

"That's a very good idea," said Ms. Pryce.

They sat down at a table, and Ben got out a notebook and pen. They stared at the blank page.

"How should we start?" he said.

"Uh, write 'Dear Charlotte,'" said Akemi.

Ben wrote "Dear Charlotte" at the top of the page, and then they stared at it some more.

"We were so busy figuring out what was going on with the Sneaks that we missed what was going on with you," suggested Akemi.

Ben thought of Charlotte pinning her hair back fiercely with those white bow barrettes, her rice-pudding face as Danny Farkas taunted her, her avid curiosity as the truth about other universes began to unfold before them. She had done something terrible, leading them to Sabrin, but Ben meant it when he said he forgave her. Charlotte Moss's dreams of other worlds and her bleak life in *this* world were too vivid to him to hold on to any real anger. He wanted a second chance to be her friend so badly that it hurt.

The rest of the letter came quickly. Ben tore the page out of his notebook. Akemi folded it up and handed it to Damon.

"I'll be sure to deliver this," he said. "No matter what happens."

"What do you mean? What could happen?" asked Akemi, looking alarmed.

"Damon is . . . under review," said Ms. Pryce. "For his interference in Gael House without authorization."

"You mean for *saving* us?" said Ben.

"Yes," said Damon. "I was not authorized to enter the house or take any kind of action at that point. My superiors feel that my work across the multiverse has suffered because of my particular interest in this planet . . . and they may be right. I will accept their judgment, whatever it is. I came to say goodbye, actually. I'm to be summoned any moment, but I did want to say . . ." He looked at Ms. Pryce.

"I'm so sorry," she said.

"I wanted to say it was worth it," he told her simply.

A blue sphere of light, about the size of a fist, opened up in the air next to Damon's head. They all stared at it—like a hole in the fabric of what ought to be.

"There it is," he said. "Don't worry—I'll take a quick de-
tour and deliver your letter. Good luck to you all."

"Damon," said Ms. Pryce.

"Worth it," Damon said again, and smiled. Then he touched
a finger to the blue sphere. It snapped shut, and Damon was
gone.

Ms. Pryce looked down at her desk.

"Will he be all right?" asked Akemi.

"I don't know," said Ms. Pryce. Her voice had lost its crisp
edge. She took off her glasses for a moment, which made her
look very young and sad, and wiped a finger under each eye.
Then she put her glasses back on and looked up at them, fully
their school librarian again. She picked up their town history
project from a stack on her desk. "I'm afraid I've given you a
C-minus," she said.

"*What?*" squawked Akemi. "But *you* know why we didn't
do a better job!"

"You barely completed the monument section," said Ms.
Pryce. "You've had two weeks. Time management is an important skill. I don't make exceptions."

Ben and Akemi gaped at each other.

"If you want to do a makeup project for a better grade, I
will allow it," she continued. "You could finish up with Agatha,
if you wanted, now that she's back home." Her eyes twinkled
a little behind her glasses. "You could ask her about her life—
her *real* life. She has some remarkable stories that you might
appreciate hearing. The project would be for my eyes only.

315

The Gateway Society is always recruiting, and it's never too early to start training for this line of work. You were both very impressive on Friday."

"How is Agatha, anyway?" asked Ben, trying to recover from the shock of Ms. Pryce giving them a C-minus after they'd stopped a monstrous Eater of Worlds from ravaging the planet.

"She seems well," said Ms. Pryce. "Her nephew is returning this week and will stay until she makes a full recovery. You may be interested in meeting him, too. Good luck at the basketball game against Rylant this evening, Miss Hanamura. We'll be there to cheer you on. Ms. Kennedy has strong-armed me into coming with her."

"Really?" said Akemi, surprised.

"Oh, yes," said Ms. Pryce. "She's obsessed with basketball."

She handed them their project, with the big red C− on it.

✱

Ben's parents were still in overeager parenting mode, and came with Ben and Leo to the basketball game. Ms. Pryce was sitting straight-backed and unsmiling with Ms. Kennedy, who was waving team colors and had painted her face green. Mr. Susskind was there too, occasionally waving a tiny Livingston Middle School flag and clapping at the wrong moments.

It was an exciting game, the score staying close throughout. Livingston Middle School pulled ahead in the final minutes, when Jessica Masterson brilliantly faked a shot but then passed to Akemi, who sank the ball from fifteen feet. Jessica and Akemi high-fived almost before they realized what they were doing. Then they both looked awkward and turned away from each other while the rest of the team swarmed Jessica.

Leo was sitting in front of Ben with his friends—Christina on one side of him and Jordan on the other—and they all screamed themselves hoarse.

"I don't *get* basketball," Ben heard his mother whisper to his father.

✳

"This is my dad," said Akemi, when they had all gathered at Perera's after the game, introducing a tired-looking man in a rumpled suit to Ben's parents. He sat down with them, smiling a creaky sort of smile that looked not much in use. Ms. Kennedy came over, beaming, to join them.

"What an *amazing, thrilling* game!" she cried. Ben had never seen their teacher so excited. "Your daughter is a *gift*, Mr. Hanamura, a *gift*! We *whupped* those Rylant kids!"

Mr. Hanamura looked stunned by this short, green-faced, frizzy-haired woman hollering at him. He glanced nervously at Akemi.

"This is my homeroom teacher, Dad," she said, trying not to laugh.

"Oh! Glad to meet you!" He shook her hand.

"A *gift!*" Ms. Kennedy repeated.

Akemi tugged on Ben's sleeve, and they moved away, leaving the adults.

"Your dad came!" said Ben.

"I know. I can't believe it," she said wryly, but she looked pleased.

At the next table, Leo and his friends were demolishing their pizza cheerfully. Christina looked imperious, and Jordan looked scared, but it was a start.

As they passed the table where Jessica Masterson sat with Jake, Lekan, Jae, Audrey, and Briony, Ben made a point of saying, "Hey. Good game, Jessica."

The others all looked at him in surprise, but Jessica Masterson just smiled and said, "Thanks." She nodded at Leo's table. "Looks like things are going okay over there."

"I hope so," said Ben. "Thanks for helping him."

"Tell me how it turns out," she said.

"I will."

"Ben," said Akemi, jerking her chin toward the door. Damon was there, looking around, a bouquet of flowers in one hand and a silver briefcase in the other. He saw Ms. Pryce across the pizzeria, and they both smiled.

Ben and Akemi got Cokes at the counter and then joined Ms. Pryce and Damon at Ms. Pryce's table just as Damon was saying, "I didn't have time to get flowers before—though I understand it is . . . ah, customary, when a person has been ill or injured?"

"Thank you," said Ms. Pryce, taking the flowers and looking embarrassed. Some of the other kids were looking over at them, giggling and whispering.

"Congratulations on the game," said Damon to Akemi. "I caught the end of it. Very exciting. Did you know that in other universes, in similar worlds, similar sports have evolved, but *basket-and-ball* is unique to this world in the entire multiverse?"

"Huh," she said. "I . . . didn't know that. Um, it's just called 'basketball.'"

"Sugar gliders are another example—an animal that has evolved nowhere else. There are some interesting, unique points in this world. I presented the Cartographers with a list, hoping to raise the status of this planet."

He glanced at Ms. Pryce as he said this.

She smiled and said, "I'm not sure I'd put basketball and sugar gliders at the top of that list, but I appreciate it."

He beamed at her, and then held out the briefcase to Ben. "And I brought this for the two of you. Hopefully you won't need it, but . . . well, just in case. It's a gift."

"Thanks," said Ben.

Charles Perera brought a pizza to the table. Ben tucked the briefcase under his feet.

"I don't suppose you have any idea of what happened to the Sneak going by the name of Spatula, do you?" asked Damon.

Ben shook his head. "Last I saw, he was a dragonfly."

Damon sighed. "I don't like the idea of a Level-Four Sneak

roaming about freely, but at least it will be trouble on a local rather than a global level. Still—you may have bitten off more than you can chew, releasing him into the world."

"What about Charlotte?" asked Ben.

"She has refused to speak with me, but I delivered your letter before my, ah, sentencing," said Damon.

"Sentencing?" said Akemi. "Did you get in trouble?"

"Well, yes," said Damon awkwardly. "I've been fired, in fact."

"*What?*" they all exclaimed together.

"I can't blame them," said Damon. "I broke a number of laws and ignored protocol and became far too preoccupied with this world. I'm being punished in a manner that the Cartographers feel is best suited to my crimes."

"What does that mean?" asked Ben.

"It means I've been reduced, ahem, so they would put it, to . . . well, a mortal. A human being. I am . . . imprisoned here, I suppose. To lead an ordinary life, grow old, and die, in the form that was once my human-visiting guise. I cannot leave this planet. I cannot change this body. I cannot do . . . *anything.*"

They were all silent for a long time.

"I'm so sorry," whispered Akemi at last.

"Me too," said Ben.

Ms. Pryce closed her eyes briefly and opened them again.

"It could be worse," said Damon, with a kind of forced brightness. "It will take a good deal of getting used to, natu-rally. I'm no longer immortal—that's a bit of a shock. But I've watched all of you deal with the death sentence that comes with being human, and I admire it greatly, the way you just . . . live for the now, so to speak. Obviously, this planet holds its charms for me. I shall just have to figure out how to live as a man. And, I suppose, find a job. . . ."

"We'll help you," said Ms. Pryce, reaching across the table and squeezing his hand.

"My replacement is . . . Well, I don't want to bias you. We have rather different styles. The Cartographers felt a change was needed. At some point he'll probably pay Agatha a courtesy visit." He shrugged off the cosmic change in his status and smiled brightly.

"Try this," Ms. Pryce said to Damon, putting a slice of pizza on a plate for him. "It's pineapple pizza."

He looked faintly disgusted as he took a bite, but he said, "Delicious." He put down the slice and said cheerfully to Ms. Pryce, "So! You enjoy this game, this hoop-and-ball game, do you?"

Ms. Pryce gave him an amused look.

"I was really good at basketball, once upon a time," she said.

"You *were?*" said Akemi.

A paper napkin inched across the table. All of Ben's nerves jolted alive. He grabbed his Coke and dumped what was left over the napkin. Everybody stopped talking and looked at him. He stared at the paper napkin disintegrating in the puddle of Coke.

"I think the ceiling fan was just blowing it," said Akemi.

He could hear from her voice that she was trying not to laugh.

"Yeah," he said, wiping up the mess with the extra napkins. "Oops."

"It may take some time for things to feel properly normal again," said Ms. Pryce kindly.

The conversation carried on. Akemi grinned at Ben. He grinned back sheepishly.

"Let's go outside," she said.

He grabbed the briefcase, and they left Ms. Pryce and Damon gazing into each other's eyes over the pizza. The fresh air and quiet outside came as a relief.

"Wow, no more Locksmith Damon," Ben was saying, when Akemi made a sound like a sob and grabbed his arm.

He looked up.

On the corner across the street, under the streetlight, one hand raised in an uncertain little wave, stood Charlotte Moss. Traffic whizzed by, blocking her from view, and Ben was afraid she'd be gone when the light changed, but she was still there, not moving, just watching them, as if waiting to see what they would do. She didn't look like rice pudding. She looked very alert.

The walk signal flashed, and they raced toward her.

✳

In the gap between the universes, where a pathway built for one person only is slowly disintegrating, a piece of paper drifts through the air, read and reread many times over, damp with tears. . . .

Dear Charlotte,

We were so busy figuring out what was going on with the Sneaks that we missed what was going on with you, but now we think we understand a little bit. Sabrin lied to you, and we aren't angry. We just want you back.

Your grandmother is doing better, and Ms. Pryce thinks you'll be able to live with her again. Other than that, I guess the world is pretty much the same as it was before all this happened and maybe that doesn't seem like a good thing to you, but no matter what, you do have friends. You don't have to face any of it alone.

We let you down, and then you let us down, but we won't let you down again. We were a pretty great team for a while, and this isn't over yet. We really need your help. You saw how hopeless the Gateway Society guys are! We might still need to save the world. We can save each other too.

Your friends,
if you'll give us the chance,
Ben and Akemi

Acknowledgments

Endless gratitude, as always, to my agent, Steve Malk, for your insight and your wisdom as I flail around, sending you manuscripts and trying to figure out what I'm doing with my life. Thank you to my editor, Nancy Siscoe, who sees both the big picture and the small details so clearly, for being so kind, and for being right every time. Thank you to the whole team at Knopf Books for Young Readers—in particular, the copy editors, who have bettered this book immeasurably: Artie Bennett, Jim Armstrong, and Lisa Leventer. Thank you to Bob Bianchini for the wonderful cover design! Thank you to Kevin Cornell for capturing these characters just *brilliantly* on the cover and fitting in so many little details from the book.

Thank you, Dana Alison Levy, for being the first person to read a very early draft and reassuring me that, yes, it was A Book. Mick Hunter, David Egan, and my parents, Kieran and Susanna Egan, thank you for reading the next draft and offering your insights. I am so grateful to have you in my corner—I'd be cornerless without you. And thank you, James and Kieran, for being this book's biggest cheerleaders.

For reading things I write and, most of all, for listening to me rationalize and reimagine The Writing Life and how it fits together with *my* life, my gratitude and my love to Basak Kus, Rhonda Roumani, Samantha Cohoe, and Gillian Bright.

And thank you to every young reader who picks up this book. We still need to save the world, and we can save each other too. xo